SYSTEMATIC QUALITATIVE ANALYSIS

SYSTEMATIC QUALITATIVE ANALYSIS

By

K.L. Kapoor
M.Sc., Ph.D.
D.N. College
(Meerut University)
&
G.S. Johar
Ph.D., D.Sc.
V.S.S.D. College
Kanpur University

DISCOVERY PUBLISHING HOUSE PVT. LTD.
INDIA

Received by
D P Goel
M.Sc., Ph.D
St. Stephen's College
(Delhi University)

First Published - 1989
Reprinted - 2022

ISBN: 978-81-7141-066-8

Systematic Qualitative Analysis

Published by:
DISCOVERY PUBLISHING HOUSE PVT. LTD.
4383/4B, Ansari Road, Darya Ganj
New Delhi-110 002 (India)
Phone: +91-11-23279245; 23253475; 43596065
E-mail: discoverybooksindia@gmail.com
discoverypublishinghouse@gmail.com
namitwasan9@gmail.com
web: www.discoverypublishinggroup.com

Printed at:
Infinity Imaging Systems
Delhi

FOREWORD

It gives me a great pleasure to write the foreword of the book *Systematic Qualitative Analysis* written by my worthy colleagues Dr. G.S. Jauhar and Dr. Keemti Lal Kapoor.

The practical training in a chemical laboratory has undergone great changes during the last two decades and in order to grasp the fundamentals of the qualitative analysis in a systematic manner, it is essential that a simple but systematic approach be presented to the students right from the undergraduate level.

In the present book the authors have tried to explain every step in qualitative analysis in a simple manner so that a student can understand and analyse the mixture in his way. Considering the difficulties of the qualitative analysis, in light of the above, the authors are to be congratulated for highly successful attempt in a lucid and clear presentation of the subject matter.

It is my earnest hope that the book will be found very suitable for the undergraduate students and will lead to a more widespread adoption of the newer methods of qualitative analyses.

DR. R.K. AGARWAL
Editor-in-Chief
Asian Journal of Chemistry
Department of Chemistry
Lajpat Rai Post-Graduate College
(Meerut University)
Sahibabad-201005
(Ghaziabad)

CONTENTS

1

INTRODUCTION

QUALITATIVE ANALYSIS

QUALITATIVE analysis is mainly concerned with the detection and identification of constituents of an inorganic substance or a mixture of substances. The inorganic mixture given for analysis is made from such components which, on dissolving in water, split up into two types of charged particles, one type carrying a negative charge called the anion or negative ion and the other carrying a positive charge known as cation or positive ion. The cation is also called a basic radical whereas the anion is called the acidic radical. In potassium chloride, potassium ion is a basic radical whereas the chloride ion is an acidic radical.

In order to carry out a qualitative analysis of an inorganic mixture, a number of experiments are carried out to detect the presence of basic and acidic radicals present in it. These experiments are known as tests. Tests are of two types, positive and negative. While doing a test, one is concerned with the formation or the disappearance of (i) colour, (ii) a precipitate, and (iii) a gas. If a test is done and it gives the same result as given in the procedure, it means that the test is a positive one and shows the presence of a certain radical.

Chemical reagents The identification of the constituents of the inorganic substance or mixture is achieved with the help of another substance of known nature when the former is converted into a suitable product. This substance by means of which the reaction is brought about is known as a reagent.

Group Reagent As the number of substances is very large, these have been divided into various groups based on their similarity on treatment with certain chemical reagents called group reagents. After knowing the group in which a particular substance is present, one proceeds to identify the individual ions, cations or anions.

The basic difference between the identification of components of a single substance (salt) and of a mixture lies in the fact that in the latter case a particular cation has to be completely removed before proceeding in the succeeding stages of analysis.

Dry Tests These tests are carried out with dry solid inorganic mixture. Although dry tests do not lead to very useful conclusions yet these furnish certain valuable information which could be helpful at a latter stage in the correct identification of acid and basic radicals by wet tests.

Wet Tests These are applied to substances in solution by adding a reagent to the solution of the substance which is under analysis.

Types of Qualitative Analysis

Various techniques employed in qualitative analysis depend upon the quantity of the sample used for analysis (Table 1.1).

TABLE 1.1

Method of analysis	*Amount of sample taken*
Macro	0.5–1.0 g
Semimicro	10–100 mg
Micro	1–10 mg
Ultramicro	<1 mg
Spot test	10^{-6} g

Physico-chemical Principles

Some physico-chemical principles involved in qualitative analysis are discussed here, the knowledge of which will be very useful for understanding of the reactions and tests to be performed in the laboratory.

Ionization When a salt is dissolved in water it ionizes into cation and anion. This phenomenon is called ionization. Thus, sodium chloride ionizes into sodium ion and chloride ion.

$$NaCl \rightleftharpoons Na^+ + Cl^-$$

$$NaCl \rightleftharpoons \underset{\text{(cation)}}{Na^+} + \underset{\text{(anion)}}{Cl^-}$$

In the same way acids and bases ionize in water. If the extent of ionization of an acid or base is relatively large, it is termed strong acid or base, e.g. HCl or NaOH respectively. On the other hand, CH_3COOH or NH_4OH is a weak acid or base due to less ionization. In general strongly ionized acids, bases and salts are called strong electrolytes and the feebly ionized ones are called weak electrolytes.

Law of Mass Action

The law of mass action states, 'The rate at which a substance reacts is proportional to its active mass and the rate of a chemical reaction is proportional to the product of the active masses of the reacting substances.'

The term active mass means molecular concentration, i.e., the number of gram molecules of substance per unit volume. To illustrate it, let us consider a general reaction:

$$A + B \rightleftharpoons C + D$$

Let [A], [B], [C] and [D] represent the molar concentrations of A, B, C and D respectively at the equilibrium point. According to the mass law:

Rate of forward reaction, $r_f \propto [A]\,[B]$
Rate of backward reaction, $r_b \propto [C]\,[D]$

or
$$r_f = k_1\,[A]\,[B]$$
$$r_b = k_2\,[C]\,[D]$$

k_1 and k_2 are called the velocity constants.

At equilibrium, the rates of the forward and backward reactions are equal. It means: $r_f = r_b$

Therefore, $k_1\,[A]\,[B] = k_2\,[C]\,[D]$

$$\frac{k_1}{k_2} = \frac{[C]\,[D]}{[A]\,[B]} = K$$

K is called the equilibrium constant. Its value is characteristic of the reaction and has a fixed value for a particular reaction at a given temperature. The value is independent of the initial concentrations of the reactants taken.

For a more complicated reaction, the law of mass action is modified to state that the rate of a chemical reaction is proportional to the product of the molar concentrations of the reactants, each raised to the power of its coefficient in a balance equation. Thus for the reaction:

$$nA + mB \rightleftharpoons pC + qD$$
$$r_a = k_1\,[A]^n\,[B]^m$$
$$r_b = k_2\,[C]^p\,[D]^q$$

Therefore, $k = \dfrac{[C]^p\,[D]^q}{[A]^n\,[B]^m}$

Solubility Product

Insoluble substances like AgCl, $BaSO_4$, $PbCl_2$, etc. are in fact not completely insoluble when present in aqueous solution. A very small amount of these dissolves and is present as ions. Further, there exists an equilibrium between the undissolved and the dissolved salt. For AgCl, the equilibrium equation may be written as:

$$AgCl(s) \rightleftharpoons AgCl(aq) \rightleftharpoons Ag^+(aq) + Cl^-(aq)$$

$$AgCl(s) \rightleftharpoons Ag^+(aq) + Cl^-(aq)$$

Applying the mass law,

$$K = \frac{[Ag^+]\,[Cl^-]}{[AgCl]}$$

[AgCl] is assumed to be constant because of the fact that very little of this solid dissolves in aqueous solution (by definition).

Thus, $K \times [AgCl] = K_{sp} = [Ag^+]\,[Cl^-]$

The new constant, K_{sp} is called solubility product. The solubility product for CaF_2 may be written as:

$$CaF_2(s) \rightleftharpoons Ca^{2+}(aq) + 2F^-(aq)$$

$$K_{sp} = [Ca^{2+}]\,[F^-]^2$$

The different insoluble substances are characterized by definite values of solubility product at a given temperature (Table 1.2). The value of the solubility product can be calculated from the knowledge of the solubility of the given insoluble substance at a given temperature.

TABLE 1.2

Salt	K_{sp}	*Salt*	K_{sp}
AgCl	1.7×10^{-10}	CuS	8.0×10^{-37}
AgBr	5.0×10^{-13}	ZnS	7.0×10^{-26}
AgI	8.5×10^{-17}	HgS	1.6×10^{-54}
$PbCl_2$	1.7×10^{-5}	CdS	1.4×10^{-28}

Common Ion Effect

Consider the dissociation of a weak acid, e.g., HCN.

$$HCN + H_2O \rightleftharpoons H_3O^+ + CN^-$$

It mean that $K_a = \frac{[H_3O^+][CN^-]}{[HCN]}$ has a constant value at any given temperature. If HCl is added to the above equilibrium, then the concentration of H_3O^+ is greatly increased. In order that K_a remains constant, the value of CN^- should decrease and that of undissociated HCN should increase. In other words, the above equilibrium will shift towards the left, thereby, reducing the dissociation of HCN. In a similar manner, the ionization of HCN is suppressed in the presence of NaCN which furnishes a large excess of CN^- ions. Thus, the dissociation of HCN is suppressed in the presence of both H^+ and CN^- ions. It implies that the dissociation of a weak acid is suppressed by the addition of a substance capable of furnishing a large excess of ions common to either of the ions of the acid. Arguing in a similar manner, it can be concluded that the dissociation of a weak base, e.g., NH_4OH will be suppressed by the addition of either NH_4Cl or NaOH. This effect is called the common ion effect. It may be summarized as: 'The dissociation of a weak electrolyte is suppressed (reduced) on addition of a solution of a strong electrolyte having as ion common with that of the weak electrolyte'.

With the help of the concepts of the solubility product and common ion effect we can classify the more common cations into six groups which are discussed in detail in the Unit on identification of cations.

Complex Ion Formation (Complexation)

Sometimes it is observed that a precipitate dissolves on adding excess of the precipitating reagent. For example, on adding ammonium hydroxide to a solution of copper sulphate the blue precipitate of $Cu(OH)_2$ dissolves readily in excess of ammonium hydroxide forming an intense blue coloured solution. Thus, it follows that the Cu(II) ions react with ammonia to form a new species:

$$Cu^{2+} + 4NH_3 \rightleftharpoons [Cu(NH_3)_4]^{2+}$$

tetraammine Copper (II)

This new species formed, is known as a complex ion.

Transition metal ions (elements of d-block) readily form stable complexes because of availability of vacant d-orbitals of suitable energy. The complex ion formation is applied for separation of Cu $^{+}$ from Cd^{2+} and Co^{2+} from Ni $^{+}$ by means of KCN, etc.

pH Value

The acidic or basic character of a solution can be given in terms of the H_3O^+ ion concentration of the solution. To express it more conveniently, Sorensen suggested the use of the pH scale. Thus the pH of a solution is defined as the negative logarithm (to the base 10) of the H_3O^+ ion concentration in mol L^{-1}

Mathematically, $pH = \log_{10} [H_3O^+]$

For pure water, $[H_3O^+] = 10^{-7}$

or, $pH = 7$

Thus, when the pH is <7, the solution is acidic and when it is >7, the solution is basic (Table 1.3).

TABLE 1.3

pH	*$[H_3O^+]$*	*Character*	*pH*	*$[H_3O^+]$*	*Character*
0	1.0	Increasingly	7	10^{-7}	Neutral
1	10^{-1}	acidic	8	10^{-8}	│
2	10^{-2}	│	9	10^{-9}	│
3	10^{-3}	│	10	10^{-10}	│
4	10^{-4}	│	11	10^{-11}	│
5	10^{-5}	│	12	10^{-12}	↓
6	10^{-6}	↓	13	10^{-13}	Increasingly
7	10^{-7}	Neutral	14	10^{-14}	basic

Buffer Solutions

The solutions which resist pH change when small amounts of acids or bases are added to them are called 'buffer solutions'. They contain a weak acid and its salt with a strong base (e.g., $CH_3COOH+CH_3COONa$) or a weak base and its salt with a strong acid (e.g., NH_4OH+NH_4Cl).

Let us see how such a solution works taking an example of $CH_3COOH-CH_3COONa$ buffer. The species present in solution are:

$$CH_3COOH+H_2O \rightleftharpoons CH_3COO^-+H_3O^+$$

$$CH_3COONa \rightleftharpoons CH_3COO^-+Na^+$$

The ionization of acetic acid is very small due to the presence of a large excess of its common ion, i.e. acetate ions. Thus the buffer solution contains a large amount of unionized acetic acid, large amount of acetate ions and a small amount of H_3O^+ ions. If a strong acid like HCl is added to this solution, H^+ ions from HCl will combine with the acetate ions present in the solution to form unionized acetic acid. Hence, H_3O^+ ion concentration (or $pH=-\log[H_3O^+]$) of the solution remains essentially the same as that of the original solution. On the other hand, when a strong base like NaOH is added to the buffer solution; OH^- ions from NaOH react with H_3O^+ ions present in the solution to form unionized water. The decrease in the concentration of H_3O^+ ions is made up by the tendency of the acetic acid equilibrium ($CH_3COOH+H_2O \rightleftharpoons CH_3COO^- +H_3O^+$) to get readjusted. Arguing in the same manner, it can be inferred that a mixed solution of NH_4OH and NH_4Cl will resist any change in its pH value on addition of an acid or a base.

Oxidizing and Reducing Agents

Oxidation is any reaction in which an atom or ion loses electrons. Reduction is any reaction in whichan atom or ion gains electrons. Therefore oxidation and reduction may be referred as de-electronation and electronation respectively. Thus,

$Co^{2+} \rightarrow Co^{3+}$	+1 electron, i.e. oxidation
$As^{3+} \rightarrow As^{5+}$	+2 electrons, i.e. oxidation
$Cu^{2+} \rightarrow Cu^{+}$	−1 electron, i.e. reduction
$Fe^{3+} \rightarrow Fe^{2+}$	−1 electron, i.e. reduction

The oxidizing agent is a substance which brings about oxidation. It means the substance which picks up electrons is an oxidizing agent. In the same way a reducing agent is a substance which brings about reduction. It may also be explained as a substance which supplies electrons.

The overall reaction, in which reduction and oxidation are coupled, is called redox reaction. For example,

$$5Fe^{2+} \rightarrow 5Fe^{3+} + 5e^{-} \qquad \text{Oxidation}$$

$$MnO_4^{-} + 8H^{+} + 5e^{-} \rightarrow Mn^{2+} + 4H_2 \qquad \text{Reduction}$$

$$MnO^{-}_4 + 8H^{+} + 5Fe^{2+} \rightarrow 5Fe^{3+} + Mn^{2+} + 4H_2O \qquad \text{Redox}$$

2

IDENTIFICATION OF ANIONIC RADICALS

THE anions cannot be divided into groups in the same systematic way as the cations are divided. However, the acidic radicals or anions may be divided into three following groups:

1. *Dil. sulphuric acid group* This group includes the following radicals:

Carbonate, sulphide, sulphite, thiosulphate, nitrite, acetate and cyanide.

2. *Conc. sulphuric acid group* This group includes the following radicals:

Chloride, bromide, iodide, fluoride, nitrate, oxalate, tartrate, citrate, and chlorate.

3. *Anions not covered by dil. or conc. sulphuric acid* This group includes the following radicals:

Sulphate, phosphate, borate and chromate or dichromate.

The anions given in the above classification will be systematically studied in the following pages.

1. Action of Dil. H_2SO_4. Treat about 0.2 to 0.3 g of the mixture in a test tube with 2-3 mL of dil. H_2SO_4. Note the reactions in the cold and then warm it gently. Identify the gases evolved and refer to Table 2.1.

TABLE 2.1

Dilute Sulphuric Acid Test

S.No.	*Observation*	*Test*	*Inference*
1.	Brisk effervescence in the cold with the evolution of a colourless and odourless gas (CO_2)	The gas (CO_2) when passed through lime water turns it milky due to the formation of $CaCO_3$. However, if excess of this gas is passed, the milkiness of lime water disappears due to the formation of soluble $Ca(HCO_3)_2$.	Carbonate CO_3^{-2}
2.	Evolution of a colourless gas having a smell of rotten eggs (H_2S)	(a) The gas (H_2S) turns lead acetate paper black (b) The gas (H_2S) also turns alkaline sodium nitroprusside paper purple.	Sulphide S^{2-}
3.	Effervescence	The gas (SO_2) turns acidified potassium dichromate paper green.	Sulphite SO_3^{2-}
4.	Effervescence and in addition to this reacting solution becomes white changing to yellow.	Add a few drops of ferric chloride solution, a violet red colour which soon fades away.	Thiosulphate $S_2O_3^{2-}$
5.	A light brown gas evolves.	(a) The gas (NO) turns ferrous sulphate solution black (b) The gas (NO) turns acidified KI-starch blue.	Nitrite NO_2^-
6.	Colourless gas with vinegar like odour (CH_3COOH)	Add neutral ferric chloride solution. A red colour appears.	Acetate CH_3COO^-

7.	Evolution of a colourless gas having a smell of bitter almonds (HCN).	The gas (HCN) turns brown suspension of CuS on filter paper to colourless.	Caynide CN^-

Notes 1. Dissolve 0.2 g of $CuSO_4$ in 100 mL of water and add a few drops of NH_4OH. Pass H_2S gas through it. The final solution is called suspension of CuS.

2. If the mixture contains lead, the dilute acid test should be repeated with dil. nitric acid.

3. Many sulphides like antimony sulphide do not give H_2S gas with dil. acid. In such cases the gas is evolved on heating with conc. hydrochloric acid alone.

4. Some basic carbonates, e.g. of Bi and Pb do not evolve CO_2 with effervescence but gradually.

CHEMISTRY FOR THE TESTS OF ANIONIC RADICALS OF DIL. SULPHURIC ACID GROUP

1. *Carbonates* When treated with dil. H_2SO_4, all carbonates decompose, causing effervescence due to the evolution of CO_2 gas.

$$Na_2CO_3+H_2SO_4 \rightarrow Na_2SO_4+H_2O+CO_2$$

This gas when passed through lime water turns it milky due to the formation of solid calcium carbonate.

$$\underset{\text{(lime water)}}{Ca(OH)_2}+CO_2 \rightarrow \underset{\text{(milky white ppt.)}}{CaCO_3}$$

If excess of CO_2 gas is passed through this lime water, the milkiness disappears owing to the formation of soluble calcium bicarbonate.

$$CaCO_3+H_2O+CO_2 \rightarrow \underset{\text{(soluble)}}{Ca\ (HCO_3)_2}$$

2. *Sulphides* When treated with dil. H_2SO_4, all sulphides

evolve H_2S gas which is a colourless gas having a characteristic odour of rotten eggs.

$$\underset{\text{dilute}}{MS+H_2SO_4}\rightarrow MSO_4+H_2S \text{ (where } M=\text{bivalent metal)}$$

This gas turns lead acetate paper black due to the formation of black lead sulphide.

$$(CH_3COO)_2Pb+H_2S\rightarrow \underset{\text{(black)}}{PbS}+CH_3COOH$$

This gas also turns alkaline sodium nitroprusside paper purple due to the formation of $Na_4Fe(CN)_5NOS$.

$$Na_2Fe(CN)_5NO+2NaOH+H_2S\rightarrow \underset{\text{(purple)}}{Na_4Fe(CN)_5NOS}+2H_2O$$

3. *Sulphites* When treated with dil. H_2SO_4, all sulphites decompose to evolve SO_2 gas. This is a colourless gas having characteristic smell of burning sulphur.

$$MSO_3+H_2SO_4\rightarrow MSO_4+SO_2+H_2O \text{ (}M=\text{bivalent metal)}$$

This gas turns potassium dichromate paper green due to the reduction of Cr(VI) to Cr(III) ions.

$$K_2Cr_2O_7+H_2SO_4+3SO_2\rightarrow \underset{\text{(green)}}{Cr_2(SO_4)_3}+K_2SO_4+H_2O$$

or

$$Cr_2O_7^{2-}+2H^++3SO_2\rightarrow \underset{\text{(green)}}{2Cr^{3+}}+3SO_4^{2-}+H_2O$$

4. *Thiosulphates* When treated with dil. H_2SO_4, all thiosulphates decompose to evolve SO_2 gas and give a ppt. of sulphur.

$$Na_2S_2O_3+H_2SO_4\rightarrow Na_2SO_4+H_2O+SO_2+S$$

5. *Nitrites* When treated with dil. H_2SO_4, nitrites decompose to evolve nitric oxide gas which reacts with atmospheric oxygen to yield reddish brown fumes of nitrogen dioxide.

$$NaNO_2+H_2SO_4 \rightarrow NaHSO_4+HNO_2$$

$$3HNO_2 \rightarrow HNO_3+H_2O+2NO$$

$$2NO+\underset{(air)}{O_2} \rightarrow NO_2$$

The nitric oxide gas turns ferrous sulphate solution brownish-black due to the formation of $[Fe(H_2O)_5NO]SO_4$.

$$FeSO_4+NO+5H_2O \rightarrow \underset{(brownish\text{-}black)}{[Fe(H_2O)_5NO]SO_4}$$

The nitric oxide gas also liberates iodine from KI of KI-starch paper which becomes blue due to the formation of absorption complex.

$$2KI+2NO+\underset{(air)}{O_2} \rightarrow 2KNO_2+I_2$$

$$I_2+Starch \rightarrow \underset{(blue)}{Strach\text{-}iodine\ adsorption\ complex}$$

6. *Acetates* When treated with dil H_2SO_4, acetates decompose to form acetic acid.

$$2CH_3COONa+H_2SO_4 \rightarrow Na_2SO_4+2CH_3COOH$$

This acetic acid reacts with ferric chloride solution to form red colour of ferric acetate.

$$3CH_3COOH+FeCl_3 \rightarrow \underset{(red)}{Fe(CH_3COO)_3}+3HCl$$

7. *Cyanides* When treated with dil. H_2SO_4, cyanides decompose to give HCN gas. This is a colourless gas having smell of bitter almonds.

$$2NaCN+H_2SO_4 \rightarrow Na_2SO_4+2HCN$$

(HCN is an extremely poisonous gas and should never be inhaled.)

Action of conc. H_2SO_4 Treat about 0.5 g of mixture in a dry test tube with 2-3 mL of conc. H_2SO_4. Note the reaction in cold and then heat it gently. Identify the gases evolved with the help of Table 2.2.

TABLE 2.2

Concentrated Sulphuric Acid Test

S. No.	*Observation*	*Tests*	*Inference*
1.	Colourless pungent smelling gas which fumes in air.	When a glass rod dipped in NH_4OH is placed over the mouth of the test tube, dense white fumes due to the formation of NH_4Cl are obtained.	Chloride Cl^-
2.	Reddish-brown heavy fumes; the evolution of fumes increases on adding MnO_2	(a) The brown fumes (Br_2) turn starch paper yellow. (b) The brown fumes (Br_2) turn fluorescent paper red.	Bromide Br^-
3.	Violet vapours of iodine, the evolution of vapours is increased on adding MnO_2.	The violet vapours (I_2) turn starch paper deep blue.	Iodide I^-
4.	Colourless pungent smelling gas with greasy drops in the test tube.	The glass rod moistened with water is brought in contact with the vapour (HF), a waxy deposit is obtatined on glass rod.	Fluoride F^-
5.	Light brown fumes which increase on heating the reaction mixture with copper chips or paper pellets.	The brown fumes (NO_2) turn ferrous sulphate solution black.	Nitrate NO^{3-}
6.	Colourless gas which burns with a pale blue flame.	The gas turns lime water milky,	Oxalate $C_2O_4^{2-}$

7. Colourless gases (CO, CO_2 and SO_2), occurring rapid charring and smell of burnt sugar.	(a) The gas (CO) burns with pale blue flame. (b) The gas (SO_2) turns acidified dichromate paper green.	Tartrate $C_4H_4O_6^{2-}$
8. Colourless gases (CO, CO_2 and SO_2) and occurring slow charring. The solution darkens slowly.	As above	Citrate $C_6H_5O_7^{3-}$
9. Evolution of yellow gas with smell of Cl_2 gas in cold.	On warming the solution cracking sound is heard.	Chlorate ClO_3^-

Notes 1. As soon as the test is complete, one should not throw contents directly into the sink. Cool the tube, dilute with water and then throw into the sink.

2. Never heat the contents of the test tube to boiling because otherwise H_2SO_4 will decompose to liberate SO_2 that makes the identification of other gases quite difficult.

CHEMISTRY FOR THE TESTS OF ANIONIC RADICALS OF CONC. SULPHURIC ACID GROUP

1. *Chloride* When treated with conc. H_2SO_4, chlorides yield HCl gas.

$$NaCl+H_2SO_4 \rightarrow NaHSO_4+HCl$$

With ammonia, HCl gas gives dense white fumes due to the formation of NH_4Cl

$$NH_3+HCl \rightarrow NH_4Cl$$

The gas turns moist blue litmus paper red.

2. *Bromide* When bromides are heated with conc. H_2SO_4 reddish brown fumes with a penetrating odour are evolved due to the formation of a mixture of HBr and Br_2.

$$KBr+H_2SO_4 \rightarrow KHSO_4+HBr$$
$$2HBr+H_2SO_4 \rightarrow Br_2+SO_2+2H_2O$$

The evolution of brown fumes with MnO_2 increases due to the formation of excess bromine from the oxidation of HBr with MnO_2.

$$MnO_2+2HBr+H_2SO_4 \rightarrow MnSO_4+2H_2O+Br_2$$

When a paper dipped in starch is brought over the mouth of the test tube from which brown fumes are coming out, it turns yellow owing to the formation of starch-bromide adsorption complex.

$$Br_2+\text{Starch} \rightarrow \text{Starch-bromide adsorption complex (yellow)}$$

3. *Iodide* When iodides are heated with conc. H_2SO_4, violet vapours of iodine evolve. Some HI is also produced but most of the HI reduces the sulphuric acid into SO_2, H_2S and sulphur.

$$KI+H_2SO_4 \rightarrow KHSO_4+HI$$

$$H_2SO_4+2HI \rightarrow I_2+SO_2+2H_2O$$

$$H_2SO_4+6HI \rightarrow 3I_2+S+4H_2O$$

$$H_2SO_4+8HI \rightarrow 4I_2+H_2S+4H_2O$$

By adding MnO_2 in the test tube containing the mixture and conc. H_2SO_4, the evolution of iodine vapours is increased because the HI formed decomposes readily.

$$MnO_2+H_2SO_4+2HI \rightarrow MnSO_4+2H_2O+I_2$$

When a paper dipped in starch is brought over the mouth of the test tube from which violet vapours are coming out, it turns blue owing to the formation of starch-iodide adsorption complex.

$$I_2+\text{Starch} \rightarrow \text{Starch-iodine adsorption complex (blue)}$$

4. *Fluoride* When fluorides are heated with conc. H_2SO_4, pungent smelling gas, HF evolves. The gas reacts with silica to form SiF_4 which further reacts with water to give a mixed deposit of H_4SiO_4 and H_2SiF_6.

$$CaF_2 + H_2SO_4 \rightarrow CaSO_4 + 2HF$$

$$SiO_2 + 4HF \rightarrow SiF_4 + 2H_2O$$

$$3SiF_4 + 4H_2O \rightarrow H_4SiO_4 + 2H_2SiF_6$$

5. *Nitrate* When nitrates are treated with conc. H_2SO_4, they yield light-brown vapours of nitrogen dioxide which are produced due to the decomposition of nitric acid formed first.

$$NaNO_3 + H_2SO_4 \rightarrow NaHSO_4 + HNO_3$$

$$4HNO_3 \rightarrow 4NO_2 + O_2 + 2H_2O$$

By adding copper turnings or paper pellets in the test tube, the brown colour deepens because the nitric acid formed decomposes readily.

$$Cu + 4HNO_3 \rightarrow Cu(NO_3)_2 + 2NO_2 + 2H_2O$$

$$3Cu + 8HNO_3 \rightarrow 3Cu(NO_3)_2 + 2NO + 4H_2O$$

$$2NO + O_2 \rightarrow 2NO_2$$

$$C + 4HNO_3 \rightarrow 2H_2O + 4NO_2 + CO_2$$

(from paper)

When brown vapours of NO_2 are passed through acidified ferrous sulphate, the latter reduces the nitrogen dioxide to nitric oxide. This oxide is then absorbed by the unoxidized portion of ferrous sulphate to give a brownish black solution.

$$2FeSO_4 + H_2SO_4 + NO_2 \rightarrow Fe_2(SO_4)_3 + NO + H_2O$$

$$FeSO_4 + NO + 5H_2O \rightarrow [Fe(H_2O)_5NO]SO_4$$

(brownish black)

6. *Oxalate* When oxalates are heated with conc. H_2SO_4, the colourless and odourless gas evolved by their decomposition is a mixture of CO and CO_2. While CO_2 turns lime water milky, CO burns with a blue flame.

$$Na_2C_2O_4 + H_2SO_4 \rightarrow CO + CO_2 + H_2O + Na_2SO_4$$

$$CO_2 + Ca(OH)_2 \rightarrow CaCO_3 + H_2O$$

$$2CO + O_2 \rightarrow 2CO_2$$

7. *Tartrate* When tartrates are heated with conc. H_2SO_4, the colourless and smell of burnt sugar-like gas evolves with rapid charring.

$$\begin{array}{l} CH(OH)COOK \\ | \\ CH(OH)COOK \end{array} + H_2SO_4 \rightarrow K_2SO_4 + 2H_2O + 4CO_2 + CO + 2C$$

$$C + 2H_2SO_4 \rightarrow CO_2 + 2H_2O + 2SO_2$$

8. *Citrate* When citrates are heated with conc. H_2SO_4, the colourless gas with slow charring evolves. The solution darkens slowly due to the liberation of CO, CO_2 and some SO_2.

$$2Na_3C_6H_5O_7 + 3H_2SO_4 \rightarrow \underset{\text{citric acid}}{2H_3C_6H_5O_7} + 3Na_2SO_4$$

$$\begin{array}{l} CH_2COOH \\ | \\ C(OH)COOH \\ | \\ CH_2COOH \end{array} \rightarrow CO + H_2O + \underset{\text{acetone dicarboxylic acid}}{\begin{array}{l} CH_2COOH \\ | \\ CO \\ | \\ CH_2COOH \end{array}}$$

$$\begin{array}{l} CH_2COOH \\ | \\ CO \\ | \\ CH_2COOH \end{array} \rightarrow \underset{\text{acetone}}{CH_3COCH_3} + 2CO_2$$

9. *Chlorate*. When chlorates are treated with conc. H_2SO_4, a yellow gas having smell similar to Cl_2 evolves in cold and gives cracking sound on heating.

$$3KClO_3 + 3H_2SO_4 \rightarrow 2ClO_2 + HClO_4 + 3KHSO_4 + H_2O$$

Action of acidified potassium permagnate Take about 0.2-0.3 g of the mixture in a test tube. To this add 3-4 mL of dil. H_2SO_4. Boil the solution gently till no more gas evolves. Cool the reaction mixture to room temperature and add 2-3 mL of dil. sulphuric acid followed by potassium permanganate solution drop by drop till pink colour persists. Now heat and note if further decolorization occurs or not. Also, look for the evolution of gas or vapour. Draw the appropriate inference by using Table 2.3.

TABLE 2.3

Acidified Potassium Permanganate Test

S. No.	*Observation*	*Test*	*Inference*
1.	Decolorization of potassium permanganate in cold accompanied by evolution of gas as follows:		
	(*i*) Evolution of chlorine gas having pale-greenish colour	The gas has a characteristic smell and bleaches litmus paper	Chloride Cl^-
	(*ii*) Evolution of reddish-brown bromine gas (the solution in the test tube becomes reddish brown)	The gas turns starch paper yellow	Bromide Br^-
	(*iii*) Evolution of violet iodine vapours	The vapours turn starch paper blue	Iodide I^-
2.	Pink colour of $KMnO_4$ is discharged in cold without the evolution of any gas	—	Ferrous ion Fe^{2+}
3.	Pink colour of $KMnO_4$ is discharged on heating with brisk effervescence due to the evolution of CO_2 gas.	The CO_2 gas turns lime water milky	Oxalate $C_2O_4^{2-}$
4.	Pink colour of $KMnO_4$ is not discharged at all.	—	Oxalate, chloride, bromide and iodide are absent.

CHEMISTRY FOR THE TESTS OF ACID RADICALS Cl^-, Br^-, I^- AND $C_2O_4^{2-}$ WITH ACIDIFIED POTASSIUM PERMANGANATE

The potassium permanganate test is useful in the detection of chloride, bromide, iodide, ferrous (Fe^{2+}) and oxalate radicals.

In the presence of dil. sulphuric acid, potassium permanganate acts as an oxidizing agent due to the liberation of nascent oxygen.

$$2KMnO_4+3H_2SO_4 \rightarrow K_2SO_4+2MnSO_4+3H_2O+5(O)$$

The nascent oxygen is able to oxidize chloride, bromide, iodide, ferrous and oxalate ions and in the process the pink colour of potassium permanganate gets discharged. In addition, the characteristic gases also evolve in many cases. These observations provide useful indication about the presence or absence of radicals.

$$CaCl_2+H_2SO_4+(O)\xrightarrow{\text{cold}}CaSO_4+H_2O+Cl_2$$

$$2KBr_2+H_2SO_4+(O)\xrightarrow{\text{cold}}K_2SO_4+H_2O+Br_2$$

$$2NaI_2+H_2SO_4+(O)\xrightarrow{\text{cold}}Na_2SO_4+H_2O+I_2$$

$$2FeSO_4+H_2SO_4+(O)\xrightarrow{\text{cold}}Fe_2(SO_4)_3+H_2O$$

$$\begin{array}{l}COONa\\ |\\ COONa\end{array}+H_2SO_4+(O)\xrightarrow{\text{hot}}2CO_2+Na_2SO_4+H_2O$$

Notes 1. Heavy metal chlorides decolorize acidified $KMnO_4$ very slowly.

2. The order of oxidation by acidified permanganate solution is iodide, bromide, chloride, ferrous and oxalate radicals.

Other anions not covered by dil. or conc. H_2SO_4 There are certain anions which do not give any useful reaction either with dil. or conc. H_2SO_4. For such radicals, certain other reagents are employed. These are described in Table 2.4.

TABLE 2.4

Preliminary Tests for Sulphate, Phosphate, Borate and Chromate

S. No.	*Experiment*	*Observation*	*Inference*
1.	Take 0.5 g of the mixture in a test tube. To this add 2-4 mL of dil. HCl. Boil the contents to expel all the gases. Filter and to the filtrate add $BaCl_2$ solution.	A white ppt. of $BaSO_4$ is obtained which is insoluble in conc. HCl or conc. HNO_3	Sulphate SO_4^{2-}
2.	Take 0.5 g of the mixture in a test tube. To this add 3-4 mL of conc. HNO_3 and ammonium molybdate solution.	A yellow ppt. or colouration due to the formation of ammonium phosphomolybdate is obtained.	Phosphate PO_4^{3-}
3.	Take 0.5 g of the mixture in a china dish. To it add 3 mL of H_2SO_4 and 2 mL of ethyl alcohol. Heat the china dish and ignite the vapours over the china dish.	A green edged flame is seen.	Borate BO_3^{3-}
4.	Mix 0.5 g of the mixture with 0.5 g of sodium chloride. To this add 3 mL of conc. H_2SO_4. Heat the mixture gently. Deep red vapours are obtained. Pass these vapours into NaOH solution contained in a test tube. A yellow solution is obtained. Neutralize it with dil. acetic acid and add lead acetate solution.	A yellow ppt. is obtained.	Chromate CrO_4^{2-} or Dichromate $Cr_2O_7^{2-}$

CHEMISTRY FOR THE TESTS OF ACID RADICALS, SO_4^{2-}, PO_4^{3-}, BO_3^{3-} and CrO_4^{3-} or $Cr_2O_7^{2-}$ (TABLE 2.4)

1. *Sulphate* When the mixture is boiled with dil. HCl, carbonates, sulphides and sulphites are decomposed and further addition of dil. HCl ensures that the solution is sufficiently acidic so that only barium sulphate is precipitated.

$$Ba^{2+} + SO_4^{2-} \rightarrow \underset{\text{(white ppt.)}}{BaSO_4}$$

2. *Phosphate* When a mixture having phosphate is boiled with nitric acid followed by the addition of ammonium molybdate, a yellow coloration or ppt. due to the formation of ammonium phosphomolybdate is obtained.

$$Na_2HPO_4 + 12(NH_4)_2MoO_4 + 23HNO_3 \rightarrow (NH_4)_3PMo_{12}O_{40} + 2NaNO_2 + 21NH_4NO_3 + 12H_2O$$

3. *Borate* The test given in Table 2.4 is based on the formation of volatile ethylborate which burns with a green-edged flame.

$$H_3BO_3 + 3C_2H_5OH \rightarrow (C_2H_5)_3BO_3 + 3H_2O$$

4. *Chromate or dichromate* When a mixture having chromate or dichromate is mixed with sodium chloride and heated with conc. sulphuric acid, chromyl chloride gas evolves. The gas is passed into sodium hydroxide. It gives yellow solution due to sodium chromate formation. Chromate gives yellow ppt. of lead chromate with lead acetate.

$$4NaCl + K_2Cr_2O_7 + 3H_2SO_4 \rightarrow K_2SO_4 + 2Na_2SO_4 + 3H_2O + 2CrO_2Cl_2 \text{ (red vapours)}$$

$$CrO_2Cl_2 + 4NaOH \rightarrow \underset{\text{(yellow soln.)}}{Na_2CrO_4} + 2NaCl + 2H_2O$$

$$Na_2CrO_4 + Pb(CH_3COO)_2 \rightarrow \underset{\text{(yellow ppt.)}}{PbCrO_4} + CH_3COONa$$

Identification of Acidic Radicals by Wet Tests

Tests indicated in the preliminary tests do not give very conclusive information. Hence, wet tests are to be performed for the confirmation of such anions which may or may not be indicated by preliminary tests. These anions must be free from heavy metal ions.

Preparation of Solution for the Wet Tests of Acidic Radicals

It is evident that the first step in the detection of acid radicals by wet tests is the preparation of the solution of the mixture. While some mixtures may be quite soluble in water whereas others may be partially soluble or completely insoluble in water. Thus, depending upon the solubility of the given mixture, we may prepare the aqueous solution or sodium carbonate extract for carrying out the wet tests.

1. *Preparation of water extract* As ail common nitrites and nitrates are soluble in water, the confirmatory tests for such anions can be performed with the water extract of the mixture.

In order to prepare the water extract, boil 1-2 g of mixture with 10-20 mL of distilled water for two or three minutes. If the mixture dissolves completely, add more of the mixture in small quantities to obtain a concentrated solution. The solution so obtained is called a "water extract."

2. *Preparation of sodium carbonate extract* If the mixture under examination is partially or completely insoluble in water, sodium carbonate extract is prepared.

In order to prepare sodium carbonate extract, mix intimately about 1-2 g of the solid mixture powder with 3-5 g of pure Na_2CO_3 powder. Place this mixture in a 50 mL china dish. Add about 20-25 mL of distilled water and boil for at least 10 min [Fig. 2.1 (a)]. Filter and wash the residue upon the filter paper with a little hot water. The filtrate so obtained is called sodium carbonate extract or soda extract [Fig. 2.1(b)].

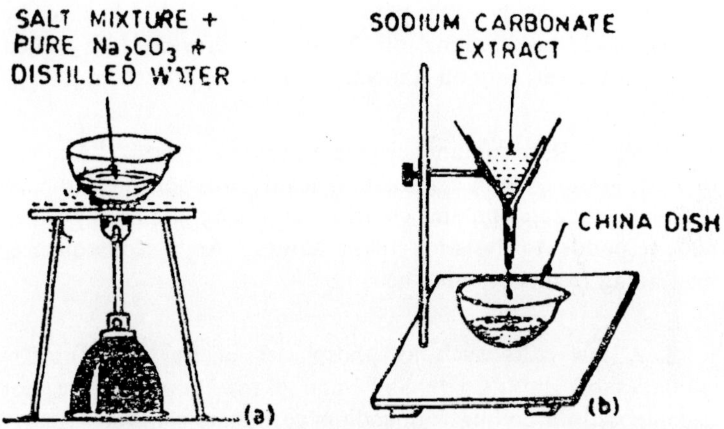

Fig. 2.1. Preparation of sodium carbonate extract.

Explanation Certain cations interfere with the confirmatory tests of certain acid radicals when present in the solution. Such cations are eliminated in the form of insoluble carbonates as a result of treatment with sodium carbonate. These insoluble carbonates are removed by filtration.

$$MA_2 + Na_2CO_3 \rightarrow MCO_3 + 2NaA$$

Examples

$$\underset{}{Ca_3(PO_4)_2} + 3Na_2CO_3 \rightarrow \underset{\text{(ppt.)}}{3CaCO_3} + \underset{\text{(soln.)}}{2Na_3PO_4}$$

$$CaSO_3 + Na_2CO_3 \rightarrow \underset{\text{(soln.)}}{Na_2SO_3} + \underset{\text{(ppt.)}}{CaCO_3}$$

The filtrate containing sodium salts of acid radicals, will be used for identifying the various acid radicals, while the insoluble residue may be used for the identification of basic radicals.

How to use sodium carbonate extract. Sodium carbonate extract contains an excess quantity of unreacted sodium carbonate which may interfere in the usual tests of acid radicals. Therefore, it becomes essential to destroy excess sodium carbonate. This is done by acidifying the extract with some acid (the choice depends upon the nature of the acid radical to be tested) and then boiling off the carbon dioxide. It is cooled and used for carrying out the various tests.

Notes 1. Pure sodium carbonate should be used. "Analar" or A.R. grade sodium carbonate is highly satisfactory. Ordinary sodium carbonate contains chloride and sulphate as impurities and responds to tests for these anions. As a consequence, misleading results are obtained.

2. A few salts such as phosphates of Fe^{3+} and Al^{3+}; sulphides of Zn^{2+}, Ca^{2+}, Sb^{3+} and a few fluorides are not decomposed on boiling with sodium carbonate solution. Hence, these anions are not present in the "sodium carbonate extract", their confirmatory tests must be performed with the residue or mixture.

3. Some cations such as Cu^{2+}, As^{3+} and Sb^{3+} form soluble complexes with sodium carbonate and hence these cations partly go into the sodium carbonate extract. These should be preferably removed by acidifying extract with dil. HCl and passing H_2S gas. Excess of H_2S can be eliminated by boiling and then the solution can be tested for various anions except Cl^- and S^{2-}.

4. If ammonium is present in the mixture it must be expelled completely because it tends to complex copper, cadmium, nickel, etc. into the soluble ammine which goes into the filtrate.

5. Some of the cations like As^{3+}, Sb^{3+}, Sn^{2+}, etc. partly go into the filtrate due the amphoteric nature of the parent metals. These should be completely removed by adding dil. HCl followed by passing H_2S gas and rejecting the precipitate. H_2S is boiled off from the filtrate.

6. Sometimes tartrate and oxalate form soluble complexes with certain cations like Cu^{2+}, Fe^{3+}, Cr^{3+} and Al^{3+} and these go into the sodium carbonate extract. Remove copper by passing H_2S. Boil off H_2S from the filtrate and render it ammoniacal. A precipitate is formed due to the hydroxides of the iron, chromium or aluminium. Reject the ppt. and expel ammonia from the filtrate by boiling. Use the resulting solution for the detection of anions.

Confirmation of carbonate and bicarbonate Take 0.5 g of the mixture in a test tube containing 4-5 mL of distilled water. Warm and Filter.

Filtrate	*Residue*
Filtrate may contain soluble carbonate. Divide the filtrate into two portions: (*a*) To part I, add dil. HCl. A brisk effervescence due to the liberation of CO_2 which turns lime water milky indicates soluble carbonate or bicarbonate	Residue may have insoluble carbonate. To this add dil. HCl. A brisk effervescence with the evolution of CO_2 which turns lime water milky confirms carbonate.
$CO_3^{2-}+2H^+ \rightarrow H_2O+CO_2$ $HCO_3^-+H^+ \rightarrow H_2O+CO_2$	$CO_3^{2-}+2H^+ \rightarrow H_2O+CO_2$
It no ppt. appears in cold, heat it to boiling. Formation of white ppt. confirms bicarbonate $Mg^{2+}+2HCO_3^- \rightarrow Mg(HCO_3)_2$ $Mg(HCO_3)_2 \rightarrow MgCO_3+H_2O+CO_2$	
(*b*) To part II, add $MgSO_4$ solution. If a white ppt. is obtained in cold, it confirms carbonate $Mg^{2+}+CO_3^{2-} \rightarrow MgCO_3$ (white ppt.)	

Confirmatory Tests of Sulphide

Experiment	*Observation*
1. To 1 mL of sodium carbonate extract, add a few drops of freshly prepared sodium nitroprusside solution.	The formation of violet or purple coloration confirms sulphide $Na_2S + Na_2Fe(CN)_5NO \rightarrow Na_4Fe(CN)_5NOS$ (purple of violet colouration)
2. Acidify 1 mL of sodium carbonate extract with dil. acetic acid and boil the solution to expel CO_2. To this add 1 mL of lead acetate solution.	The formation of black ppt. (PbS) confirms the presence of sulphide. $Na_2S + (CH_3COO_3Pb \rightarrow PbS + 2CH_3COONa$ (black ppt.)
3. Shake 2 mL of sodium carbonate extract with 0.2 g of cadmium carbonate.	The formation of yellow ppt. (CdS) confirms the presence of sulphide. $Na_2S + CdCO_3 \rightarrow CdS + Na_2CO_3$ (yellow ppt.)

Confirmatory Tests of Sulphite

Experiment	*Observation*
To 5 mL of sodium carbonate extract, add excess of $BaCl_2$. The precipitate formed may be due to sulphite, sulphate or excess of sodium carbonate present in the solution. $Na_2SO_3 + BaCl_2 \rightarrow BaSO_3 + 2NaCl$ (ppt.) Filter the ppt. and divide the ppt. into three equal parts;	

(*a*) To part I, add dil. HCl	If there is evolution of SO_2 which turns acidified dichromate paper green, it confirms sulphite. $BaSO_3 + 2HCl \rightarrow BaCl_2 + H_2O + SO_2$ $K_2Cr_2O_7 + 4H_2SO_4 \rightarrow K_2SO_4 + Cr_2(SO_4)_3 + 4H_2O + 3(O)$ $SO_2 + H_2O + (O) \rightarrow H_2SO_4$
(*b*) To part II, add a few drops of potassium permanganate solution followed by the addition of 3 mL of dil. H_2SO_4	If the pink colour of the permanganate is discharged, it confirms sulphite. $BaSO_3 + H_2SO_4 \rightarrow BaSO_4 + H_2O + SO_2$ $\underset{\text{(colourless)}}{K_2SO_4} + \underset{\text{(colourless)}}{2MnSO_4} + 2H_2SO_4$
(*c*) To part III, add bromine water and warm the solution	If sulphite is present, the colour of bromine gets discharged and a white ppt. ($BaSO_4$) insoluble in acids is obtained $BaSO_3 + Br_2 + H_2O \rightarrow \underset{\text{(ppt.)}}{BaSO_4} + 2HBr$

Confirmatory Tests of Thiosulphate

Experiment	*Observation*
1. Add 2-3 mL of silver nitrate solution to 1 mL of 'water extract' or 'sodium carbonate extract' which is already neutralized with dil. acetic acid.	Appearance of white ppt. turning yellow, orange, brown and finally black in quick succession confirms thiosulphate $Na_2S_2O_3 + 2AgNO_3 \rightarrow Ag_2S_2O_3 + 2NaNO_3$

	The white ppt. of $Ag_2S_2O_3$ is soluble in excess of thiosulphate. At first a sparingly soluble complex $NaAgS_2O_3$ is formed which dissolves in excess of thiosulphate forming a soluble complex $Na_4Ag_2(S_2O_3)_3 \rightarrow Ag_2S_2O_3 + Na_2S_2O_3 + 2NaAgS_2O_3$ $2NaAgS_2O_3 + Na_2S_2O_3 \rightarrow Na_4Ag_2(S_2O_3)_3$
2. Acidify 1-2 mL of sodium carbonate extract with dil. acetic acid and add few drops of ferric chloride solution.	A violet red colour which soon fades away confirms thiosulphate $FeCl_3 + 2Na_2S_2O_3 \rightarrow 3NaCl + NaFe(S_2O_3)_2$ $Fe(S_2O_3)_2^- + Fe^{3+} \rightleftharpoons 2Fe^{2+} + S_4O_6^{2-}$

Confirmatory Tests of Nitrite

Experiment	*Observation*
1. Acidify 1-2 mL of sodium carbonate extract with dil. acetic acid or dil. sulphuric acid and boil the solution to expel CO_2. Add a crystal of KI and 1 mL of starch solution. Also, add a few drops of dil. sulphuric acid	A deep blue coloration confirms nitrate. $NaNO_2 + CH_3COOH \rightarrow HNO_3 + CH_3COONa$ $3HNO_2 \rightarrow HNO_3 + H_2O + 2NO$ $2NO + O_2 \rightarrow 2NO_2$ $2KI + 2NO_2 \rightarrow 2KNO_2 + I_2$ I_2 + Starch $\rightarrow$ Starch-iodine adsorption complex (blue)
2. Acidify 2-3 mL of sodium carbonate extract with dil. acetic acid. Boil off CO_2. To this add a pinch of thiourea. a few drops of dil. HCl and ferric chloride solution	A blood red coloration indicates the presence of nitrite. $NaNO_2 + CH_3COOH \rightarrow CH_3COONa + HNO_2$ $HNO_2 + H_2NCSNH_2 \rightarrow N_2 + HCNS + 2H_2O$ $FeCl_3 + 3HCNS \rightarrow Fe(CNS)_3 + 3HCl$ (blood red colouration)

3. Acidify 1-2 mL of sodium carbonate extract with dil. acetic acid and boil to expel CO_2. To this add a few drops of m-phenylenediamine hydrochloride solution followed by a few drops of hydrochloric acid.	The formation of brown ppt. confirms nitrite. $NaNO_2+CH_3COOH \rightarrow CH_3COONa+HNO_2$ $2C_6H_4\begin{matrix}\diagup NH_2\\ \diagdown NH_2\end{matrix} + HNO_2 \rightarrow$ $C_6H_4\begin{matrix}\diagup NH_2\\ \diagdown N{=}N{-}C_6H_3\begin{matrix}\diagup NH_2\\ \diagdown NH_2\end{matrix}\end{matrix}$

Confirmatory Tests of Acetate

Experiment	*Observation*
1. Heat a pinch of dry mixture with a few drops of conc. H_2SO_4 and 0.5 mL of ethyl alcohol.	A pleasant pear-like fruity smell shows the presence of acetate. $CH_3COOH+C_2H_5OH \rightarrow CH_3COOC_2H_5+H_2O$
2. To 1 mL of water extract (or 1 mL of sodium carbodate extract neutralized with dil acetic acid) add carefully neutral $FeCl_3$ solution.	A red colouration may be due to acetate. Now dilute and boil the liquid. A brown ppt. of basic ferric acetate is formed. $3CH_3COOH+FeCl_3 \rightarrow Fe(CH_3COO)_3+3HCl$ $Fe(CH_3COO)_3+2H_2O \rightarrow Fe(OH)_2CO.COCH_3+2CH_3COOH$
3. Mix a pinch of solid mixture with equal volume of pure $Ca(OH)_2$ and heat the test tube strongly. Pass the evolved vapours into a solution of of 2,4-dinitrophenylhydrazine.	The formation of a yellow ppt. or turbidity confirms acetate $Ca(OH)_2+2CH_3COOH \rightarrow 2H_2O+Ca(CH_3COO)_2 \rightarrow CH_3COCH_3$ $\begin{matrix}CH_3\diagdown\\ CH_3\diagup\end{matrix}CO+H_2N.NH.C_6H_3.(NO_3)_2 \rightarrow$ $\begin{matrix}CH_3\diagdown\\ CH_3\diagup\end{matrix}C{=}N.NH.C_6H_3(NO_3)_2$

4. Take a small quantity of the mixture and oxalic acid on the palm and moisten it with water and then rub between the thumb and the fore-finger.	If vinegar smell is given out, it confirms acetate. $2CH_3COONa + H_2C_2O_4 \rightarrow Na_2C_2O_4 + 2CH_3COOH$

Note 2,4-Dinitrophenylhydrazine can be prepared by dissolving 0.25 g solid 2,4-dinitrophenylhydrazine in a mixture of 42 mL of conc. HCl and 50 mL of water by warming on a water bath, then diluting it to 250 mL with water.

Confirmatory Tests of Cyanide

Experiment	*Observation*
1. Neutralize 2 mL sodium carbonate extract with dil. acetic acid and add a little yellow ammonium sulphide solution. Evaporate the solution to dryness in a china dish. Acidify the solution with dil. HCl and add few drops of $FeCl_3$.	A blood red colour appears, it confirms cyanide. $CN^- + (NH_4)_2S \rightleftharpoons SCN^- + (NH_4)_2S$ $Fe^{3+} + 3SCN^- \rightleftharpoons Fe(SCN)_3$
2. Acidify 2 mL sodium carbonate extract with dil. acetic acid. Add NaOH solution and $FeSO_4$ solution, now boil the solution and add dil. HCl followed by $FeCl_3$ solution.	A blue coloration or ppt. confirms cyanide.
3. Place a drop of the suspension of CuS on filter paper. To this add a drop of sodium carbonate extract.	If the brown colour of CuS disappears, it confirms cyanide. $2CuS + 10NaCN \rightarrow 2Na_3Cu(CN)_4 + 2N_2S + (CN)_2$

This test can be carried out in the presence of Br^-, I^-, $Fe(CN)_6^{4-}$ and $Fe(CN)_6^{3-}$.

Note Dissolve 0.2 g of $CuSO_4$ in 120 mL of water. To this add a few drops of ammonia solution. Pass H_2S gas through it. The final solution is called suspension of copper sulphide.

Confirmatory Tests of Chloride

	Experiment	*Observation*
1.	Acidify 2-3 mL of sodium carbonate extract with dil. HNO_3. Boil the solution to expel CO_2. To this add silver nitrate solution.	If a white ppt. is obtained, this confirms chloride provided it is soluble in ammonia but insoluble in conc. HNO_3. $AgNO_3+NaCl \rightarrow AgCl+NaNO_3$ (white ppt.) $AgCl+2NH_3 \rightarrow [Ag(NH_3)_2]Cl$ (soluble)
2.	Take 0.2 g of the mixture in a dry test tube. To this add a pinch of manganese dioxide and 2-3 mL of conc. H_2SO_4. Heat the test tube.	Evolution of greenish yellow gas having a pungent irritating odour which turns moist starch iodide paper blue confirms chloride. $MgCl_2+H_2SO_4 \rightarrow MgSO_4+2HCl$ $MnO_2+H_2SO_4 \rightarrow MnSO_4+H_2O+(O)$ $2HCl+(O) \rightarrow H_2O+Cl_2$ (greenish yellow gas)
3.	*Chromyl chloride test* Take 0.5 g of the dry mixture in a dry test tube. To this add 0.5 g of powdered $K_2Cr_2O_7$ and 2 mL conc. H_2SO_4. Heat the tube and pass the red vapours of chromyl chloride through dil. NaOH solution.	If a yellow solution is obtained, acidify this with acetic acid and add 1-2 mL of lead acetate solution. The formation of a yellow ppt. of lead chromate soluble in NaOH confirms chloride. $4NaCl+K_2Cr_2O_7+3H_2SO_4 \rightarrow K_2SO_4+2Na_2SO_4+3H_2O+2CrO_2Cl_2$ (red vapours) $CrO_2Cl_2+4NaOH \rightarrow Na_2CrO_4+2NaCl+2H_2O$ (yellow sol.) $Na_2CrO_4+(CH_3COO)_2Pb \rightarrow PbCrO_4+2CH_3COONa$ (yellow ppt.)
4.	*Sodium arsenite test* Acidify 2-3 mL of sodium carbonate extract with dil. HNO_3. Boil the solution to expel CO_2 and add $AgNO_3$ solution.	A white ppt. obtained is treated with sodium arsenite solution when formation of a yellow ppt. confirms chloride. $Na_3AsO_3+3AgCl \rightarrow Ag_3AsO_3+3NaCl$ (yellow ppt.)

Notes (1) Chromyl chloride test fails in such mixtures which contain heavy metal chlorides like $HgCl_2$, Hg_2Cl_2, $SnCl_2$, AgCl, etc. In such cases, the test can be performed from the residue obtained after evaporating 10 mL of sodium carbonate extract in a china dish.

(2) The mixture which contains iodide does not respond to this test. In such cases, only the liberation of chlorine will occur which confirms the presence of chloride.

(3) This test serves as a distinctive test for chloride because silver bromide and silver iodide are not affected by sodium arsenite solution.

Confirmatory Tests of Bromide

	Experiment	*Observation*
1.	Acidify 2-3 mL of sodium carbonate extract with dil. HNO_3. Boil off CO_2. To this add $AgNO_3$ solution.	The formation of a light yellow ppt. sparingly soluble in dil. ammonia confirms bromide. $NaBr + AgNO_3 \rightarrow AgBr + NaNO_3$ (light yellow ppt.)
2.	Neutralize 2 mL of sodium carbonate extract with dil. HCl. Boil off CO_2. To this add 2 mL of CS_2 or CCl_4 or $CHCl_3$. Then to this add chlorine water drop by drop and shake.	The formation of yellow or orange colour in organic solvent confirms bromide. $2NaBr + Cl_2 \rightarrow 2NaCl + Br_2$; $Br_2 + CS_2$; Orange colour in CS_2 layer.
3.	Heat 0.5 g of the mixture with 0.5 g of MnO_2 and 3-4 mL of conc. H_2SO_4.	Brown vapours of bromine are evolved which turn moist starch paper yellow. This confirms bromide. $2KB_2 + H_2SO_4 \rightarrow K_2SO_4 + 2HBr$; $MnO_2 + H_2SO_4 \rightarrow MnSO_4 + H_2O + (O)$; $2HBr + (O) \rightarrow H_2O + Br_2$ (brown vapours)

Confirmatory Tests of Iodide

	Experiment	*Observation*
1.	Neutralize 2 mL of sodium carbonate extract with dil. HNO_3. Boil off CO_2. To the remainder add $AgNO_3$ solution.	The formation of pale yellow ppt. insoluble in ammonia solution confirms iodide. $NaI + AgNO_3 \rightarrow AgI + NaNO_3$ (pale yellow ppt.)

2. Acidify 2 mL of sodium carbonate extract with dil. HCl. Boil off CO_2. To this add, in drops, 2 mL of CS_2 or $CHCl_3$ or CCl_4 and chlorine water. Shake the test tube.	The formation of violet colour in organic layer which disappears on the addition of excess of chlorine water confirms iodide. $2NaI + Cl_2 \rightarrow 2NaCl + I_2$ $I_2 + CS_2$; violet colour in CS_2 layer. $5Cl_2 + I_2 + 6H_2O \rightarrow 2HIO_3 + 10HCl$
3. Heat 0.5 g of the mixture with 0.5 g of solid MnO_2 and 3-4 mL of conc. H_2SO_4.	The formation of violet vapours of iodine which turn starch paper blue confirms iodide. $2KI + H_2SO_4 \rightarrow K_2SO_4 + 2HI$ $MnO_2 + H_2SO_4 \rightarrow MnSO_4 + H_2O +$ (O); $2HI + (O) \rightarrow H_2O + I_2$ (violet vapours)

Confirmatory Tests of Fluoride

Experiment	*Observation*
1. Acidify 2-3 mL of sodium carbonate extract with dil. acetic acid, boil off CO_2 and add $CaCl_2$ solution.	A white ppt. insoluble in dil. H_2SO_4 confirms fluoride. $Ca^{2+} + 2F^- \rightarrow CaF_2$ (white ppt.)
2. Take a small amount of the Mixture in dry test tube and add an equal amount of sand and 1-2 mL of conc. H_2SO_4.	A white waxy ppt. deposits on the glass rod confirms fluoride $SiO_2 + 4H^+ + 4F^- \rightarrow SiF_4 + 2H_2O$ $3SiF_4 + 4H_2O \rightarrow H_4SiO_4 + 2H_2SiF_6$ silicic acid (white waxy ppt.) hydrofluo silicic acid

Confiramatory Tests of Nitrate

Experiment	*Observation*
1. *Diphenylamine Test* To the water extract (all nitrates are water soluble) or	If a blue ring is formed at the zone of the contact of the two liquids, this confirms nitrate.

sodium carbonate extract (2 mL) neutralized with dil. H_2SO_4 add a few mL of diphenylamine reagent in a test tube.

$$2(C_6H_5)_2NH+(O)\rightarrow(C_6H_5)_2N-N(C_6H_5)_2+H_2O$$
(blue)

2. *Ring Test*

To 2-3 mL of water extract or 2-3 mL of sodium carbonate extract neutralized with dil. H_2SO_4, add 2-3 mL of reshly prepared ferrous sulphate solution. Pour conc. H_2SO_4 slowly in a thin stream along the sides of the test tube (Fig. 2.3).

A brown black ring at the junction of two layers confirms nitrate.

$$Cu(NO_3)_2+H_2SO_4\rightarrow CuSO_4+2HNO_3$$

$$6FeSO_4+2HNO_3+3H_2SO_4\rightarrow 3Fe_2(SO_4)_3+2NO+4H_2O$$

$$FeSO_4+NO\rightarrow FeSO_4.NO$$
(dark brown ring)

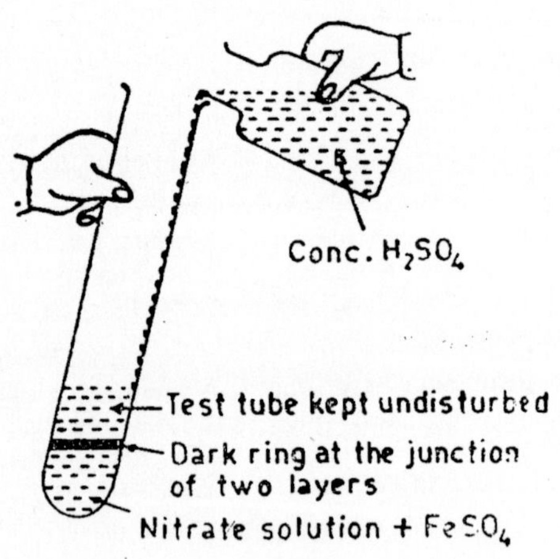

Fig. 2.3. Ring test for nitrate.

Notes (1) The ring test fails when nitrite is present even in traces. This happens because nitrite forms a black solution when ferrous sulphate solution is added.

(2) The ring test also fails in the presence of bromide or iodide or both when present along with nitrate in the mixture.

(3) Diphhenylamine reagent is prepared by dissolving 0.4 g of diphenylamine in 80 mL of conc, sulphuric acid followed by the addition of 20 mL of water.

Confirmately Tests of Oxalate

Experiment	Observation
1. Acidify 2-3 mL of sodium carbonate extract with very dil. acetic acid and boil off CO_2. To this add $CaCl_2$ solution. If a white ppt. is obtained, dissolve it in minimum quantity of dil. H_2SO_4 and to this add a few drops of $KMnO_4$ solution.	If pink colour is discharged on warming, it confirms oxalate. $\begin{array}{l}COONa\\ \vert\\ COONa\end{array} + CaCl_2 \rightarrow \begin{array}{l}COO\\ \vert\\ COO\end{array}\!\!>Ca + 2NaCl$ (white ppt.) $\begin{array}{l}COO\\ \vert\\ COO\end{array}\!\!>Ca + H_2SO_4 \rightarrow \begin{array}{l}COOH\\ \vert\\ COOH\end{array} + CaSO_4$ $2MnO_4^- + 6H^+ + 5H_2C_2O_4 \rightarrow 2Mn^{2+} + 10CO_2 + 8H_2O$ (colourless)
2. Acidify sodium carbonate extract with dil. acetic acid Boil off CO_2. To this add ferrous sulphate solution.	If a yellow ppt. is formed, it confirms oxalate. $2C_2O_4^{2-} + Fe^{2+} \rightarrow Fe(C_2O_4)_2^{2-}$

Confirmatory Tests of Tartrate

Experiment	Observation
1. Neutralize 2-3 mL of sodium carbonate extract with dil. acetic acid and boil off CO_2. Add NH_4OH till it smells of ammonia, boil the solution from some time to expel excess of NH_3. Take a little $AgNO_3$ solution in a clean test tube and add very dil. NH_4OH until the ppt. Ag_2O is nearly, but not quite redissolved. Mix the two solutions and warm the solution gradually nearly to the boiling point.	A bright silver mirror deposition on the inner surface of the tube confirms tartrate. $2Ag^+ + 2OH^- \rightarrow Ag_2O + H_2O$ $5Ag_2O + CuH_4O_6^{2-}$ $10Ag + 4CO_2 + H_2O + 2OH^-$ (silver mirror)

2. Neutralize 2-3 mL of sodium carbonate extract as above and add 1-2 drops of saturated solution of $FeSO_4$ followed by the addition of 2 drops of 20 vol. H_2O_2 and excess of NaOH solution and a drop of $FeCl_3$ solution.	A deep-violet or blue colouration confirms tartrate.

Confirmatory Tests of Citrate

Experiment	*Observation*
1. Neutralize 2-3 mL of sodium carbonate extract as in case of tartrate and add $CaCl_2$ solution. Boil the solution for several minutes. *Note* In the case of tartrate ppt. appears in cold.	A crystalline white ppt. confirms citrate. $3Ca^{2+} + 2C_6H_5O_7^{3-} \rightarrow Ca_3(C_6H_5O_7)_2$
2. Prepare neutral solution of sodium carbonate extract as above and add $AgNO_3$ solution. A white ppt. (silver citrate) is obtained which is dissolved in NH_4OH. Heat the solution at 60°C; no silver mirror is obtained. Boil the solution. *Note* In tartrate silver mirror is readily obtained.	A bright silver mirror is gradually produced.
3. Acidify 2-3 mL of sodium carbonate extract with dil acetic acid and boil off CO_2. To this add 0.5 mL of Deniges Reagent, boil the solution and add few drops of 0.1N $KMnO_4$ solution.	The purple colour of $KMnO_4$ is discharged and a white ppt of $HgSO_4.2HgO.2CO(CH_2COO)_2Hg$ is obtained.

This test is very sensitive but the interference is caused by the presence of halides.

Note Deniges reagent may be prepared by dissolving 1 g of mercuric oxide in 20 mL of water and 4 mL of conc. sulphuric acid.

Confirmatory Tests of Chlorate

	Experiment	*Observation*
1.	Add 1 mL of conc. H_2SO_4 to the water extract or sodium carbonate extract (1-2 mL) followed by 2-3 mL of aqueous solution of aniline sulphate	A deep blue colouration confirms chlorate.
2.	Neutralize 2 mL of sodium carbonate extract with dil. HNO_3 and add 1-2 mL of $AgNO_3$ solution and H_2SO_3 solution (Na_2SO_3+HCl).	A white ppt. confirms chlorate $NaClO_3+3H_2SO_3 \rightarrow NaCl+2H_2SO_4$ $NaCl+AgNO_3 \rightarrow AgCl+NaNO_3$
3.	Add zinc dust and NaOH solution into sodium carbonate extract, boil the solution and remove uncreated zinc dust. Acidify the filtrate with dil. HNO_3 and add $AgNO_3$ solution.	A white ppt confirms chlorate $ClO_3^-+Zn+2OH^- \rightarrow Cl^-+(ZnO_2)_2^-+H_2O$ $Cl^-+Ag^+ \rightarrow AgCl$

Confirmatory Tests of Sulphate

	Experiment	*Observation*
1.	*$BaCl_2$ test* Acidify 2 mL of sodium carbonate extract with dil. HCl. Boil off CO_2. To this add $BaCl_2$ solution.	A white ppt. (insoluble in conc. HCl or conc. HNO_3) confirms sulphate. $MgSO_4+BaCl_2 \rightarrow BaSO_4+2MgCl_2$
2.	*Lead acetate test* Acidify 2 mL of sodium carbonate extract with dil. acetic acid. Boil off CO_2. To this and lead acetate solution	A white ppt. (soluble in excess of hot ammonium acetate solution) confirms sulphate. $MgSO_4+(CH_3COO)_2Pb$ $PbSO_4+(CH_3COO)_2Mg$ (white ppt.)

3. *Match-stick test* Acidify 2 mL of sodium carbonate extract with dil HCl. Boil off CO_2. To this add $BaCl_2$ solution. Filter the solution. Reject the filtrate and mix the ppt. with solid Na_2CO_3 to get a paste. Apply this paste on the end of a carbonized match-stick and fuse this end in the reducing flame. Dip the fused mass into sodium nitroprusside solution taken in a china dish.	If violet streaks are produced, this confirms sulphate. $BaCl_2+ZnSO_4 \rightarrow BaSO_4+ZnCl_2$ $Na_2CO_3+BaSO_4 \rightarrow Na_2SO_4+BaCO_3$ $Na_2SO_4+C \rightarrow Na_2S+4CO$ $Na_2S+Na_2[Fe(CN)_5NO] \rightarrow Na_4[Fe(CN)_5NOS]$ (violet).

Confirmatory Tests of Phosphate

Experiment	*Observation*
1. *Ammonium molybdate test* Acidify 2-3 mL of sodium carbonate extract with dil. nitric acid. To this add 2-3 mL of conc. nitric acid followed by the addition of 5 mL of ammonium molybdate solution.	A slow formation of canary yellow ppt. confirms the presence of phosphate $Na_2HPO_4+12(NH_4)_2MoO_4 +23HNO_3 \rightarrow (NH_4)_3PMO_{12}O_{40}+2NaNO_2+$ (canary yellow ppt.) $21NH_4NO_3+12H_2O$
2. *Magnesis mtxture test* To 2-3 mL of sodium carbonate extract add 2-4 mL of magnesia mixture. A white ppt. is obtained. Treat this ppt. with silver nitrate solution containing a few drops of acetic acid.	If ppt. turns yellow, it confirms phosphate. $Na_2HPO_4+Mg(NO_3)_2+NH_3 \rightarrow Mg(NH_4)PO_4+2NaNO_3$ (white ppt.)

Confirmatory Tests of of Borate

Expertment	*Observation*
1. *Glycerine-methyl alcohol test* Mix 0.2 g of the mixture with 1 mL of glycerine in a test tube.	If the gas evolved burns with green flame, borate is confirmed.

To this add 1 mL of methyl alcohol. Heat the test tube on a free flame and ignite the issuing gas (Fig. 2.4).

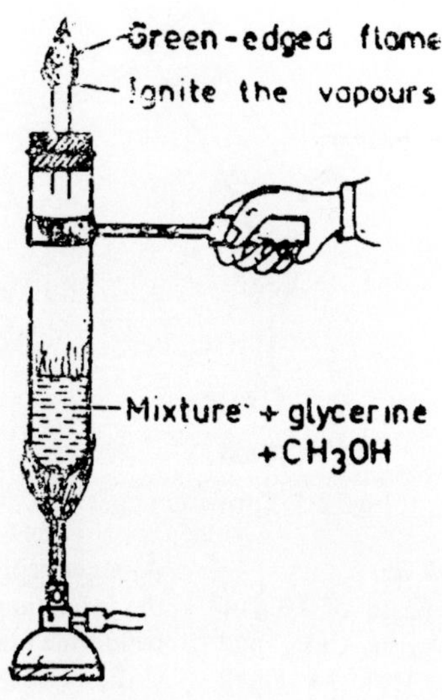

Fig. 2.4 Test for borate.

2. *Silver nitrate test*
Neutralize 2 mL of sodium carbonate extract with dil. HNO_3 To this add $AgNO_3$ solution.

If a white ppt. is obtained which on boiling turns brown or black, this identifies borate

$$Ag^+ + BO_2^- \rightarrow AgBO_2 \text{ (white ppt.)}$$

$$2AgBO_2 + 3H_2O \rightarrow Ag_2O \text{ (brown or black ppt.)} + 2H_3BO_3$$

3. *Turmeric paper test*
Dissolve 0.2 g of the mixture in minimum quantity of dil. HCl. Dip a piece of turmeric paper into this solution. Dry it by wrapping it round a test tube containing boiling water (Fig. 2.5).

The colour of the turmeric paper turns brown. Place a drop of sodium hydroxide solution on the dried turmeric paper. A green or dirty blue spot on the paper identifies borate.

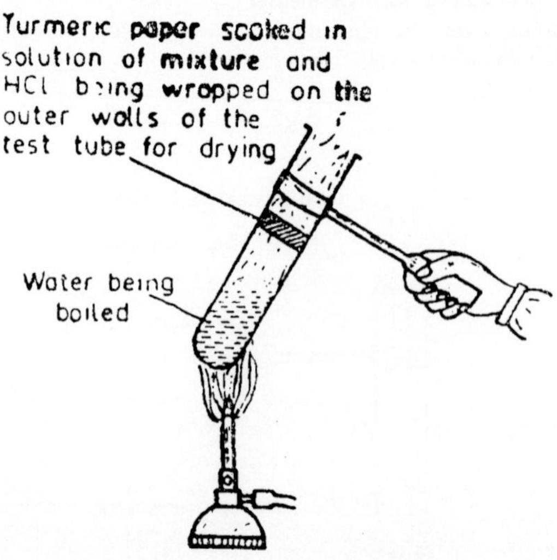

Fig. 2.5 Turmeric paper test.

4. *Calcium fluoride test* Make a thin paste of 0.2 g of solid mixture with CaF_2 and conc. H_2SO_4. Hold a small quantity of this paste at the end of a glass rod and put it near the edge of the flame of a Bunsen burner.	A green coloured flame due to the formation of volatile brown trifluoride identifies borate. $CaF_2+H_2SO_4 \rightarrow CaSO_4+2HF$ $H_3BO_3+3HF \rightarrow BF_3+3H_2O$ (volatile)

Confirmatory Tests of Chromate

Experiment	*Observation*
1. Neutralize 0.2 mL of sodium carbonate extract with acetic acid and add $AgNO_3$ solution.	A brownish red ppt. insoluble in dil. HNO_3 and NH_4OH $CrO_4^{2-}+2Ag^+ \rightarrow Ag_2CrO_4$
2. Neutralize 2 mL of sodium carbovate extract with acetic acid and add lead acetate solution	A yellow ppt. insoluble in acetic acid but soluble in dil. HNO_3 and NaOH confirms chromate $Pb^{2+}+CrO_4^{2-} \rightarrow PbCrO_4$
3. Acidify the water extract with dil. H_2SO_4 and add 2 mL of amyl alcohol and 1 mL of H_2O_2 dropwise	On shaking organic layer turns blue, it confirms chromate $Cr_2O_7^{2-}+4H_2O_2+2H^+ \rightarrow 2CrO_5+5H_2O$

Confirmatory Tests of Dichromate

Experiment	*Observation*
1. Acidify water extract with dil. H_2SO_4 and add $FeSO_4$ solution.	A green colouration confirms dichromate. $Cr_2O_7^{2-} + 6Fe^{2+} + 14H^+ \rightarrow 2Cr^{3+} + 6Fe^{3+} + 7H_2O$
2. Add $AgNO_3$ solution into water extract.	A reddish brown ppt. confirms dichromate which on boiling changes into less soluble Ag_2CrO_4. $2Ag^+ + Cr_2O_7^{2-} \rightarrow Ag_2Cr_2O_7$ $2Ag_2Cr_2O_7 + H_2O \rightarrow 2Ag_2CrO_4 + H_2Cr_2O_7$

Confirmatory Tests of Thiocyanate

Experiment	*Observation*
1. Acidify 2 mL sodium cabonate extract with dil. HCl and add $FeCl_3$ solution; it gives blood red colour. Add NH_4F or $HgCl_2$ or $Na_2C_2O_4$.	Blood red colour disappears, it confirms thiocyanate. $Fe(SCN)^{2+} + 6F^- \rightarrow FeF_6^{3-} + SCN^-$
2. Neutralize sodium carbonate extract with dil. HCl and add dil. solution of a mixture of pyridine and copper sulphate followed by chloroform.	On shaking well chloroform layer turns green. $Cu^{2+} + 2C_5H_5N + 2SCN^- \rightarrow Cu(C_5H_5N)_2(SCN)_2$
3. Acidify 2 mL sodium carbonate extract with dil. HCl and add $Co(NO_3)_2$ solution and amyl alcohol.	On shaking amyl alcohol layer turns blue. $Co^{2+} + 4SCN^-$ $Co(SCN)_4^{2-}$

Confirmatory Tests of Ferrocyanide

Experiment	*Observation*
1. Acidify 2 mL sodium carbonate extract with dil. H_2SO_4 and	A white ppt. of ferrous-ferric cyanide changing into pale biue ppt.

add few drops of $FeSO_4$ solution.	of ferric ferrocyanide, it confirms ferrocyanide.
2. Acidify 2 mL sodium carbonate extract with dil. HCl and add ammonium molybdate solution.	A brown ppt. of molybdenyl ferrocyanide confirms ferrocyanide.
3. Acidify 2 mL sodium carbonate extract with dil. HCl and add $FeCl_3$ solution.	A blue ppt. insoluble in dil. HCl but soluble in conc. HCl confirms ferrocyanide. $Na^+ + Fe^{3+} + Fe(CN)_6^{4-} \rightarrow NaFe[Fe(CN)_6]$ $NaFe[Fe(CN)_6] + 3OH^- \rightarrow Fe(OH)_3 + Fe(CN)_6^{4-} + Na^+$

Confirmatory Tests of Ferricyanide

Experimeet	*Observation*
1. The water extract of the mixture is treated with a solution of $FeSO_4$.	A deep blue ppt. confirmrs ferricyanide.
2. The water extract is treated with $AgNO_3$ solution dropwise.	A brick red ppt. appears, which is insoluble in cold dil. HNO_3 but soluble in NH_4OH. $Fe(CN)_6^{3-} + 3Ag^+ \rightarrow Ag_3Fe(CN)_6$ it confirms ferricyanide.
3. Acidify 2 mL sodium carbonate extract and add $FeCl_3$ solution.	A brown colouration confirms ferricyanide. $Fe(CN)_6^{3-} + Fe^{3+} \rightarrow Fe[Fe(CN)_6]$

Confirmatory Tests of Arsenite

Experiment	*Observation*
1. Add $BaCl_2$ solution into neutral solution of sodium carbonate extract.	A white ppt. soluble in dil. HCl confirms arsenite. $3Ba^{2+} + 2AsO_3^{3-} \rightarrow Ba(AsO_3)_2$

2. Add 2 mL of conc. HCl to a few drops of test solution. Now add saturated solution of $SnCl_2$ and heat gently.	The solution brown to black confirms arsenite. $AsO_3^{3-} + 6H^+ \rightarrow As^{3+} + 3H_2O$ $2As^{3+} + 3Sn^{3+} \rightarrow 2As + 3Sn^{4+}$
3. Add. $AgNO_3$ solution to the neutral solution of the test sample.	A yellow ppt. soluble in NH_4OH and HNO_3 confirms arsenite. $AsO_3^{3-} + 3Ag^+ \rightarrow Ag_3AsO_3$ $Ag_3AsO_3 + 6NH_3 \rightarrow [Ag(NH_3)_2]_3AsO_3$ $Ag_3AsO_3 + 3H^+ \rightarrow H_3AsO_3 + 3Ag^+$

In the presence Cl^-, Br^- and I^-, the test is made as follows:

Acidify the test solution with HNO_3 and add $AgNO_3$ solution in excess Filter the precipitated silver salts and make the filtrate neutral by adding ammonia. At the neutral zone formed by ammonia above the acid solution a yellow precipitate of silver arsenite will be formed.

Confirmatory Tests of Arsenate

Experiment	*Observation*
1. Add $AgNO_3$ solution to the neutral solution of the test solution.	A redeish brown ppt. soluble in NH_4OH and HCl confirms arsenate $AsO_4^{3-} + 3Ag^+ \rightarrow Ag_3AsO_4$ $Ag_3AsO_4 + 3H^+ \rightarrow H_3AsO_4 + 3Ag^+$ $Ag_3AsO_4 + 6NH_3 \rightarrow [Ag(NH_3)_2]_3.AsO_4$
2. Acidify 2 mL of sodium carbonate extract with conc. HCl and pass H_2S gas for long time in hot.	A yellow ppt. confirms arsenate $2H_3AsO_4 + 5H_2S \rightarrow As_2S_5 + 8H_2O$
3. Acidify 2 mL of sodium carbonate extract with dil. HNO_3 and add ammonium molybdate solution and boil.	A yellow ppt. soluble in NH_4OH and NaOH confirms arsenate. $AsO_4^{3-} + 12(NH_4)_2MoO_4 + 24H^+ \rightarrow (NH_4)_3AsO_4.12MoO_3 + 12H_2O + 12NH_4^+$

TESTS OF SPECIAL COMBINATION OF ANIONIC RADICALS

A given mixture may contain a combination of two or more and such anionic radicals which connot be confirmed by their usual tests because the presence of one anion may interfere in the tests of other anions. Some of these combinations are given below:

1. *Carbonate in the presence of Sulphite* Sulphite interferes in the lime-water test for carbonate because both SO_2 and CO_2 turn lime-water milky.

$$Ca(OH)_2 + CO_2 \rightarrow CaCO_3 + H_2O$$

$$Ca(OH)_2 + SO_2 \rightarrow CaSO_3 + H_2O$$

The following procedure is odopted for the identification of carbonate in presence of sulphite.

Take a small amount of mixture (solid) and an equal quantity of solid $K_2Cr_2O_7$ in a test tube. Now add dil. H_2SO_4, heat and pass the evolved gas through lime-water. If the lime water turns milky, carbonate or bicarbonate is present.

Turning of solution (in the test tube which is being heated) green, confirms sulphite.

$$Cr_2O_7^{2-} + 2H^+ + 3SO_2 \rightarrow \underset{\text{(green)}}{2Cr^{3+}} + H_2O + 3SO_4^{2-}$$

2. *Nitrate in the presence of Nitrite* Both nitrite and nitrate liberate NO_2 gas. Hence nitrite must be removed completely before testing for nitrate.

Acidify Na_2CO_3 extract with dil. H_2SO_4 and heat with excess of solid urea or NH_4Cl. Nitrite will be decomposed into N_2.

$$2NO_2^- + NH_2CONH_2 + 2H^+ \rightarrow 2N_2 + 3H_2O + CO_2$$

$$NO_2 + NH_4^+ \rightarrow N_2 + 2H_2O$$

Divide the solution into two parts for testing nitrate.

(a) To part I, ring test is carried out as described earlier.

(b) To part II add dil. H_2SO_4 in order to make it acidic. Add a crystal of KI and 1 mL of starch solution. Absence of blue colour shows the complete removal of nitrite. Now add zinc dust and heat. Appearance of blue colour confirms nitrate.

$$Zn \rightarrow Zn^{2+} + 2e^-$$
$$NO_3^- + 2H^+ + e^- \rightarrow NO_2^- + H_2O$$
$$I^- + H^+ \rightarrow HI$$
$$2HI + 2NO_2^- + 2H^+ \rightarrow 2NO + I_2 + 2H_2O$$
$$I_2 + \text{Starch} \rightarrow \text{Blue coloured complex}$$

3. *Nitrate in the presence of Bromide and/or Iodide* The ring test of nitrate is interfered by iodide and to a smaller extent by bromide due to the colour of the liberated iodine/bromine. In such cases halogen shold be removed before proceeding for ring test.

Method I To the water extract of mixture add excess of ammoniacal silver sulphate solution. Filter the ppt. containing AgBr and/or AgI. Perform ring test in the filtrate.

$$Ag^+ + X^- \rightarrow AgX \qquad (X^- = Br^-, I^-)$$

Method II Boil the water extract with excess of Cl_2 water in a dish, till no more Br_2 or I_2 evolves. Now perform the ring test.

$$2X^- + Cl_2 \rightarrow 2Cl^- + X_2 \qquad (X = Br, I)$$

Alternative procedure Acidify Na_2CO_3 extract with dil. H_2SO_4. Add a few crystals of KI and starch solution followed by the addition of zinc. Appearance of blue colour indicates nitrate.

4. *Chloride, bromide and iodide in presence of each other* These anionic constituents are detected in presence of each other in the following ways.

Mathod I Neutralize sodium carbonate extract with dil. H_2SO_4, add solid $NaNO_2$ and boil the contents. Appearance of violet vapour of iodine indicates iodide.

Go on adding $NaNO_2$ till the of iodine is completely removed. (This is indicated by the appearence of brown vapours of NO_2). Continue heating to get a clear solution. Cool and add $NaHCO_3$ (solid) so that solution becomes alkaline. Now add conc. HNO_3 and heat the solution when it becomes brown; bromide is present.

Next boil the above solution by adding more of conc. HNO_3 to expel as much of bromine as possible. Now add $AgNO_3$ solution. A white curdy ppt. (AgCl) soluble in NH_4OH confirms chloride.

Method II Chromyl chloride test is performed for Cl^- as described earlier while iodide and bromide can be identified as follows:

Take Na_2CO_3 extract, acidify with dil. HCl, add a few drops of CCl_4 or CS_2. Now add Cl_2 water drop by drop with shaking. If CCl_4/CS_2 layer turns violet, iodide is present.

Add successively Cl_2– water and convert iodide completely to iodate on shaking. Violet colour in CCl_4/CS_2 fades away and ultimately CCl_4/CS_2 layer becomes colourless when bromide is absent, or reddish brown when bromide is present.

Method III Acidify Na_2CO_3 extract with dil. H_2SO_4. Now add solid ferric ammonium sulphate and heat. Appearance of violet vapours of I_2 confirms I^-.

Expel completely I_2 gas from the mixture by heating and add a crystal of $KMnO_4$ and heat again. Br_2 gas is evolved.

After expelling all the Br_2 gas, filter and test the filtrate for Cl^- with $AgNO_3$ solution.

5. *Sulphide, sulphite, sulphate and thiosulphate in presence of each other* If a mixture containing these anionic constituents is treated with dil. H_2SO_4, H_2S is evolved from sulphide while SO_2 is liberated from sulphite and thiosulphate. These different gases are evolved at the same time and their identification is difficult. Following method is adopted for identifying these radicals:

Take Na_2CO_3 extract and shake it with $Cd(NO_3)_2$ or $CdCO_3$ solution. Heat for 2-3 min and filter.

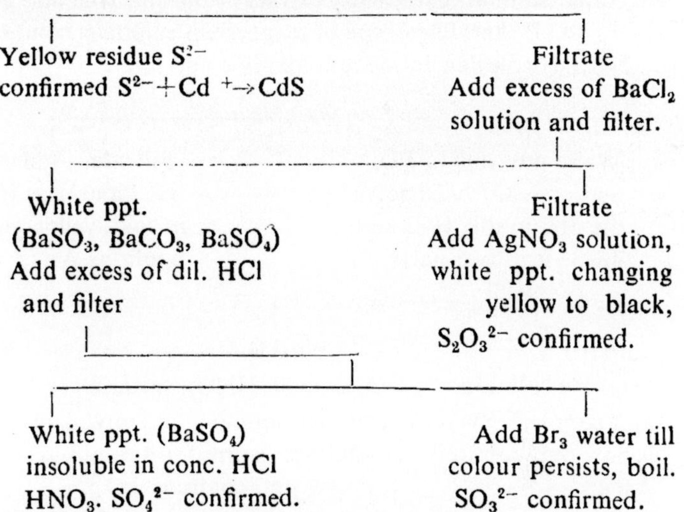

6. *Carbonate in the presence of oxalate* Both carbonate and oxalate are decomposed by conc. H_2SO_4. Carbonates are also decomposed by dilute acids. Therefore, oxalates can be analysed by first destroying carbonates.

Heat the mixture with excess of dil. H_2SO_4 till there is no effervescence. Now add MnO_2 powder. Fresh effervescence starts due to the decomposition of oxalate.

$$C_2O_4^{2-}+MnO_2+4H^{+}\rightarrow Mn^{2+}+2H_2O+2CO_2$$

7. *Oxalate in the presence of fluoride* Both oxalate and fluoride yield a white ppt. with $CaCl_2$ solution.

Acidify Na_2CO_3 extract with acetic acid and add $CaCl_2$ solution. A white ppt. of CaC_2O_4 and CaF_2 is obtained. The ppt. is treated with hot dil. H_2SO_4 in which CaC_2O_4 is soluble. Filter the solution and test the residue for fluoride. To the filtrate add few drops of $KMnO_4$ solution which is decolourized in the presence of oxalate.

8. *Phosphate in the presence of arsenite and arsenate* All these anions give yellow ppt. with conc. HNO_3 and ammonium molybdate.

Acidify sodium carbonate extract with dil. HCl and add NH_4Cl (solid) and few drops of magnesium sulphate solution. Add NH_4OH solution to make it alkaline and filter.

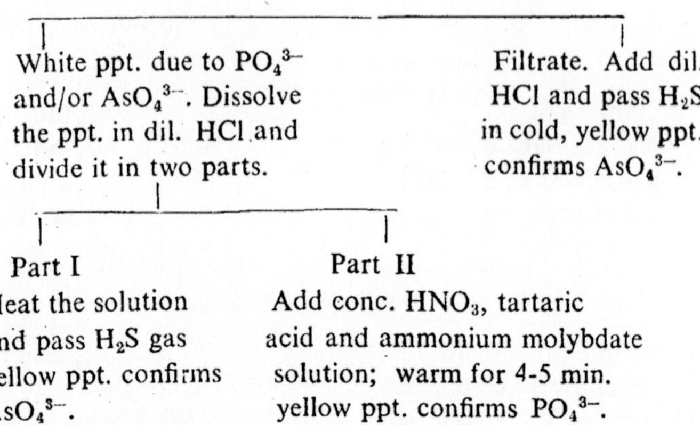

Note If AsO_4^{3-} is absent there is no need of adding tartaric acid.

INTERFERING RADICALS AND THEIR REMOVAL

Oxalate, tartrate, borate, fluoride and phosphate are known as interfering radicals because these radicals interfere in the regular course of detection of cations after II group. Infact the salts of these acidic radicals are soluble in acidic medium and become insoluble in neutral or alkaline medium.

Theory of Interference

The theory of interference can be explained on the basis of electrolytic dissociation. Consider calcium oxalate which is a salt of weak acid. The solution is acidic upto II group. Therefore CaC_2O_4 dissociates as follows:

$$CaC_2O_4 \rightarrow Ca^{2+} + C_2O_4^{2-}$$
$$2HCl \rightarrow 2Cl^- + 2H^+$$

$$\text{or} \quad Ca^{2+} + 2Cl^- \rightarrow \underset{\text{(highly ionized)}}{CaCl_2}$$

$$2H^+ + C_2O_4^{2-} \rightarrow \underset{\text{(feebly ionized)}}{H_2C_2O_4}$$

It is clear from the above reactions that oxalic acid forms which is feebly ionized and in the presence of HCl (highly ionized) the dissociation of $H_2C_2O_4$ is suppressed duo to common ion effect. Thus $[Ca^{2+}][C_2O_4^{2-}]$ is decreased and the CaC_2O_4 does not precipitate and remains in solution.

On the other hand, the solution in III group is alkaline on the addition of NH_4Cl and NH_4OH. NH_4OH and $H_2C_2O_4$ dissociate as follows:

$$2NH_4OH \rightarrow 2NH_4^+ + 2OH^-$$

$$H_2C_2O_4 \rightarrow C_2O_4^{2-} + 2H^+$$

$$\text{or} \quad 2NH_4^+ + C_2O_4^{2-} \rightarrow \underset{\text{(highly ionized)}}{(NH_4)_2C_2O_4}$$

$$2H^+ + 2OH^+ \rightarrow \underset{\text{(feebly ionized)}}{2H_2O}$$

Thus the ionization of $H_2C_2O_4$ is highly increased and $[C_2O_4^{2-}]$ is also increased in the solution. Due to this $[Ca^{2+}]$ $[C_2O_4^{2-}]$ is also increased and exceeds the solubility product of CaC_2O_4 so that it gets precipitated.

$$Ca^{2+} + (NH_4)_2C_2O_4 \rightarrow \underset{\text{(ppt.)}}{CaC_2O_4} + 2NH_4^+$$

The above theory of intereference of the oxalate is also applicable to other basic radicals as well as to other interfering radicals.

Removal of Oxalate and Tartrate

These can be removed simultaneously by the following method: Boil off H_2S from the filtrate of group II, if group II is present, by evaporating to dryness; otherwise, use the original mixture. Now add 4-5 mL conc. HNO_3 in paste (or mixture) taken in a porcelain dish and heat till it is almost dry. Repeat the same treatment 3-4 times. Extract the residue with dil. HCl and filter if necessary, use the filtrate for group III and others.

Theory Oxalate and tartrate changed into oxalic acid and tartaric acid respectively by the reaction with conc. HNO_3. These acids are easily decomposed in the presence of conc. HNO_3 as follows;

$$CaC_2O_4 + 2HNO_3 \rightarrow Ca(NO_3)_2 + H_2C_2O_4$$
$$CaC_4H_4O_6 + 2HNO_3 \rightarrow Ca(NO_3)_2 + H_2C_4H_4O_6$$
$$2HNO_3 \rightarrow H_2O + 2NO_2 + O$$
$$H_2C_2O_4 + O \rightarrow H_2O + 2CO_2$$
$$H_2C_4H_4O_6 + 4(O) \rightarrow 3H_2O + 3CO_2 + CO$$

Removal of Borate and Fluoride

These can be removed by the following method:

Boil off H_2S from the filtrate of group II by evaporating to dryness in a porcelain dish. Treat this residue or mixture with 3-4 mL conc. HCl and evaporate to almost dryness. Repeat the same treatment 3-4 times. Dissolve the residue in dil. HCl and filter if necessary, use the filterate for group III and others.

Theory Borate and fluoride change into boric acid and hydrofluoric acid respectively which volatilize

$$CaF_2 + 2HCl \rightarrow CaCl_2 + 2HF \uparrow$$
$$Ca_3(BO_3)_2 + 6HCl \rightarrow 3CaCl_2 + 2H_3BO_3 \uparrow$$

Removal of Phosphate

Phosphate is removed from the filtrate of group II. One of the following methods is used for the removal of phosphate.

(*i*) *Ferric Chloride Method* Test about 1-2mL of the filtrate of group II for iron. Boil off H_2S from the filtrate of group II and add few drops of conc. HN_3 (to change ferrous into ferric ion, if present) and heat the solution for 2 min.

To the solution, add NH_4Cl (solid) and NH_4OH till a clear smell of ammonia is obtained. It no ppt. is obtained then there is no need of removing phosphate. Now to the solution containing ppt. add 2-3 g of sodium acetate and glacial acetic acid till the smell of acetic acid is obtained. Add neutral ferric chloride solution dropwise with stirring until the solution acquires tea-colour. Now add to it NH_4OH till the smell of ammonia is obtained. Boil and filter.

Residue	*Filtrate* Concentrate to 10-15 mL and add 2 g of NH_4Cl and NH_4OH in slight excess. Boil and filter.	
Group III is present and test as usual. If no residue is obtained group III is absent	*Residue* Test for Al^{3+} and Cr^{3+} if not tested earlier.	*Filtrate* Test for groups IV, V and VI.

Theory The phosphates of group III (Al, Cr and Fe) are insoluble in sodium acetate and acetic acid buffer solution while phosphates of the group IV, V and VI are soluble. By adding neutral ferric chloride phosphate ions are removed as ferric phosphate.

$$Fe^{3+} + PO_4^{3-} \rightarrow FePO_4 \downarrow$$

The excess of iron is removed as basic ferric acetate by dilution and boling.

$$Fe^{3+} + 3CH_3COO^- \rightarrow Fe(CH_3COO)_3$$

$$Fe(CH_3COO)_3 + 2H_2O \rightarrow \underset{\text{basic ferric acetate}}{Fe(OH)_2.CH_3COO} + 2CH_3COOH$$

Ferric ion has been selected because:

(i) $FePO_4$ is the least soluble under the above conditions.

(ii) It is easy to test Fe^{3+} in the filtrate from the group II.

(iii) Excess of Fe^{3+} ion can be detected from the colour of the solution in filtrate.

Notes

(i) Avoid large evcess of $FeCl_3$ because $FePO_4$ is soluble in $FeCl_3$.

(ii) Use freshly prepared neutral ferric chloride solution.

(iii) Neutral ferric chtoride solution can be prepared by adding dil. NH_4OH (prepared by diluting 1mL of shelf NH_4OH with about 15-20 mL of water) to 2-3 drops of shelf $FeCl_3$ solution with shaking till a light ppt. persists. Boil, filter and the filtrate will be neutral ferric chloride solution.

(*ii*) *Zirconyl nitrate method* Boil off H_2S from the filtrate of group II and concentrate to almost dryness. Extract the residue, into 10 mL dil. HCl. Add 1 g of NH_4Cl and zirconyl nitrate solution dropwise with stirring until the precipitation is complete. Heat the solution to boil and filter.

Residue White ppt. of zirconyl phosphate, reject it.	*Filtrate* Test for eomplete precipitation of PO_4^{3-} by adding few drops of zirconyl nitrate. Filter the ppt. if any and add 1 g NH_4Cl in the filtrate and boil. Make the solution alkaline by adding NH_4OH, boil and filter.	
	Residue May contain hydroxides of group III and test for group III.	*Filtrate* Proceed for groups IV, V and VI in the systematic way

Theory Zirconyl nitrate is a specific reagent for PO_4^{3-} and forms the white ppt. of zirconyl phosphate and thus removes the intesfering phosphate.

$$Ca_3(PO_4)_2 + 2HCl \rightarrow 2Ca(HPO_4) + CaCl_2$$

$$ZrO(NO_3)_2 + 2Ca(HPO_4)_2 + 2HCl \rightarrow \underset{\text{(white ppt.)}}{ZrO(H_2PO_4)_2} + CaCl_2 + Ca(NO_3)_2$$

The excess of zirconyl ions is removed by adding NH_4OH,

$$ZrO(NO_3)_2 + 2NH_4OH \rightarrow \underset{\text{(white ppt.)}}{ZrO(OH)_2} + 2NH_4NO_3$$

Notes

(i) Dil. HCl should not be less than 1 N otherwise the precipitation will not be complete.

(ii) Excess of the reagent should be avoided otherwise there may by formation of colloidal solution.

(iii) Zirconyl nitrate solution is prepared by dissolving 10 g of zirconyl nitrate $ZrO(NO_3)_2.2H_2O$ in 6.5 mL of conc. HNO_3 and diluting to 100 mL with water. Boil the solution with stirring and keep for 25 h. Decant the solution clear and filter.

VIVA-VOCE

Q. 1 What do you understand by qualitative and quantitative analysis?

Ans. Qualitative analysis is to detect the constituents (ions or radicals) present in a substance. Quantitative analysis is to determine the amount of the individual components of a substance.

Q. 2 What is a salt?

Ans. Salt is formed by the interaction of an acid with a base for example.

$$HCl + NaOH \rightarrow NaCl + H_2O$$
$$\text{(acid)} \quad \text{(base)} \rightarrow \text{(salt)} \quad \text{(water)}$$

The salt has two parts (cation and anion), cation is called basic redical while anion is called acid or anionic radical.

Q. 3 What is mixture?

Ans. Mixture is a combination of two or more salts in any ratio.

Q. 4 Is there any difference between a base and an alkali?

Ans. Yes, the substance having a tendency of giving electrons is called base, e.g. alcohols, ethers, etc. Bases which are derived from alkali (Li, Na, K) or alkaline earth metals (Ca,Sr, Ba) and a few other similar to bases are called alkalis.

Q. 5 Name the burner which you use in the laboratory.

Ans. Bunsen burner.

Q. 6 Which gas do you use in the laboratory and how is it prepared?

Ans. Oil gas is used in the laboratary. It is a mixture of methane, ethane, ethylene and other hydrocarbons. It is produced by the cracking of petrol, kerosene oil or solvent oil in a gas generator.

Q. 7 What do you mean by an analytical reaction and reagent?

Ans. The chemical reaction taking place is known as an analytical reaction and the subtance causing it is called a reagent.

Q. 8 What do you understand by the terms specific and selective reagents or reactions?

Ans. Specific reagents (or reactions) are those, which are indicative of only one ion (or subtance) under experimental conditions. Selective reagents (or reactions) are those, which give a similar effect with only limited number of ions (or substances).

Q. 9 What do you mean by marco-, micro-, semimicro- and ultramicro-methods of qualitative analysis ?

Ans. See text.

Q. 10 What is a buffer solution?

Ans. See text.

Q. 11 What is common ion effect?

Ans. See text.

Q. 12 What do you mean by pH?

Ans. See text.

Q. 13 What do you understand by complex ion formation?

Ans. See text.

Q. 14 What is water extract and how is it prepared?

Ans. See text.

Q. 15 What for this extract is used?

Ans. It is generally used for the testing of nitrite, acetate, thiosulphate and nitrate ions because their salts are usually soluble in water.

Q. 16 What are the advantages of sodium carbonate extract?

Ans. See text.

Q. 17 Can we use sodium bicarbonate in place of sodium carbonate in preparing extract for acid radicals?

Ans. Sodium bicarbonate cannot be used because the bicarbonates of metals are water soluble and pass into the filtrate along with sodium salts of the anions present in the mixture.

Q. 18 What is lime-water?

Ans. Solution of calcium hydroxide $Ca(OH)_2$ is known as lime-water.

Q. 19 Can we use any other solution in place of lime water for detection of carbonates?

Ans. Yes, we can use $Mg(OH)_2$ solution in place of lime-water.

Q. 20 Why does potassium dichromate paper turn green in the test of a sulphite?

Ans. Due to the formation of green chromium sulphate.

$$K_2Cr_2O_7 + 3SO_2 + H_2SO_4 \rightarrow K_2SO_4 + Cr_2(SO_4)_3 + H_2O$$

Q. 21 What is the nature of the brown ring formed in the test nitrates?

Ans. The brown ring is due to the formation of $FeSO_4.NO$ or more accurately $[Fe(H_2O)_5NO]SO_4$.

Q. 22 Why is freshly prepared solution used for the test of nitrate and nitrite?

Ans. $FeSO_4$ solution on keeping is converted into basic ferric sulphate which is not suitable for the testing of nitrate and nitrite.

Q. 23 Can a paper dipped in $AgNO_3$ be used in place of a lead acetate paper in the detection of a sulphide?

Ans. Yes, a paper dipped in $AgNO_3$ when exposed to the vapours of H_2S turns black due to the formation of silver sulphide.

$$2AgNO_3 + H_2O \rightarrow Ag_2S + 2HNO_3$$

Q. 24 Why do bromides and iodides not respond to the chromyl chloride test?

Ans. Because chromyl bromide and chromyl iodide are not known. Instead bromine and iodine are evolved.

Q. 25 What are the substances which interfere in the chromyl chloride test?

Ans. Flouride (gives CrO_2F_2), nitrate and nitrate (give NOCl) and chlorate interfere. Chlorides of mercury due to insignificant ionization do not give this test.

Q. 26 Why is it that in the chloroform test of halides only the organic layer is coloured and not the aqueous layer?

Ans. Because bromine and iodine have much more solubility in organic solvents ($CHCl_3$, CCl_4, or CS_2) than in water.

Q. 27 Why should conc. HCl not be used in the test for a sulphate?

Ans. Barium chloride which is used for testing a sulphate may get precipitated in the presence of conc. HCl. The precipitated barium chloride may be mistaken for the ppt. of sulphate.

Q. 28 Why does there appear sometimes a white ppt. when the mixture is heated with conc. H_2SO_4 for testing acid radicals?

Ans. This suggests the presence of Ba^{2+}, Sr^{2+} and Pb^{2+} in the mixture because their sulphates being insoluble appear as a white ppt.

Q. 29 Can we use $BaCl_2$ in place of $Ba(NO_3)_2$ in the detection of sulphate?

Ans. Yes, we can use $Ba(NO_3)_2$ instead of $BaCl_2$ because only Ba^{2+} ions are required for the precipitation of sulphate as barium sulphate.

$$K_2SO_4+BaCl_2 \rightarrow BaSO_4+2KCl$$

$$K_2SO_4+Ba(NO_3)_2 \rightarrow \underset{\text{(ppt.)}}{BaSO_4}+2KNO_3$$

Q. 30 Why is silver nitrate solution kept in coloured bottles?

Ans. Silver nitrate solution is decomposed in direct sunlight into its oxide. Therefore, a coloured bottle is used to store silver nitrate to avoid its decomposition.

Q. 31 Why do you use a stoppered bottle for ammonium hydroxide solution?

Ans. Because ammonia will escape out leaving a dilute solution.

Q. 32 How do you account for a yellow ppt. obtained even in the absence of phosphate when the mixture is treated with conc. HNO_3 and ammonium molybdate?

Ans. The yellow ppt. is also obtained in case arsenic is present in the mixture.

Q. 33 What is chlorine water?

Ans. The solution of chlorine gas in water is called chlorine water.

$$H_2O+Cl_2 \rightarrow 2H^++Cl^-+ClO^-$$

Q. 34 Why do you use a stoppered bottle for lime-water?

Ans. Because it will turn milky by the atmospheric carbon dioxide.

$$Ca(OH)_2+CO_2 \rightarrow CaCO_3+H_2O$$

Q. 35 What are the interfering radicals?

Ans. See text.

Q. 36 How will you remove interfering radicals?

Ans. See text.

Q. 37 Why should neutral ferric chloride solution be used in the removal of phosphate?

Ans. Ferric chloride solution of the shelf usually contains free HCl which leads to incomplete precipitation of ferric phosphate.

Q. 38 Can $AlCl_3$ or $CrCl_3$ be used in place of $FeCl_3$ for the removal of PO_4^{3-}?

Ans. See text.

3

IDENTIFICATION OF CATIONIC RADICALS

SYSTEMATIC IDENTIFICATION OF CATIONS

The tests for cations i.e. basic radicals have been considered under the following hands:

(a) Preliminary tests (Dry tests)

(b) Tests in solution (Wet tests).

Preliminary Tests for Cation Although these tests may not lead to very conclusive results, yet these afford correct valuable information which may be helpful for the correct identification of cationic consituents by wet tests. Preliminary tests comprise the following:

Physical examination Examine the mixture carefully and draw inference, if any, as following:

(a) *Study of colour of the mixture* Observe the colour of the mixture.

Colour	*Inference*
Blue	**Copper salts**
Green	**Copper, nickel, ferrous, chromium salts**

Yellow	Ferric, cadmium, arsenic sulphide salts. lead iodide, chromate salts.
Red	Lead oxide (Pb_3O_4), HgO, AgI
White	Salts of K, NH_4, Mg, Ca, Ba, Sr, Zn, Pb, Cd, Al, etc.
Pink	Cobalt, manganese salts
Brown	Oxides of Pb, Fe, Cd, Bi
Black	Oxides of Cu, Co, Ni, Fe, Mn, sulphides of Pb, Bi, Cu, Hg, Co, Ni, and Ag

Note If the colour of mixture is white, it reveals that the salts of copper, iron, and nickel are absent.

(b) *Smell* From the smell of mixture, draw the inference as follows:

Smell	*Inference*
(i) Ammoniacal smell	Ammonium redical (NH_4^+)
(ii) Smell like that of rotten eggs	Sulphide (S^{2-})
(iii) Vinegar smell	Acetate (CH_3COO^-)

Note No characteristic smell should be inferred for the absence of these radicals.

(c) *Density* After feeling the weight of the mixture, draw the inference as follows:

Observation	*Inference*
(i) The mixture is too heavy	Salts of lead of barium
(ii) The mixture is too light or a fluffy power	Carbonates of zinc, magnesium and aluminium
(iii) The mixture is neither heavy nor light	Salts of lead, barium, aluminium magnesium and calcium may be absent.

(d) *Dry heating* Take a small quintity (0.5 g) of the mixture in a dry test tude. Hold the test tube in a horizontal position with its mouth slightly upwards (Fig. 3.1) first heat the test tube gently and then strongly and make necessary observations as given in the following table.

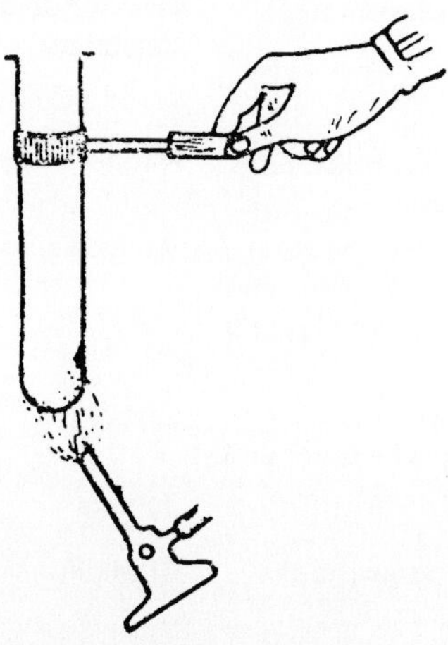

Fig. 3.1. Dry heating test.

Observation	*Inference*
1. Melting of the mixture takes place	Hydrated salts
2. Swelling of the mixture takes place	Borate, phosphate or alums
3. The mixture decrepitates (gives crackling sound on heating)	Lead nitrate, barium nitrate and potassium bromide
4. A sublimate is formed, its colour may be	
(a) White	Compounds of ammonium, arsenic and mercury
(b) Yellow	Arsenious sulphide, HgI_2
(c) Black	Arsenic, iodine and HgS
5. The mixture changes its colour:	
(a) Yellow when hot while white when cold	Zinc salt
(b) Dark brown when hot while yellow when cold	Lead, bismuth and tin salts
(c) The original salt is green which becomes dirty white or yellow on heating	Salts of nickel and ion(II)

(d) The original salt is blue which becomes white on heating and on cooling turns again blue	Copper sulphate
(e) Black residue	Salts of copper, nickel, etc.
(f) Mixture glows when heated	Salts of calbium, magnesium and aluminium
6. A gas is given out	
(a) Reddish brown gas which turns $FeSO_4$ dark brown	Nitrates of heavy metals
(b) Colourless gas which has characteristic ammoniacal odour, turns red litmus blue, turns Nessler's solution brown	Ammonium salts
(c) Colourless gas which has no odour but turns lime water milky	Carbonates
(d) Violet vapours	Iodides
7. Water drops are deposited in the test tube	Crystalline salt.

Note (i) A dry test tube is used for heating the mixture.
(ii) While heating, the mouth of the test tube should be kept away from face.
(iii) A small quantity of salt is used for dry heating.

Definitions (i) Swelling Certain salts such as alums and phesphates when heated swell up to form voluminous mass. This phenomenon, known as **intumescence,** is due to loss of water of crystallization and change in molecular structure.

(ii) Decrepitation Crystals of certain salts do not contain any water of crystallization. Yet they contain a small quantity of mother liquor entraped in their crystals. When such salts are heated, the entrapped liquid vaporizes and, thereby, causes the crystals to break. This produces a *crackling sound* known as **decrepitation.** For example, lead nitrate undergoes decrepitation.

CHEMISTRY OF THE HEATING TEST

1. Melting When the hydrated salts are heated, they lose

their water of crystallization and they dissolve in it, giving the appearance as if these have melted.

2. *Swelling* Borate, phosphate or alums on heating lose water of crystallization and swell up. This phenomenon of swelling up of a substance on heating is known as *intumescence.*

3. *Decrepitation* Crystals of substances like $Pb(NO_3)_2$, $Ba(NO_3)_2$, etc. do not contain the water of crystallization but enclose small quantities of the mother liquor. Such crystals on heating decrepitate, i.e. fly to pieces with a sharp crackling sound on account of vaporization of the enclosed moisture.

4. *Formation of a sublimate* When heated, certain salts vaporize or give out volatile products which get condensed on the upper part of the test tube in the from a sublimate (e.g., ammonium and arsenic salts).

5. *Colour changes* When heated, certain salts are partially converted into oxides. The latter have different colours, fusibilities, etc. from the original salts. For example,

$$CaCO_3 \rightarrow CaO + CO_2 \uparrow$$
(white) (glows on heating)

$$CuCO_3 \rightarrow CuO + CO_2$$
(bluish green) (black)

$$2Zn(NO_3)_2 \rightarrow 2ZnO + 4NO_2 + O_2$$
(white) (yellow when hot while white when cold)

$$2Pb(NO_3)_2 \rightarrow 2PbO + 4NO_2 + O_2$$
(brown when hot while yellow when cold)

Certain salts change their colour due to loss of water of crystallization. For example,

$$CuSO_4 5H_2O \rightarrow CuSO_4 + 5H_2O$$
(blue) (white)

$$NiCl_2 . 6H_2O \rightarrow NiCl_2 + 6H_2O$$
(green) (yellow)

6. *Evolution of gases* When the nitrates of non-alkali metals are heated, a mixture of nitrogen dioxide and oxygen is evolved.

$$2Zn(NO_3)_2 \rightarrow 2ZnO + 4NO_2 + O_2$$

When the ammonium salts of polybasic acids (having more then one replaceable hydrogen atom) are heated, they decompose to evolve ammonia gas.

$$(NH_4)_2SO_4 \rightarrow NH_4HSO_4 + NH_3 \uparrow$$

When carbonates are heated, they decompose to evolve corbon dioxide.

$$BaCO_3 \rightarrow BaO + CO_2 \uparrow$$
$$CaCO_3 \rightarrow CaO + CO_2 \uparrow$$

7. *Condensation of water drops* When salts having water of crystallization are heated, they lose water vapours which are condensed in the form of droplets on the upper part of the test tube.

Flame Test Certain metallic salts (especially chlorides) when heated strongly in a non-luminous flame get thermally ionized. The ions become excited by promoting electrons to higher energy levels. When they come back to the ground state, they emit radiations which, if they come in the visible region of the spectrum, impart characteristic colours to the flame. The colour so produced is characteristic of the cationic constituent present in the vaporized salt.

Procedure (i) Make a circular loop at the end of a platinum wire. Clean it by repeatedly dipping it in conc. HCl and heating it in the oxidizing flame (this is obtained by keeping the air holes of the burner entirely open). The wire is said to be cleaned when it imparts no colour to the flame.

(ii) Prepare a paste of mixture in conc. HCl on a watch glass.

(iii) Take a small quanitity of the paste on the loop of the platinum wire and put it into the base of the *non-luminous* or the *oxidizing flame* and keep it for some time (Fig. 3.2)

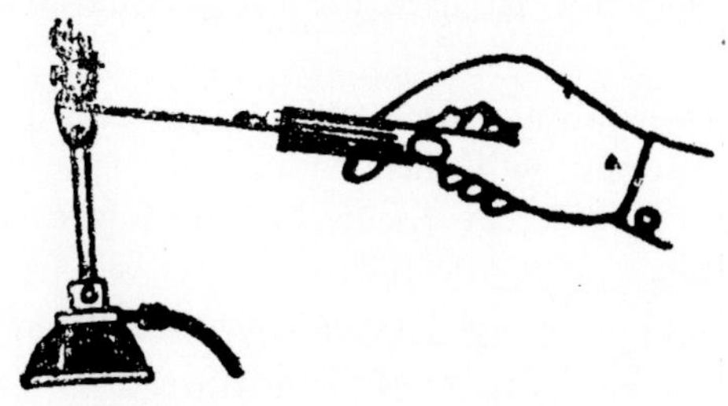

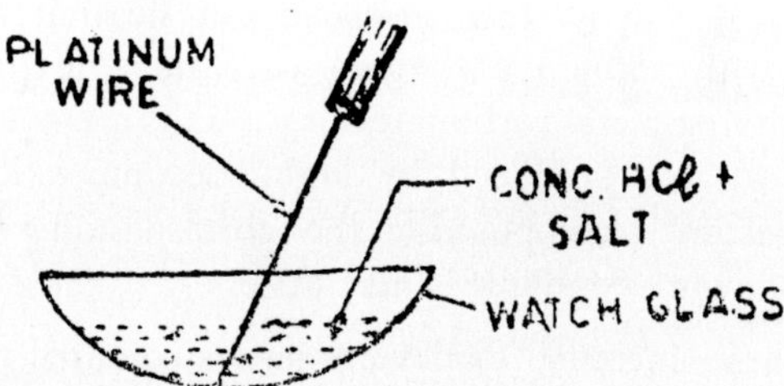

Fig. 3.2. Flame test.

(iv) Observe the colour imparted to the flame as such and also through a deep blue glass (cobalt glass) and draw the inference from Table 3.1.

TABLE 3.1 Flame Test

Flame colour as viewed through the naked eye	*Flame colour through cobalt blue glass*	*Inference*
Lilac (pink-violet)	Pink	K^+
Flickering brick red	Light green	Ca^{2+}
Crimson (deep red)	Purple	Sr^{2+}
Grassy green	Bluish green	Ba^{2+}
Dark green	Bluish green	Cu^{2+}
Bright green	—	Borate
Green flashes	—	Zn^{2+}
Yellow sparks	—	Fe or NH_4^+ salt
Bluish white	White	As^{3+}, Sb^{3+}, Bi^{3+}, Hg^{2+}, Sn^{4+}, Pb^{2+}, etc.

Notes (i) The flame test should not be performed if the mixture contains phosphate.

(ii) If the mixture contains Pb, Sn, Bi and As, the platinum wire should not be used because it forms an alloy with these metals.

(iii) It is always preferable to perform the flame tests for various cations with their individual precipitates obtained in wet tests in different groups and not to proceed directly with the mixture.

(iv) Do not use the acid employed for cleaning the platinum wire, for making a paste of the mixture.

Charcoal Cavity Test *Principle* On heating the salt or mixture with sodium carbonate or fusion mixture, first the corresponding metal carbonates (if the salts are not originally as carbonates) are produced by double decomposition and these carbonates are decomposed to the corresponding oxides. One of the following possibilities may arise:

(i) These metallic oxides are left as coloured residues. The colour of the residue is characteristic of the basic radical present.

(ii) These metallic oxides undergo reduction to the metallic state by the reducing action of the carbon of charcoal resulting in the formation of metallic beads if easily fusible.

(iii) The metal so formed in (ii) volatilizes in the form of vapours which burn in air to form an oxide. The oxide gets deposited in the form of a layer or crust around the cavity (*incrustation*).

Examples. (i) $ZnSO_4 + Na_2CO_3 \longrightarrow ZnCO_3 + Na_2SO_4$

$ZnCO_3 \longrightarrow ZnO + CO_2\uparrow$

(yellow when hot and white when cold)

(ii) $CdSO_4 + Na_2CO_3 \longrightarrow CdCO_3 + Na_2SO_4$

$CdCO_3 \longrightarrow CdO + CO_2\uparrow$

(reddish brown residure)

$$\text{(iii) } CuSO_4 + Na_2CO_3 \longrightarrow CuCO_3 + Na_2SO_4$$

$$CuCO_3 \longrightarrow CuO + CO_2$$

$$CuO + C \longrightarrow \underset{\text{(red)}}{Cu} + CO$$

Procedure (i) Make a small cavity (2 mm deep) in the clean charcoal block with the help of a cavity borer (ii) Fill the mixture of 1 part of mixture of salts and 2 parts of the fusion mixture ($Na_2CO_3 + NaNO_3$) in the cavity.

(iii) Press the mixture with a spatula and moisten the contents of the cavity with a drop of water.

(iv) Hold the charcoal block in the left hand and play upon the reducing flame very gently with the help of a blow pipe for about two minutes (Fig. 3.3).

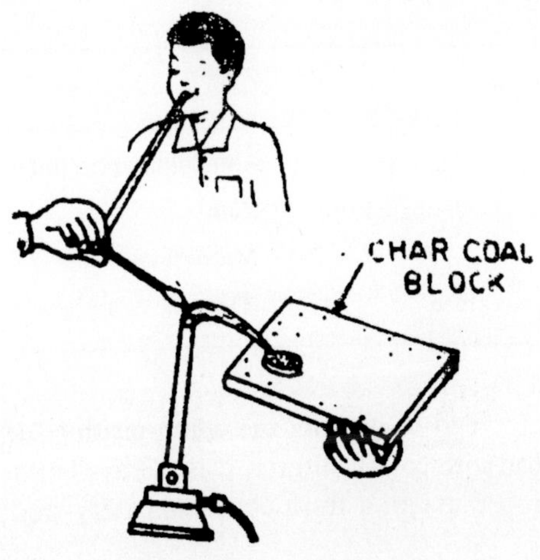

Fig. 3.3. Charcoal cavity test.

(v) Observe the colour of residue (in hot and in cold), the colour of the incrustation (if any) and the bead formation. Draw the inference as provided in Table 3.2.

Notes (i) For a new salt, one should bore a new cavity in the charcoal.

(ii) When the substance in the charcoal cavity is heated it should be completely covered by the reducing flame.

(iii) Sometimes there occurs the burning of charcoal due to deflagration of the salt. This shows that the mixture contains nitrate.

Cobalt Nitrate Test When a charcoal cavity test is carried out, a white residue may be obtained. In such a case, add a drop of cobalt nitrate solution over the white residue. Heat it again in the oxidizing flame by means of blow pipe. Note the colour of the residue and make the inference as given in Table 3.3.

TABLE 3.3

Cobalt Nitrate Test

Colour of residue	*Inference*
(i) Blue	Aluminium, phosphate and borate
(ii) Green	Zinc
(iii) Pink	Magnesium
(iv) Dirty bluish green	Tin

Notes (i) Instead of heating the white residue of the charcoal cavity test with cobalt nitrate, it is always better to place a little of the substance in a fresh charcoal cavity and apply the cobalt nitrate test.

(ii) One should avoid the addition of excess of cobalt nitrate. If it is in excess, a black mass due to the formation of cobalt oxide is obtained.

Chemical reactions involved During the cobalt nitrate test, cobalt nitrate first decomposes into cobaltous oxide which

TABLE 3.2
Charcoal Cavity Test

	Incrustation Residue or Both		*Bead*	*Inference*
	In hot	*In cold*		
1.	Yellow residue and incrustation	White residue and incrustation	None	Zinc
2.	Reddish brown residue and incrustation	Reddish brown residue and incrustation	None	Cadmium
3.	Reddish brown residue and incrustation	Yellow residue and incrustation	White, malleable metallic bead which marks paper	Lead
4.	Orange residue and incrustation	Yellow residue or incrustation	White brittle lead	Lead
5.	Red residue	Red residue	Reddish scales	Copper
6.	White residue	White incrustation	Shining white metallic hard bead which does not mark paper	Silver
7.	Black residue	Black residue	None	Iron, cobalt, nickel and managanese
8.	White residue	White residue	None	Calcium, barium, strontium, aluminium and magnesium

reacts with the metal oxides to form a compound or a solid solution with characteristic colour.

$$2Co(NO_3)_2 \longrightarrow 2CoO + 4NO_2 + O_2$$

$$CoO + ZnO \longrightarrow CoZnO_2$$ (cobalt zincate) (Rinmann's green)

$$CoO + Al_2O_3 \longrightarrow Co(AlO_2)_2$$ cobalt meta-aluminate (Thenard's blue)

$$CoO + MgO \longrightarrow CoO.MgO$$ (dirty pink)

Filter-Ash Test In place of the cobalt nitrate test, the filter-ash test can be employed. This test can be performed as follow:

(i) Mix the original solution of mixture with cobalt nitrate solution.

(ii) Take a piece of filter paper and dip in solution (i).

(iii) Take out the wet filter paper. Place it on a wire gauze and burn to ash. From the colour of the ash (which is same as in cobalt nitrate test) a useful inference can be drawn.

The chemistry of this test remains the same as in the cobalt nitrate test.

Borax Bead Test *Principle* When borax is heated, it first loses its water of crystallization and then decomposes to give a clear and transparent bead consisting of boric anhydride and sodium metaborate.

$$Na_2B_4O_7.10H_2O \longrightarrow Na_2B_4O_7 + 10H_2O$$

$$Na_2B_4O_7 \longrightarrow 2NaBO_2 + B_2O_3$$

Boric anhydride being less volatile displaces more volatile acidic anhydrides from their salts to form metaborates which possess characteristic colours.

$$B_2O_3 + CuSO_4 \longrightarrow Co(BO_2)_2 + SO_3$$

In certain cases metaborates of two different colours are produced in oxidizing and reducing flames.

$$B_2O_3+CuSO_4 \longrightarrow Cu(BO_2)_2+SO_3$$

(green when hot and blue when cold in oxidizing flame)

$$2Cu(BO_2)_2+C \longrightarrow 2Cu(BO_2)+B_2O_3+CO$$

(colourless in reducing flame)

In some cases, the bead becomes opaque in the reducing flame. This happens if too much of the metal metaborate is there and its reduction to the metallic state is possible.

$$2CuBO_2+C \longrightarrow 2Cu+B_2O_3+CO$$

(reddish brown when hot)

Procedure

(i) Make a loop at the free end of the platinum wire.

(ii) Heat the wire red hot and dip it into powdered borax and again heat to get small transparent bead in the loop of the wire. Ensure that the bead is clear and transparent. In case the bead is opaque, it is removed and the process is repeated to get transparent glassy bead (Fig. 3.4)

(iii) Touch the hot bead with a little of the mixture. Heat it again in the oxidizing flame, cool and examine the colour.

(iv) Observe the colour when hot and also when cold.

(v) Heat it again in the reducing flame and examine the colour of the bead when hot and also when cold.

(iv) Draw the inference from Table 3.4.

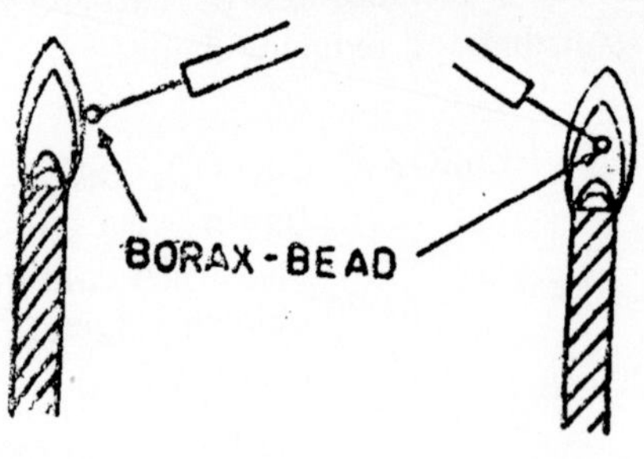

Fig. 3.4 Borax bead test.

TABLE 3.4

Borax Bead Test

	Colour of the bead in oxidizing flame		*Colour of the bead in reducing flame (when cold)*	*Inference*
	When hot	*When cold*		
1.	Brown	Pale brown	Grey or black opaque	Nickel
2.	Deep green	Deep green	Deep geen	Chromium
3.	Pinkish	Pinkish	Colourless or opaque	Manganese
4.	Green	Light blue	Red (opaque) or colourless	Copper
5.	Yellowish brown	Pale yellew	Bottle green	Iron
6.	Deep blue	Deep blue	Blue	Cobalt

Notes (i) The borax bead test must be applied when the mixture given is a coloured salt.

(ii) The borax bead produced should be perfectly colourless. If it is coloured, jerk it off and prepare a fresh bead.

(iii) In this test, only a minute amount of the mixture should be used otherwise bead will become dark and opaque in subsequent treatment.

Microcosmic Bead Test The microcosmic salt, $Na(NH_4)HPO_4.4H_2O$ behaves as borax, therefore, it can be used as borax.

Principle When microcosmic salt is heated, it loses water and ammonia and give a clear and transparent bead consisting of sodium metaphosphate.

$$Na(NH_4)HPO_4.4H_2O \longrightarrow NaPO_3 + 5H_2O + NH_3 \uparrow$$

Sodium metaborate combines with metal oxides to form orthophosphate which possess characteristic colours.

$$2\ Cu(NO_3)_2 \longrightarrow 2CuO + 4NO_2 + O_2$$

$$NaPO_3 + CuO \longrightarrow NaCuPO_4$$

copper orthophosphate
(green when hot and blue when cold in oxidizing flame)

Procedure Procedure is the same as for borax bead text. Draw the inference from Table 3.5.

TABLE 3.5

Microcosmic Bead Test

Colour of the bead in oxidizing flame		*Colour of the bead in reducing flame*		*Inference*
When hot	*When cold*	*When hot*	*When cold*	
1. Green	Blue	Colourless	Red	Copper
2. Green	Green	Green	Green	Chromium
3. Blue	Blue	Blue	Blue	Cobalt
4. Yellowish brown	Yellow	Yellow	Yellow	Iron
5. Vilolet	Violet	Colourless	Colourless	Manganese
6. Brown	Brown	Grey	Grey	Nickel

Detection of Cations (Basic Radicals) by Wet Tests

1. *Introduction* By the term *wet test* we mean the detection of cations (and anions) of the mixture in the solution state. For this a suitable reagent called a *group reagent* is added to the solution of mixture and the formation of a precipitate is noted. This ppt. is further analysed to draw the inference regarding the presence or absence of cation or cations.

For the sake of convenience, cations have been divided into six groups on the basis of the difference in solubility of their chlorides, sulphides, hydroxides, carbonates and phosphates. These precipitates are obtained by adding group reagents under the careful control of pH.

Table 3.6 gives briefly the classification of basic radicals into groups, their group reagents and the form in which they are precipitated.

Note The NH_4^+ radical is not included in the above six groups. However, it is included in group zero which is tested in the original mixture in the beginning of the analysis of the cations. The reagent for this is NaOH.

2. *Preparation of original solution* The first step before proceeding for the indentification of cationic constituents by wet test analysis is to prepare a clear and transparent solution of mixture under investigation. The following solvents are tried one by one in a systematic order by taking 0.1 g of the mixture each time, treating with 2 mL of the solvent and heating if needed for 1-2 minutes before trying the next solvent.

TABLE 3.6

Classification of Cations into Groups

Group	*Cations in group*	*Group reagent*	*Group precipitation*
I (Lead Group)	Pb^{2+}, Ag^{+}, Hg_2^{2+}	Dil. HCl	Chlorides insoluble in cold dil. HCl
II 'A' (Copper Group)	Hg^{2+}, Pb^{2+}, Bi^{3+}, Cu^{2+}, Cd^{2+}	H_2S in the presence of dil. HCl	Sulphides insoluble in HCl
II 'B' (Arsenic Group)	As^{3+}, Sb^{3+}, Sn^{2+} or Sn^{4+}	-do-	-do-
III (Iron Group)	Fe^{3+}, Al^{3+} and Cr^{3+}	NH_4OH in the presence of excess of NH_4Cl	Hydroxides insoluble in ammoniacal medium
IV (Zinc Group)	Ni^{2+}, Co^{2+}, Mn^{2+} and Zn^{2+}	H_2S in ammoniacal medium	Sulphides insoluble in ammoniacal medium
V (Calcium Group)	Ba^{2+}, Sr^{2+} and Ca^{2+}	$(NH_4)_2CO_3$ in the presence of NH_4Cl and NH_4OH	Carbonates insoluble in ammoniacal medium
VI (Magnesium group)	Mg^{2+}, Na^{+} and K^{+}	For Mg^{2+}, ammonium phosphate	Magnesium ammonium phosphate insoluble in ammoniacal medium
		For K^{+} and Na^{+} no specific group reagent	It is tested individually after the separation of Mg^{2+}.

(i) Distilled water

(ii) Dil. HCl

(iii) Conc. HCl

If a gas is liberated on adding a solvent, ensure that the reaction is over. Add more solvent and heat. A clear solution may be formed when no gas comes out. If the solution has been formed on heating, it should be cooled to the room temperature before assuming that the solvent is satisfactory.

After finding out the appropriate solvent, prepare the *stock solution* or the *original solution* by dissolving 1 g of mixture in 10-15 mL of the solvent.

Notes (i) The original solution must be clear and transparent.
(ii) It may not be colourless.

Analysis of Group Zero Cation (Ammonium) NH_4^+

Identification Heat 0.5 g of the mixture with 3-5 mL of NaOH. liberation of NH_3 gas indicates the presence of NH_4^+ radical. The gas evolved may be identified by the following tests.

$$NH_4Cl + NaOH \longrightarrow NH_3 + NaCl + H_2O$$

(a) Bring a piece of filter paper soaked in tumeric solution. If the paper acquires a brown colour, this confirms the presence of NH_4^+ radical.

(b) Bring a glass rod dipped in conc. HCl over the mouth of the test tube. If dense white fumes of NH_4Cl are obtained, this confirms the presence of the NH_4^+ radical.

$$NH_3 + HCl \longrightarrow \underset{\text{(dense white fumes)}}{NH_4Cl}$$

(c) Pass the evolved gas into Nessler's reagent. The formation of a reddish brown ppt. confirms NH_4^+ radical.

$$\underset{\text{(Nessler's reagent)}}{K_2HgI_4} \longrightarrow 2\ KI + HgI_2$$

$$HgI_2 + 2NH_3 \longrightarrow Hg\begin{matrix} \diagup NH_2 \\ \diagdown I \end{matrix} + NH_4I$$

$$Hg\begin{matrix} \diagup NH_2 \\ \diagdown I \end{matrix} \quad Hg\begin{matrix} \diagup NH_2 \\ \diagdown I \end{matrix} + H_2O \longrightarrow \begin{matrix} Hg\diagup NH_2 \\ \diagdown O \\ Hg\diagup \\ \diagdown I \end{matrix} + NH_4I$$

iodide of Millon's base
(reddish-brown ppt.)

Preparation of Nessler's reagent Dissolve 13 g of KI in 100 mL of water. To it add a saturated solution of $HgCl_2$ slowly until a scarlet red ppt. just appears. Filter and reject the ppt To the filtrate add a solution of 20 g of KOH is 50 mL of water and dilute to 200 mL. The reagent thus consists of an alkaline solution of potassium mercuriodide (K_2HgI_4),.

Analysis of First Group Cations (Pb^{2+}, Ag^+, Hg_2^{2+})

To about 10 mL of the solution of the mixture, add dil. HCl in a slight excess in the cold. A white ppt. indicates the pressure of group I. Filter and preserve the filtrate for the Group II. Analyse the ppt. in accordance to Table 3.6.

The white ppt. may contain $PbCl_2$, AgCl and Hg_2Cl_2. Wash the precipitate with cold water on filter paper. Transfer the ppt. in a test tube by piercing the point of filter paper with a glass rod and washing the precipitate with water into the test tube. Boil the ppt. with water. Filter hot.

Notes (i) In case the solution of the mixture is made in dil. HCl, Group I is absent. Proceed directly for Group II.

TABLE 3.6

Analysis of First Group Cations (Pb^{2+}, Hg^{+} and Hg_2^{2+})

The filtrate may contain Pb^{2+}. Divide it into 3 parts: (i) Cool part I under tap water; a white crystalline ppt. of $PbCl_2$ confirms Pb^{2+} (ii) To part II, add K_2CrO_4 solution A yellow ppt. of $PbCrO_4$ soluble in NaOH confirms Pb^{2+} (iii) To part III, while it is hot, add KI solution. A yellow ppt. which dissolves on boiling with water but separates out on cooling confirms Pb^{2+}.	*Residue* on the filter paper may contain AgCl. Wash it several times with boiling water until washings give a negative test for Pb^{2+} with K_2CrO_4. Now pour 5-8 mL of warm ammonia solution over the ppt. and collect the filtrate.	
	Filtrate May contain $[Ag(NH_3)_2]Cl$ Divide into three parts: (i) To part I, add KI solution, A pale yellow ppt. insoluble in NH_4OH and HNO_3 confirms Ag^+ (ii) To part II, add dil. HNO_3. A white ppt. of AgCl confirms Ag^+ (iii) To part III, add K_2CrO_4 solution. A brick red ppt. confirms Ag^+.	Residue if black confirms Hg_2^{2+}. Dissolve biack ppt. in aqua regia. Evaporate to dryness. Extract with water. Divide it into 3 parts: (i) Add KI solution to the first part A red ppt. dissolving in excess of KI coufirms Hg_2^{2+} (ii) Add $SnCl_2$ solution to the second part. White ppt. turning grey confirms Hg^{2+} (iii) To the third part add Cu chips. A silvery white deposit of Hg on Cu confirms Hg_2^{2+}.
Pb^{2+}	Ag^+	Hg_2^{2+}

(ii) Avoid large excess of HCl during precipitation of Group I cations because $PbCl_2$ is soluble in hot excess HCl due to the formation of complex, H_2PbCl_4.

$$PbCl_2 + 2HCl \longrightarrow H_2PbCl_4$$

(iii) If the solution is prepared in conc. HCl, dilute the solution. If the ppt. appears on dilution, test it for Group I.

(iv) Sometimes on diluting the solution mixture in conc. HCl, white ppt. appears even if the group I is absent. This is because of oxychlorides of antimony, bismuth and tin are formed by hydrolysis. Under such circumstances add some conc. HCl and warm; the ppt. due to oxychloride dissolves.

(v) If a yellow white ppt. is obtained on the addition of HCl, this is due to the formation of colloidal sulphur from thiosulphate present in the mixture. In such a case boil it with a little of solid $NaNO_3$ or NH_4NO_3.

Chemistry of the Reactions Involved

1. *Precipitation* When dil. HCl is added to original solution, the cations (Pb^{2+}, Ag^+, Hg_2^{2+}) of Group I are precipitated as their chlorides.

$$Pb^{2+} + 2Cl^- \longrightarrow PbCl_2 \downarrow$$
$$Ag^+ + Cl^- \longrightarrow AgCl \downarrow$$
$$Hg_2^{2+} + 2Cl^- \longrightarrow Hg_2Cl_2 \downarrow$$

2. *Separation* The separation of lead-, silver-, mercurous chlorides is based on the simple fact that lead chloride is soluble in boiling water whereas silver chloride and mercurous chloride are not.

3. *Identification of lead* (i) As lead chloride is soluble in hot water, it separates out on cooling in the form of needle-shaped crystals.

(ii) With pottassium chromate solution, the solution of lead chloride gives a yellow ppt. of lead chromate which is soluble in sodium hydroxide.

$$PbCl_2 + K_2CrO_4 \longrightarrow \underset{\text{(yellow ppt.)}}{PbCrO_4} + 2KCl$$

(iii) With potassium iodide solution, the solution of lead chloride gives a yellow ppt. of lead iodide.

$$PbCl_2 + 2KI \longrightarrow \underset{\text{(yellow ppt.)}}{PbI_2} + 2KCl$$

4. *Identification of silver* When ammonium hydroxide is added to silver chloride, the latter dissolves to form a colourless and soluble complex.

$$AgCl + 2NH_4OH \longrightarrow \underset{\text{(colourless)}}{[Ag(NH_3)_2]Cl} + 2H_2O$$

(i) KI solution forms a yellow ppt. of AgI

$$[Ag(NH_3)_2]Cl + KI \longrightarrow \underset{\text{(yellow ppt.)}}{AgI} + 3NH_3 + KCl$$

(ii) Dil. HNO_3 decomposes the soluble silver complex to form a white precipitate of AgCl.

$$[Ag(NH_3)_2]Cl + 2HNO_3 \longrightarrow AgCl + 2NH_4NO_3$$

(iii) K_2CrO_4 solution forms a red ppt. of silver chromate.

$$2[Ag(NH_3)_2]Cl + K_2CrO_4 \longrightarrow Ag_2CrO_4 + 2KCl + 2NH_3$$

5. *Identification of mercury* When ammonium hydroxide is added to mercurous chloride, the latter forms black and white ppt. of Hg and $Hg(NH_2)Cl$ respectively

$$Hg_2Cl_2 + 2NH_4OH \longrightarrow \underbrace{\underset{\text{(black)}}{Hg\downarrow} + \underset{\text{(white)}}{Hg(NH_2)Cl\downarrow}}_{\text{black}} + NH_4Cl + 2H_2O$$

The black residue is dissolved in aqua regia when $HgCl_2$ is obtained.

$$\underbrace{HNO_3 + 3HCl}_{\text{aqua regia}} \longrightarrow NOCl + 2H_2O + 2Cl$$

$$Hg + 2Cl \longrightarrow HgCl_2$$

$$Hg(NH_2)Cl + 2HCl \longrightarrow HgCl_2 + NH_4Cl$$

(i) KI solution forms a red ppt. of HgI_2 which dissolves in excess of KI.

$$\underset{}{HgCl_2 + 2KI \longrightarrow \underset{\text{(red ppt.)}}{HgI_2} + 2KCl}$$

$$HgI_2 + 2KI \longrightarrow \underset{\text{(soluble)}}{K_2[HgI_4]}$$

(ii) With $SnCl_2$ solution, a white ppt. turning to grey-black is obtained.

$$HgCl_2 + SnCl_2 \longrightarrow \underset{\text{(white ppt.)}}{Hg_2Cl_2} + SnCl_4$$

$$Hg2Cl_2 + SnCl_2 \longrightarrow \underset{\text{(grey)}}{2Hg} + SnCl_4$$

(iii) A grey deposit is deposited when copper chips are added to $HgCl_2$

$$HgCl_2 + Cu \longrightarrow \underset{\text{(grey)}}{Hg} + CuCl_2$$

Analysis of Group II Cations (Hg^{2+}, Pb^{2+}, Bi^{3+}, Cu^{2+}, Cd^{2+} (As^{3+}, Sb^{3+}, Sn^{2+} or Sn^{4+})

If the aqueous solution of the mixture does not yield any ppt. with dil. HCl or if the original solution has been prepared in dil. HCl, this shows the absence of Group I.

Take about 1-2 mL of the filtrate of Group 1 or take 1-2 mL of the original aqueous solution acidified with dil HCl or 1-2 mL of original solution prepared in dil. HCl (if Group I is absent) in a test tube. Warm and pass H_2S gas from the Kipp's apparatus (Fig. 3.5) through this solution. If a coloured ppt. is obtained, this shows the presence of Group II. In such a case, pass H_2S gas through the remaining portion of the solution for a sufficient time to ensure complete precipitation. Filter the solution. Preserve the ppt. for Group II.

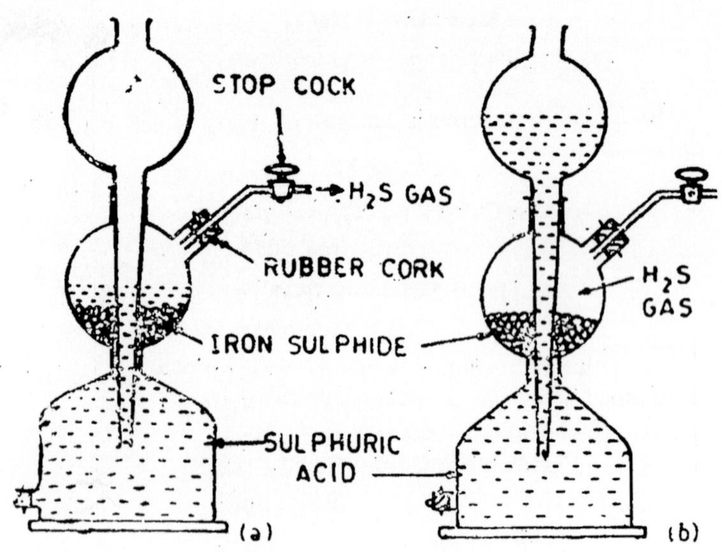

Fig. 3.5. Kipp's Apparatus.

In the filtrate, pass H_2S gas again. Repeat this process until the filtrate yields no ppt. even on dilution and heating. Collect the whole of the ppt. thus obtained and use it for the analysis of Group II. Keep the filtrate for the analysis of subsequent groups. The ppt. may consist of sulphides of

Hg, Pb, Bi, Cu,	Cd, As, Sn(IV)	Sb,	Sn(II)
(black)	(yellow)	(orange)	(brown)

Wash the ppt. with hot water and transfer it into a test tube, add about 10 mL of yellow ammonium sulphide solution. Heat with occasional shaking and filter.

Residue may contain HgS, PbS, Bi_2S_3 CuS and CdS. This constitutes Group IIA Analyse the ppt. in accordance to Table 3.7.	*Filtrate* may contain the thiosalts $(NH_4)_3AsS_4$, $(NH_4)_3SbS_4$ and $(NH_4)_3SnS_3$. This constitutes Gruop II B Analyse the filtrate in accordance to Table 3.8.

TABLE 3.7

Analysis of Group II A Cations

(Ag^{2+}, Pb^{2+}, Bi^{3+}, Cu^{2+} and Cd^{2+}

Wash the ppt. with hot water. Heat the ppt. with 5 mL of 50 per cent HNO_3 and filter.

<table>
<tr>
<td rowspan="4">Residue Black due to HgS.
Dissolve it in aqua-regia and evaporate off aqua regia. Dilute it with water. Divide it into 3 parts.
(i) To part I solution add amm. thiocyanate nnd sod. acetate followed by $Co(NO_3)_2$ solution. A deep blue colour or precipitate confirms mercury.
(ii) To part II solution add NaOH solution. A yellow precipitate confirms Hg^{2+}.
(iii) To part III solution add $SnCl_2$ solution. A white ppt.</td>
<td colspan="4">Filtrate To a portion add dil. H_2SO_4 and alcohol. If a white precipitates appears, add more alcohol and 5 NH_2SO_4 to the whole and boil till white fumes appear. Cool, add water and filter.</td>
</tr>
<tr>
<td rowspan="3">Residue White due to $PbSO_4$. Dissolve in minimum amount of ammonium acetate solution and divide it into two parts.
(i) To part I add K_2CrO_4 solution. A yellow precipitate of $PbCrO_4$ confirms Pb^{2+}.
(ii) To part II, add KI solution. A yellow ppt. is formed which dissolves in boiling water. This confirms Pb^{2+}.</td>
<td colspan="3">Filtrate Add ammonia solution dropwise till the solution is alkaline. If precipitate appears, filter.</td>
</tr>
<tr>
<td rowspan="2">Residue White. Dissolve the precipitate in conc. HCl and heat. Add to this water and divide it into 3 parts.
(i) To part I add [Preparation of sodium starnite solution. Take 1 mL of $SnCl_2$ solution and add dropwise NaOH solution until the gelatinous ppt. of $Sn(OH)_2$ first formed dissolves completly.] sodium stannite regent. A black precipitate</td>
<td colspan="2">Filtrate may contain Cu^{3+} and Cd^{2+}. Note the colour of the filtrate.</td>
</tr>
<tr>
<td>If colour is blue, it confirms Cu^{2+}.
Confirmatory tests for Cu^{3+}.
(i) Acidify a portion with acetic acid and add $K_4Fe(CN)_6$ solution. Reddish-brown ppt. confirms Cu^{2+}.
(ii) Apply flame test. Green flame confirms Cu^{2+}.</td>
<td>If the solution is blue or colourless, Cd^{2+} may be present.
Confirmatory tests for Cd^{2+}.
(i) When solution is blue, add KCN solution till the colour is discharged then pass H^3S gas through it. If yellow ppt. appears, Cd^{2+}</td>
</tr>
</table>

turning grey confirms Hg^{2+}.		confirms Bi^{3+}. (*ii*) To part II add thiourea solution. A yellow colouration appears if Bi^{3+} is present. (*iii*) To part III add excess of water. A white turbidity or ppt. ion firms Bi^{3+}.		is confirmed. [If the solution is blue, it means that Cu^{2+} is definitely present whereas Cd^{2+} may or may not be present. To test for Cd^{2+} in the presence of Cu^{2+} test in the presenee of KCN.] (*ii*) When the solution is colourless, Cu^{2+} is absent pass H_2S through the solution yellow ppt. confirms Cd^{2+}.
Hg^{2+}	Pb^{2+}	Bi^{3+}	Cu^{2+}	Cd^{2+}

Notes (i) Group II should be precipitated from a hot solution because heating favours coagulation of the sulphides and its subsequent filtration.

(ii) Use thoroughly washed tubing for passing H_2S in the mixture solution.

(iii) Pass H_2S for a sufficiently long time to ensure complete precipitation. Arsente, if present, is slowly precipitated by H_2S. In such a case reduce arsenate by heating the solution with a crystal of NH_4I.

(iv) Before passing H_2S, the solution must not be too much acidic as in that case Pb, Cd, Sn, are not completely precipitated. If acidity is too low, sulphides of Group IV may be precipitated. For correct precipitation, the acid concentration should be about 0.3 N.

(v) Sometimes on passing H_2S, the colour of the ppt. goes on changing, e.g., in case of Hg at first a dirty white, brown, then orange and finally black.

(vi) Too concentrated HNO_3, if used to dissolve the sulphides of Group IIA, will oxidize PbS to $PbSO_4$ which will remain behind with HgS. Also in this case residue may not be black but yellow due to the formation of $Hg(NO_3)_2.HgS$.

Chemistry of the Reactions Involved

1. *Precipitation* When H_2S gas is passed throug the filtrate obtained from Group I or through the original solution (it Group I is absent) the cations of Group II are precipitated.

$$M^{2+} + H_2S \rightarrow MS + 2H^+ \qquad [M = \text{Hg, Pb, Cu, Cd, Sn(II)}]$$

$$2M^{3+} + 3H_2S \rightarrow M_2S_3 + 6H^+ \qquad [M = \text{As, Sb}]$$

$$M^{4+} + 2H_2S \rightarrow MS_2 + 4H^+ \qquad [M = \text{Sn(IV)}]$$

2. *Separation of Group IIA from IIB* Group IIA cations are insoluble while Group IIB cations are soluble in yellow ammonium sulphide solution. The latter form soluble thio salts.

$$As_2S_3 + 3(NH_4)_2S + 2S \rightarrow \underset{\text{ammonium thioarsenate}}{2(NH_4)_3AsS_4}$$

$$Sb_2S_3 + 3(NH_4)_2S + 2S \rightarrow 2(NH_4)_3SbS_4$$
ammonium thioantimonate

$$(SnS + NH_4)_2S + S \rightarrow (NH_4)_2SnS_3$$
ammonium thiostannate

3. *Identification of Mercury* Mercury sulphide is insoluble in 50 per cent HNO_3 while sulphides of Pb^{2+}, Bi^{3+}, Cu^{2+} and Cd^{2+} dissolve in it to form nitrates.

$$3MS + 8HNO_3 \rightarrow 3M(NO_3)_2 + 4H_2O + 2NO + 3S$$
$$[M = \text{Pb, Cu and Cd}]$$

$$Bi_2S_3 + 8HNO_3 \rightarrow 2Bi(NO_3)_2 + 2H_2O + 2NO + 3S$$

Mercury sulphide dissolves in aqua regia to form $HgCl_2$ which is soluble.

$$HNO_3 + 3HCl \rightarrow 2H_2O + NOCl + 2Cl$$
$$HgS + 2Cl \rightarrow HgCl_2 + S$$

(i) With ammonium thiocyanate and cobalt nitrate in the presence of sod. acetate, $HgCl_2$ gives a deep blue colour or ppt.

$$Hg^{2+} + Co^{2+} + 4SCN^- \rightarrow Co[Hg(SCN)_4]$$
(deep blue ppt.)

(ii) With NaOH solution, the solution of $HgCl_2$ gives a yellow ppt. of HgO

$$Hg^{2+} + 2OH^- \rightarrow HgO + H_2O$$

(iii) $SnCl_2$ reduces $HgCl_2$ to white ppt. of Hg_2Cl_2. Excess of $SnCl_2$ reduces it to a grey ppt. of Hg.

$$2Hg^{2+} + SnCl_2 \rightarrow Hg_2Cl_2 + Sn^{4+}$$
(white ppt.)

$$Hg_2Cl_2 + Sn^{2+} \rightarrow 2Hg + Sn^{4+} + 2Cl^-$$
(grey)

4. *Identification of Lead* When the black ppt. of lead sulphide is treated with 50 per cent nitric acid, a colourless

solution due to the formation of lead nitrate is obtained. With sulphuric acid, lead nitrate solution yields a white ppt. of lead sulphate.

$$Pb(NO_3)_2+H_2SO_4 \rightarrow PbSO_4+2HNO_3$$
(white ppt.)

The ppt. of lead sulphate dissolved in ammonium acetate solution yields lead accetate.

$$PbSO_4+2CH_3COONH_5 \rightarrow (CH_3COO)_2Pb+(NH_4)_2SO_4$$

(i) With potassium chromate solution, lead acetate solution yields a yellow ppt. of lead chromate.

$$PbCl_2+K_2CrO_4 \rightarrow PbCrO_4+2KCl$$

(ii) With KI solution, lead acetate solution yields a yellow ppt. of lead iodide.

$$(CH_3COO)_2Pb+2KI \rightarrow PbI_2+2CH_3COOK$$

5. *Identification of Bismuth* On adding NH_4OH to the filtrate containing Bi^{3+}, Cu^{2+} and Cd^{2+}, only bismuth forms a white ppt. of $Bi(OH)_3$ while Cu^{2+} and Cd^{2+} form soluble complexes.

$$Bi^{3+}+3NH_4OH \rightarrow Bi(OH)_3+3NH_4^+$$
(white ppt.)

$$Cu^{2+}+4NH_4OH \rightarrow [Cu(NH_3)_4]_2^{+}+4H_2O$$
(deep blue solution)

$$Cd^{2+}+4NH_4OH \rightarrow [Cd(NH_3)]^{2+}+4H_2O$$
(colourless solution)

$Bi(OH)_3$ dissolve in dil. HCl and gives $BiCl_3$.

$$Bi(OH)_3+HCl \rightarrow BiCl_3+3H_2O$$

(i) Sodium stannite reduces Bi^{3+} to the metal (black ppt.), and sodium stannite is oxidized to sodium stannate.

$$3Bi^{3+}+3SnO_2^{2-}+6OH^- \rightarrow 2Bi+3SnO_3^{2-}+3H_2O$$
(black)

(ii) Thiourea, $CS(NH_2)_3$, forms a yellow colouration with bismuth salts in the presence of dil. HNO_3.

(iii) With excess of water $BiCl_3$ solution gives a white turbidity of bismuth oxychloride.

$$BiCl_3 + H_2O \rightarrow \underset{\text{(white turbidity)}}{BiOCl} + 2HCl$$

6 *Identification of Copper* The deep blue coloured solution of $[Cu(NH_3)_4]^{2+}$ with acetic acid gives green solution.

$$[Cu(NH_3)_4]^{2+} + 2CH_3COOH \rightarrow \underset{\text{(green solution)}}{Cu(CH_3COO)_2} + 4NH_3 + 2H^+$$

(i) With potassium ferrocyanide solution, the green solution of copper acetate yields a reddish-brown ppt. of copper ferrocyanide.

$$2Cu^{2+} + [Fe(CN_6)]^{4-} \rightarrow \underset{\text{(reddish brown ppt.)}}{Cu_2[Fe(CN_4)]}$$

7. *Identification of Cadmium*

(i) Potassium cyanide converts $[Cu(NH_3)_4]^{2+}$ and $[Cd(NH_3)_4]^{2+}$ into complex cyanides.

$$2[Cu(NH_3)_4]^{2+} + 10CN^- \rightarrow 2[Cu(CN)_4]^{3-} + (CN)_2 + 8NH_3$$

$$[Cd(NH_3)_4]^{2+} + 4CN^- + 4H_2O \rightarrow [Cd(CN)_4]^{2-} + 4NH_4OH$$

$[Cu(CN)_4]^{3-}$ ion is very stable does not ionize in solution to give sufficient concentration of Cu^{2+} ion whereas $[Cd(CN)_4^{?}]^-$ being unstable produces a much higher concentration of Cd^{2+} ion in solution. On passing H_2S gas in the solution yellow ppt. of CdS is obtained

$$[Cd(CN)_4]^{2-} \rightleftharpoons Cd^{2+} + CN^-$$

$$Cd^{2+} + S^{2-} \rightarrow \underset{\text{(yellow ppt.)}}{CdS}$$

TABLE 3.8

(As^{3+}, Sb^{3+} and Sn^{2+})

To the filtrate of Group IIB, add dil. HCl. If a coloured ppt. is obtained, it means that Group II B is present. Filter it. Reject the filtrate and test residue for Group IIB cations.

Wash residue of group IIB with hot water, filter and reject washings. Add to the residue 10 mL of conc. HCl and boil gently for 5 minutes, cool and filter.

Analysis of Group IIB Cations

<table>
<tr>
<td rowspan="2">*Residue* Dissolve the yellow ppt. by boiling in conc. HNO_3. Divide it 3 parts.
(*i*) To a part of the solution, add ammonium molybdate solution and heat. A yellow precipitate confirms As^{3+}.
(*ii*) Make second part alkaline with NH_4OH and add magnesia mixture. A white precipitate confirms As^{3+}.
(iii) To the part III (make it neutral) add $AgNO_3$ solution. A yellow ppt. soluble in HNO_3 and NH_4OH confirms, As^{3+}.
As^{3+}</td>
<td colspan="2">*Filtrate* It may have $SnCl_4$ and $SbCl_3$. Boil off H_2S. Add NH_4OH to make the filtrate alkaline. Add oxalic acid (solid), boil and pass H_2S. Filter.</td>
</tr>
<tr>
<td>*Residue* (orange). Dissolve the precipitate in conc. HCl. Boil off H_2S. Divide it in two parts.
(*i*) To one part add NH_4OH in order to neutralize the solution. Dilute with large excess of water. A white precipitate or turbidity soluble in tartaric acid confirms Sb^{3+}
(*ii*) To another part of the solution, add a small tin piece and wait for some time. A grey spongy deposit indicates Sb^{3+}.
Sb^{3+}</td>
<td>*Filtrate* It may be contain $SnCl_4$. Boil off H_2S and add Zn dust and dil. HCl. Keep it for some time. Filter and divide it into two parts.
(*i*) To one part add ammonium molybdate solution. A deep blue colouration or precipitate indicates Sn^{2+}.
(*ii*) To second part, add $HgCl_2$ solution. A white or grey ppt. confirms
Sn^{2+}</td>
</tr>
</table>

(ii) When the solution is colourless, on passing H_2S gas in this solution of $[Cd(NH_3)_4]^{2+}$ ions, yellow ppt. of CdS is obtained.

$$[Cd(NH_3)_4]^{2+} + H_2S \rightarrow \underset{\text{(yellow ppt.)}}{CdS} + 2NH_4^+ + 2NH_3$$

Notes (i) If on addition or dil. HCl, instead of yellow or orange ppt. there is white ppt., Group IIB is absent. The white ppt. is due to sulphur.

(ii) When assenic sulphide is dissolved in conc. HNO_3 a black mass floats in the test tube. This is due to sulphur. Remove it.

(iii) Antimony should be reported only if an orange ppt. is formed.

Chemistry of the Reactions Involved

Precipition When dil. HCl is added in the filtrate of Group IIB (thiosalts of As, Sb and Sn) the corresponding sulphides are pracipitated.

$$\underset{\substack{\text{thioarsenate}\\\text{ion}}}{2(AsSO_4)^{3-}} + 6H^+ \longrightarrow \underset{\substack{\text{(yellow}\\\text{ppt.)}}}{As_2S_5} + 3H_2S$$

$$\underset{\substack{\text{thioantimonate}\\\text{ion}}}{2(SbS_4)^{3-}} + 6H^+ \longrightarrow \underset{\substack{\text{(orange}\\\text{ppt.)}}}{Sb_2S_5} + 2H_2S$$

$$\underset{\substack{\text{thiostannite}\\\text{ion}}}{(SnS_3)^{2-}} + 2H^+ \longrightarrow \underset{\substack{\text{(yellow}\\\text{ppt.)}}}{SnS_2} + H_2S$$

Excess of ammonium sulphide is decomposed liberating sulphur as a light yellow ppt.

2. *Separation* Arsenic sulphide is insoluble in conc. HCl while sulphides of antimony and tin are soluble in conc. HCl and form corresponding chlorides.

$$Sb_2S_5 + 10HCl \longrightarrow 2SbCl_3 + 5H_2S + 2Cl_2$$

$$SnS_2 + 4HCl \longrightarrow SnCl_4 + 2H_2S$$

3. *Identification of Arsenic* The yellow ppt. of As_2S_5 dissolves in conc. HNO_3 forming arsenic acid.

$$As_2S_5 + 10HNO_3 + 4H_2O \longrightarrow 2H_3AsO_4 + 5S + 10NO$$

(i) Ammonium molybdate yields a yellow ppt. with arsenic solution in presence of HNO_3.

$$AsO_4^{3-} + 3NH_4^+ + 12MoO_4^{2-} + 24H^+ \rightarrow \underset{\text{(yellow ppt.)}}{(NH_4)_3AsO_4 12MoO_3} + 12H_2O$$

(ii). On adding magnesia mixture, a white crystalline precipitate is obtained.

$$H_3AsO_4 + 3MgSO_4 + 3NH_4OH \longrightarrow \underset{\text{(white ppt.)}}{Mg(NH_4)AsO_4} + (NH_4)_2SO_4 + 3H_2O$$

(iii) H_3AsO_4 forms a yellow ppt. with $AgNO_3$ solution

$$H_3AsO_4 + 3AgNO_3 \rightarrow \underset{\text{(yellow ppt.)}}{Ag_3AsO_4} + 3HNO_3$$

4. *Identification of Antimony* In the presence of NH_4OH and excess of oxalic acid, tin forms a relatively stable tin-oxalate complex ion, whereas antimony forms a much less stable antimony oxalate complex ion. Thus on passing H_2S, Sb_2S_3 is obtained.

$$Sn^{4+} + \underset{\text{oxalic acid}}{2H_2C_2O_4} \rightarrow \underset{\text{(stable not decomposed by } H_2S)}{Sn(C_2O_4)_2} + 4H^+$$

$$2Sb^{3+} + 3H_2S \rightarrow Sb_2S_3 + 6H^+$$
(orange ppt.)

(i) Sb_2S_3 dissolves in HCl forming $SbCl_3$, on dilution milkiness is produced which is soluble in tartaric acid ($C_4H_6O_6$).

$$Sb_2S_3 + 6H^+ \longrightarrow 2Sb^{3+} + 3H_2S$$

$$Sb^{3+} + Cl^- + H_2O \longrightarrow SbOCl + 2H^+$$

$$SbOCl + C_4H_6O_6 \longrightarrow C_4H_5SbO_7 + H^+ + Cl^-$$
(soluble)

(ii) On putting tin foil in $SbCl_3$ solution, a black deposit of antimony is obtained.

$$2Sb^{3+} + 3Sn \longrightarrow 3Sn^{2+} + 2Sb$$

5. *Indentification of Tin* Addition of zinc dust to the solution reduces $SnCl_4$ to $SnCl_2$.

$$Sn^{4+} + Zn^{2+} \longrightarrow Sn^{2+} + Zn^{2+}$$

(i) Ammonium molybdate forms a blue colour or precipitate with $SnCl_2$ solution.

$$Sn^{2+} + 3MoO_4^{2-} \longrightarrow Mo_3O_8 + Sn^{4+} + 5H_2O$$
(blue)

(ii) Mercuric chloride is reduced to Hg_2Cl_2 (white ppt.) and finally to grey or black precipitate of mercury.

$$Sn^{2+} + Hg^{2+} + 2Cl^- \longrightarrow Sn^{4+} + Hg_2Cl_2$$
(white ppt.)

$$Hg_2Cl_2 + Sn^{2+} \longrightarrow Sn^{4+} + 2Hg + 2Cl^-$$
(gray)

Analysis of Group III Cations (Fe^{3+}, Cr^{3+} and Al^{3+})

Boil Group II filtrate for a sufficient time in a china dish to remove H_2S completely (test with lead acetate paper). Add about 2 mL of conc. HNO_3 and boil to oxidize any Fe^{2+} to Fe^{3+} state. Add 2 mL of solid NH_4Cl, heat to boiling and and NH_4OH in slight excess until the solution smells of ammonia. Boil for a minute and filter immediately. Examine the precipitale for identifying the members of Group III and keep safe the filtrate for subsequent groups. The ppt. may consists of hydroxides of.

Fe	Cr	Al	MnO_2 H_2O
(reddish brown)	(dirty green)	(white)	(black)

Analysis the ppt. in accordance to Table 3.9.

Distinction between Ferrous (Fe^{2+}) *and Ferric* (Fe^{3+}) I. Add $K_3[Fe(CN)_6]$ solution to the original solution (O.S.). The formation of a deep blue colouration or a ppt. indicates the present of ferrous (Fe^{2+}) ion whereas the formation of brown colouration indicates ferric (Fe^{2+}) ion.

II. Add $K_4[Fe(CN)_6]$ solution to the O.S. The formation of a deep blue colouration or a ppt. indicates ferric (Fe^{3+}) ion wheares the formation of light blue colour indicates ferrous (Fe^{2+}) ion.

III. Add KSCN solution to the O.S. The formation of a blood red colouration indicates ferric (Fe^{3+}) ion.

Notes (i) Before proceeding for the analysis of Group III remove interfering redicals.

(ii) If black residue is obtained after the treatment with Na_2O_2 or NaOH—Br_2 water, both Mn^{2+} and Fe^{3+} are present.

TABLE 3.9

Analysis of Group III Cations

(Fe^{3+}, Cr^{3+} and Al^{3+})

Wash the ppt. with hot water, add little water and then add 1-2 g of Na_2O_2 or add NaOH solution and bromine water/H_2O_2. Boil and filter.

<table>
<tr><td rowspan="2">Residue Brown. Dissolve the residue in 5 N HCl and divide it in 3 parts.
(i) To Part I, add $K_4Fe(CN)_6$ a prussion blue colour or ppt. confirms Fe^{3+}.
(ii) To Part II, add KSCN solution—a blood red colour confirms Fe^{3+}.
Fe^{3+}
(iii) To the third part, add conc. HNO_3, bismuthatc solution and shake. A purple violet precipitate confirms Mn^{2+}.
Mn^{2+}</td><td colspan="2">Filtrate If colourless, Al is present and/or is absent; if yellow Cr is definitely present. Divide solution in two portions.</td></tr>
<tr><td>Tests for Cr^{3+}
(i) Acidify a part of this portion with acetic acid and add lead acetate solution. A bright yellow precipitate soluble in NaOH confirms Cr^{3+}.
(ii) Acidify another part with dil. H_2SO_4 and add ether. Add 2-3 drops of H_2O_2 and shake. A blue colour in ethereal layer confirms Cr^{3+}.
Cr^{3+}</td><td>Tests for Al^{3+}
(i) To one part add amm. acetate solution, aluminon and excess of $(NH_4)_2CO_3$ solution. A bright red lake confirms Al^{3+}
(ii) Add solid NH_4Cl to the second part and boil. A white gelationous precipitate confirms Al^{3+}.
(iii) Charcaol Cavity Test Place 2 drops of the solution and 10 mg of Na_2CO_3 in the charcoal cavity. Heat in an oxidizing flame. Add 1 drop of $Co(NO_3)_2$ to the dry mass and heat again a blue mass (Thenard's blue) confirms Al^{3+}.
Al^{3+}</td></tr>
</table>

(iii) Solid NH_4Cl should be added in excess, otherwise cations like Zn^{2+} and Mn^{2+} may be precipitated here.

(iv) If on adding a few drops of conc. HNO_3, a thick heavy ppt. settles down, the presence of Ba^{2+} is indicated. This dissolves on dilution.

(v) After the addition of NH_4Cl, the solution should be warmed but not boiled before adding NH_4OH, otherwise chromium, if present, will result in a pink coloured soluble complex $[Cr(NH_3)_6(OH)_3]$.

(vi) Too much excess of NH_4Cl should be avoided otherwise Cr^{3+} is not precipitated and $Al(OH)_3$ may from a colloidal solution.

(vii) The KSCN test for ferric (Fe^{3+}) ion is highly sensitive. A pink colour is given by it in any solution. Only a deep red colour in a dilute solution indicates ions.

(viii) Ferrous iron if present should be changed into ferric iron by boiling with a few drops of conc. HNO_3.

Chemistry of the Reactions Involved

I. If Group II filtrate is coloured, the solution should be boiled with nitric acid to oxidize the ferrous salt to ferric salt. The oxidation is necessary because ferrous hydroxide is not completely precipitated and also the colour of ferrous hydroxide is light green which is similar to that of chromium trioxide.

$$2HNO_3 \rightarrow 2NO + H_2O + 3(O)$$

$$FeCl_2 + 2HCl + (O) \rightarrow 2FeCl_3 + H_2O$$

or $$3Fe^{2+} + NO_3^- + 4H^+ \rightarrow 3Fe^{3+} + NO + 2H_2O$$

II. On treatment of the solution with NH_4Cl and NH_4OH, the cations of Group III are precipitated as hydroxides.

$$M^{3+} + 3OH^- \rightarrow M(OH)_3 \ [M = \text{Fe, Cr and Al}]$$

Indentification of Iron The brown ppt. of ferric hydroxide dissolves in dil. HCl to yield a yellow solution of ferric chloride.

$$Fe(OH)_3 + 3HCl \rightarrow FeCl_3 + 3HCl$$

(i) With potassium ferrocyanide solution, ferric ions yield a deep blue colour or a ppt. of ferric ferrocyanide or prussian blue.

$$FeCl_3+K_4[Fe(CN)_6]\rightarrow KFe[Fe(CN)_6]+3KCl$$

potassium ferric ferrocyanide (prussain blue)

(ii) With potassium sulphocyanide solution, ferric ions yield a blood-red colouration due to the formation of potassium ferric sulphocyanide.

$$EeCl_3+6KSCN\rightarrow K_3Fe(SCN)_6+3KCl$$

(blood red colour)

With potassium sulphocyanide solution, ferrous ions do not react.

(iii) With potassium ferricyanide solution, ferrous ions yield a deep blue colour or a ppt. of Turnbull's blue.

$$FeCl_2+K_3[Fe(CN)_6]\rightarrow KFe[Fe(CN)_6]+2KCl$$

(Turnbull's blue)

With potasium ferricyanide solution ferric ions yield a brown colouration.

Identification of Chromium When the dirty green ppt. of $Cr(OH)_3$ is boiled with Na_2O_2 (or $NaOH+H_2O_2$), it dissolves and forms a yellow coloured chromate.

$$2Cr(OH)_3+3Na_2O_2\rightarrow 2Na_2CrO_4+2NaOH+2H_2O$$

sodium chromate

(i) With lead acetate solution, sodium chromate solution yield a yellow ppt. of lead chromate.

$$CrO_4^{2-}+Pb^{2+}\rightarrow PbCrO_4$$

yellow ppt,

(ii) With acidified chromate solution, H_2O_2 forms a blue peroxide of chromium which is stable in other medium.

$$2Na_2CrO_4 + H_2SO_4 \rightarrow Na_2Cr_2O_7 + H_2O + Na_2SO_4$$

$$Na_2Cr_2O_7 + H_4SO_2 \rightarrow Na_2SO_2 + H_2Cr_2O_7$$

$$H_2Cr_2O_7 + 4H_2O_2 \rightarrow 2CrO_5 + 5H_2O$$

Indentification of Aluminium When the white ppt. of aluminium hydroxide is treated with NaOH solution, the ppt. dissolves due to the formation of sodium meta-aluminate.

$$Al(OH)_3 + NaOH \rightarrow \underset{\text{sodium meta-aluminate}}{NaAlO_2} + 2H_2O$$

(i) When the solution of sodium meta-aluminates is boiled with ammonium chloride, a white gelatinous ppt. of aluminium hydroxide is formed.

$$NaAlO_2 + H_2O + NH_4Cl \rightarrow Al(OH)_3 + NaCl + NH_3$$

(ii) The white precipitate of $Al(OH)_3$ absorbs the blue colouring matter of litmus and turns blue.

Analysis of Group IV Cations (Ni^{2+}, Co^{2+}, Zn^{2+} and Mn^{2+})

Concentrate the filtrate from Group III to a small volume. Take a portion of this solution. To this odd a pinch of NH_4Cl (solid) followed by a small amount of dil. ammonia (1:1) to make it ammoniacal. Now pass H_2S gas through it in excess. If ppt. is obtained, then pass H_2S through whole of solution after adding solid NH_4Cl and making it ammoniacal by adding dil. ammonia (1:1). Filter and preserve the filtrate for the next group. The ppt. may consists of sulphides of

Ni, Co	Mn	Zn
(black)	(buff)	(white)

Analyse the precipitata in accordance with Table 3.10.

TABLE 3.10

Analysis of Group IV Cations
(Ni^{2+}, Co^{2+}, Mn^{2+}, and Zn^{2+})

<table>
<tr><td colspan="4">Wash the ppt. with hot water and dissolve in very dil. HCl. Warm the solution and filter.</td></tr>
<tr><td colspan="2">Residue Black residue may have NiS, CoS. Dissolve the residue in aqua regia. Evaporate it to dryness. Note the colour of the residue. If it is blue, it indicates cobalt. If it is yellow, it indicates nickel. If green, both cobalt and nickel may be present.

Extract the residue with water and divide into five parts.</td><td colspan="2">Filtrate It may have Zn^{2+} and Mn^{2+}. Boil off H_2S and add NaOH and H_2O_2 or Br_2 water. Filter</td></tr>
<tr><td>(i) To part I add NH_4OH and dimethylglyoxime solution—a red ppt. confirms Ni^{2+}.
(ii) To part II add NaOH and Br_2 water. A black precipitate confirms Ni^{2+}

Ni^{2+}</td><td>(i) To part III add NH_4SCN solution and amyl alcohol, a blue coloured amyl alcohol layer confirms Co^{2+}.
(ii) To part IV, add NH_4Cl and NH_4OH. Then add $K_3Fe(CN)_6$ solution and warm gently. Reddish-brown ppt. or colouration indicates cobalt.

Co^{2+}</td><td rowspan="2">Residue It may be brown to black due to $Mn(OH)_2$ or MnO.OH. Dissolve the ppt. in dil HNO_3 and H_2O_2 Heat to decompose excess of H_2O_2
Divide this into four parts:
(i) To part I add Br_2 water and NaOH. Boil. A black precipitate confirms Mn^{2+}.
(ii) To part II add PbO_2 and conc. HNO_3. Boil, cool and dilute the contents. A pink colouration confirms Mn^{2+}.
(iii) To part III, add a pinch of solid sodium bismuthate. Formation of a purple colour confirms Mn^{2+}.

Mn^{2+}</td><td rowspan="2">Filtrate If may have Na_2ZnO_2. Divide this into three parts.
(i) In part I, pass H_2S gas. A white ppt. confirms Zn^{3+}.
(ii) Acidify part II with dil. H_2SO_4 and add 0.1% $CuSO_4$ solution and ammonium mercury-thiocyanate reagent. Stir. A violet ppt. confirms Zn^{2+}.
(iii) Acidify part III with dil. HCl and add $K_4Fe(CN)_6$.
A bluish white ppt. confirms Zn^{2+}.

Zn^{2+}</td></tr>
<tr><td colspan="2">Test for Co^{2+} and Ni^{2+} if present together To part V add $NaHCO_3$ and Br_2 water dropwise Shake the dish. If an apple green colour is obtained in cold, it confirms Co^{2+}. If on heating a black colour appears, it confirms Ni^{2+}.</td></tr>
</table>

Preparation of Ammonium Mercuric Thiocyanate Dissolve 1.6 g of $HgCl_2$ and 1.8 g of NH_4SCN in 20 mL of H_2O.

Notes I. For the confirmation of Group IV cations dry tests are quite reliable and must be carried out with great care.

II. Carry out the cobalt nitrate charcoal cavity test for zinc with white ppt. The formation of a green mass confirms the presence of Zn^{2+}.

III. Carry out the borax bead test with the black ppt. of nickel or the buff coloured ppt. of manganese.

IV. Pass H_2S gas in hot solution as in cold zinc and manganese sulphides form a fine suspension especially when present in small amounts.

V. The solution should be strongly ammoniacal before passing H_2S gas so that the cations of Group IV are completely precipitated.

Chemistry of the Reactions Involved

1. Precipitation When H_2S gas is passed through the ammoniacal solution, the cations of Group IV will be precipitated as sulphides.

$$M^{2+} + H_2S \rightarrow MS + 2H^+ \quad [M = Ni, Co, Mn, Zn]$$

The *solubility product* values for Group II sulphides are smaller than those for Group IV sulphides. It means that the concentration of S^{2-} ions required for Group IV cations will be high as compared to that for Group II cations.

But the concentration of S^{2-} in acidic medium is low. Therefore, the sulphides of Group IV cations will not be precipitated in Group II. However, the concentration of S^{2-} ions in acidic medium is quite sufficient to precipitate Group II cations.

$$HCl \rightleftharpoons H^+ + Cl^-$$

$$H_2S \rightleftharpoons 2H^+ + S^{2-}$$

In the presense of NH_4OH, the concentration of S^{2-} becomes appreciably large to preciptate Group IV cations.

$$NH_4OH \rightleftharpoons NH_4^+ + OH^-$$

$$H_2S \rightleftharpoons 2H^+ + S^{2-}$$

$$H^+ + OH^- \rightarrow H_2O$$

2. *Separation.* When the sulphides of Ni, Co, Mn and Zn are treated with dil. HCl only MnS and ZnS go into the solution while NiS and CoS are unaffected.

$$MnS + 2HCl \rightarrow MnCl_2 + H_2S$$
$$ZnS + 2HCl \rightarrow ZnCl_2 + H_2S$$

3. *Identification of Nickel and Cobalt* When NiS and CoS are treated with aqua regia, they dissolve to yield green solution due to the formation of hydrated chlorides of Ni and Co.

$$MS + 2HCl + \underset{\text{(from nitric acid)}}{O} \rightarrow MCl_2 + H_2O$$

$[M = \text{Ni and Co}]$

(i) Nickel chloride in ammoniacal medium forms a red ppt. (chelete) with dimethylglyoxime.

$$NiCl_2 + 2NH_4OH + 2\begin{array}{l} CH_3-C=NOH \\ \quad\quad | \\ CH_3-C=NOH \end{array} \rightarrow 2NH_4Cl + 2H_2O +$$

$$\begin{array}{ccccc} & & OH & & O \\ & & | & & \uparrow \\ CH_3-C & = & N & N & =C-CH_3 \\ | & & \searrow & \swarrow & | \\ & & & Ni & \\ | & & \nearrow & \nwarrow & | \\ CH_3-C & = & N & N & =C-CH_3 \\ & & \downarrow & | & \\ & & O & OH & \end{array}$$

bis(dimethylgyoximato)nickel(II)

(ii) Nickel chloride in presence of NaOH and Br_2 water yields black ppt. of Ni_2O_3.

$$NiCl_2 + 2NaOH \rightarrow Ni(OH)_2 + 2NaCl$$

$$2Ni(OH)_2 + H_2O + O \rightarrow 2Ni(OH)_3$$

$$2Ni(OH)_3 \rightarrow Ni_2O_3 + 3H_2O$$

(iii) Cobalt chloride forms blue coloured complex with NH_4SCN which is extractable into amyl alcohol.

$$COCl_2 + 4NH_4SCN \rightarrow (NH_4)_2[Co(SCN)_4] + 2NH_4Cl$$

(iv) $K_3Fe(CN)_6$ yields reddish brown ppt. with $CoCl_2$.

$$3CoCl_2 + 2K_3Fe(CN)_6 \rightarrow Co_3[Fe(CN)_6]_2 + 6KCl$$

(v) When the solution is treated with excess of sod. bicarbonate, cobalt forms a pink coloured complex sod. tricarbonatocobalt(II) which on treatment with bromine water is oxidized to green coloured sod. tricarbonatocobalt(III).

$$CoCl_2 + 2NaHCO_3 \rightarrow Co(HCO_3)_2 + 2NaCl$$

$$Co(HCO_3)_2 + 4NaHCO_3 \rightarrow \underset{\text{sod. tricarbonatocobalt(II) (pink)}}{Na_4Co(CO_3)_3} + 3H_2O + 3CO_2$$

$$2Na_4Co(CO_3)_3 + Br_2 \rightarrow \underset{\text{sod. tricarbonatocobalt(III) (green)}}{2Na_3Co(CO_3)_3} + 2NaBr$$

Nickel does not form a complex with $NaHCO_3$ but on heating with bromine water, it is oxidized to black nickelic oxide.

$$Br_2 + H_2O \rightarrow 2HBr + O$$

$$NiCl_2 + 2NaHCO_3 \rightarrow NiCO_3 + 2NaCl + H_2O + CO_2$$

$$2NiCO_3 + 3H_2O + O \rightarrow 2Ni(OH)_3 + 2CO_2$$

$$2Ni(OH)_3 \rightarrow \underset{\text{(black)}}{Ni_2O_3} + 3H_2O$$

4. *Identification of Manganese* To the solution of manganese chloride, sodium hydroxide solution is added. A white ppt. of manganese hydroxide is obtained which turns brown on exposure to atmospheric oxygen due to the formation of MnO(OH).

$$MnCl_2+2NaOH \rightarrow Mn(OH)_2$$

$$Br_2+H_2O \rightarrow 2HBr+O$$

$$2Mn(OH)_2+O \rightarrow 2MnO(OH)+H_2O$$

(brown ppt.)

(i) The brown ppt. of MnO(OH) on boiling with PbO_2 and conc. HNO_3 yields a pink colouration on dilution.

$$PbO_2+2HNO_3 \rightarrow Pb(NO_3)_2+H_2O+(O)$$

$$2MnO_2+H_2O+(O) \rightarrow 2HMnO_4$$

(pink colour)

(ii) With sodium bismuthate, in acidic medium, manganese(II) yields pink colour due do MnO_4^- ion.

$$2Mn^{2+}+BiO_3^-+14H^+ \rightarrow 2MnO_4^-+5Bi^{3+}+7H_2O$$

(pink colour)

5. *Identification of Zinc* When zinc. chloride solution is treated with caustic soda solution, a white ppt. of zinc hydroxide is first obtained which when treated with excess of caustic soda solution goes into solution due to the formation of soluble complex sodium zincate.

$$ZnCl_2+2NaOH \rightarrow Zn(OH)_2+2NaCl$$

(white ppt.)

$$Zn(OH)_2+2NaOH \rightarrow Na_2ZnO_2+2H_2O$$

sodium zincate
(soluble)

(i) On passing H_2S gas through sodium zincate, a white ppt. of ZnS is obtained.

$$Na_2ZnO_2+H_2S \rightarrow ZnS+2NaOH$$

(ii) Acidic solution of zinc reacts with $CuSO_4$ and $(NH_4)_2[Hg(SCN)_4]$ to yield violet ppt. of $Zn[Hg(SCN)_4]$ and $Cu[Hg(SCN)_4]$.

$$(NH_4)_2[Hg(SCN)_4] + ZnSO_4 \rightarrow Zn[Hg(SCN)_4]$$
$$(NH_4)_2[Hg(SCN)_4] + CuSO_4 \rightarrow Cu[Hg(SCN)_4]$$

(iii) When potassium ferrocyanide solution is added to zinc chloride solution, white or bluish white ppt. of zinc ferrocyanide is formed.

$$2ZnCl_2 + K_4[Fe(CN)_6] \rightarrow \underset{\text{zinc ferrocyanide}}{Zn_2[Fe(CN)_6]} + 4KCl$$

Analysis of Group V Cations (Ba^{2+}, Sr^{2+} and Ca^{2+})

As the volume of the solution obtained after the removal of Group IV cations as sulphides is very large, it becomes essential to concentrate the solution and to remove the residual H_2S. Evaporate the solution to one-third of the bulk. Make it ammoniacal and then add a concentrated solution of $(NH_4)_2CO_3$ or solid $(NH_4)_2CO_3$. Warm the solution. The formation of a white ppt. indicates the presence of Group V cations. Filter and retain the filtrate for Group VI. The white ppt. may consist of carbonates of Ba, Sr and Ca Analyse the ppt. for Group V as given in Table 3.11.

Notes (*i*) Freshly prepared concentrated solution of $(NH_4)_2CO_3$ should be used for precipitating carbonates of Group V. Use of NH_4Cl stops the precipitation of $MgCO_3$.

(*ii*) Warming of the solution is essential to make the ppt. granular. Boiling of the solution valatilizes $(NH_4)_2CO_3$.

(*iii*) White ppt. of CaC_2O_4 forms immediately from concentrated solution but slowly from dilute solutions.

(*iv*) Sr^{2+} should only be precipitated with $(NH_4)_2SO_4$ solution. Other soluble sulphates or dil. H_2SO_4 should not be used for the precipitation of $SrSO_4$. With $(NH_4)_2SO_4$, however, Ca^{2+} forms a soluble complex salt $(NH_4)_2]$ $[Ca(SO_4)_2]$ and hence remains in solution.

TABLE 3.11

Analysis of Group V Cations

(Ba^{2+}, Sr^{2+} and Ca^{2+})

Wash the ppt. with hot water and dissolve in dil. acetic acid. Boil off CO_2 and cool. Add potassium chromate solution to a part of this solution. If a yellow ppt. is obtained, this indicates the presence of Ba^{2+}. If it is so, add potassium chromate solution to the remaining solution and filter it.		
Yellow ppt. ($BaCrO_4$). Wash the ppt. with hot water and dissolve in HCl (1:1). Divide it into two parts. (i) Dilute part I with water and add dil. H_2SO_4. A white ppt. ($BaSO_4$) insoluble in acids confirms Ba^{2+}. (ii) Evaporate part II to dryness and apply the flame test. A grassy green flame confirms Ba^{2+}.	*Filtrate* May contain Sr^{2+} and Ca^{2+}. If Ba^{2+} is absent, then start directly without adding K_2CrO_4 solution. Now add $(NH_4)_2SO_4$ solution to it. Boil the solution and allow it to stand. Filter.	
	White ppt. ($SrSO_4$). Sr^{2+} may be present. Dissolve the white ppt. in conc. HCl and perform flame test. The appearance of a crimson red flame confirms Sr^{2+}	*Filtrate* May contain Ca^{2+}. Add $(NH_4)_2C_2O_4$ solution and heat it on a water bath. White crystalline ppt. indicates Ca^{2+}. Dissolve the ppt. in a few drops of conc. HCl and apply flame test. A brick red flame confirms Ca^{2+}.

Chemistry of the Reactions Involved

1. *Precipitation* When ammonium carbonate is added to the ammoniacal solution of the filtrate obtained from Group IV the carbonates of Group V cations are precipitated.

$$BaCl_2 + (NH_4)_2CO_3 \rightarrow BaCO_3 + 2NH_4Cl$$
(white ppt.)
(same with $SrCl_2$ and $CaCl_2$)

When acetic acid is added to the carbonates of Group V cations, the corresponding soluble acetates are obtained.

$$BaCO_3 + 2CH_3COOH \rightarrow (CH_3COO)_2Ba + H_2O + CO_2$$
(same with $SrCO_3$ and $CaCO_3$)

2. *Identification of Barium* With potasium chromate solution the soluble barium acetate yields yellow ppt. of barium chromate.

$$(CH_3COO)_3Ba + K_2CrO_4 \rightarrow 2CH_3COOK + BaCrO_4$$
(yellow ppt.)

3. *Identification of Strontium* When ammonium sulphate solution is added to the soluble strontium acetate, the insoluble strontium sulphate is obtained.

$$(CH_3COO)_2Sr + (NH_4)_2SO_4 \rightarrow 2CH_2COONH_4 + SrSO_4$$
(white ppt.)

4. *Identification of Calcium* When ammonium oxalate is added to soluble calcium acetate, the insoluble calcium oxalate is formed.

$$(CH_3COO)_2Ca + (NH_4)_2C_2O_4 \rightarrow 2CH_3COONH_3 + CaC_2O_4$$
(white ppt.)

Analysis of Group VI Cations (Mg^{2+}, Na^+ and K^+)

Concentrate the filtrate for Group VI by evaportion and then add $(NH_4)_2SO_4$ and $(NH_4)_2C_2O_4$ solutions if Group V is present. Now boil the solution to ensure the complete removal of

Group V cations. If a ppt. appears, filter and reject the ppt. The clear solution thus obtained is evaporated to dryness and heated until all the ammonium salts have been volatilized. Analyse the residue left in the heating dish as given in Table 3.12.

TABLE 3.12

Analysis of Group VI Cations
(Mg^{2+}, K^+ and Na^+)

Treat the residue with 15 mL of water, stir, warm for 1 min and filter.

Residue	*Filtrate*
Dissolve the residue in a few drops of dil. HCl and add 5-6 mL of water. Divide the solution into three parts:	Divide it into two portions First portion: Divide it into 3 parts.
(I) To part I add a little of NH_4Cl and NH_4OH in slight excess and then Na_2HPO_4 solution. Shake and scratch the sides of the test tube with a glass rod. A white crytalline ppt. appears after few minutes. Dissolve the above white ppt. in a little dil. HCl. To this add a few drops of magneson reagent. Now add NaOH to make the solution alkaline. A blue colour or ppt. confirms Mg^{2+}.	(I) To part I, add a saturated solution of picric acid. Formation of yellow ppt. confirms K^+.
(II) To part II add a few a drops of titan yellow solution. Make it alkaline with NaOH solution. Warm gently. A red ppt. confirms Mg^{2+}.	(II) To part II, add a few drops of sodium cobaltinitrite solution. Formation of yellow ppt. confirms K^+.
(III) To part III, add a few drops of cobalt nitrate solution. Soak a filter paper cutting into this solution and ignite this. If a pink ash of CoO.MgO. is produced, this confirms Mg^{2+}.	(III) Perform flame test with Part III. A lilac flame which appears crimson through a blue glass confirms K^+.

Residue	*Filtrate*
	Second Portion. Divide it into three parts. (i) To part I, add zinc uramyl acetate, shake it well, after few minutes yellow crystalline ppt. is formed, this confirms Na^+. (ii) To part II, add potassium pyroantimonate solution, white ppt. on scratching confirms Na^+. (iii) With part III perform the flame test. A golden yellow flame confirms Na^+. Na^+

Preparation of Sodium Cobaltinitrite Mix dil. CH_3COOH and $NaNO_2$ (solid) with a $CoCl_2$ solution and allow to stand until brown fumes have stopped to come off.

Notes (i) The precipitation of Mg^{2+} as $Mg(NH_4)PO_4$ is slow. Therefore, scratching is done and time allowed before filtration.

(ii) The filtrate of Group V should be concentrated by evaportion for testing Mg^{2+}.

(iii) For testing K^+, a freshly prepared solution of cobaltinitrite is used.

(iv) NH_4^+ gives some tests, of K^+. Hence NH_4^+ should be decomposed before testing for K^+.

(v) When both Na^+ and K^+ are identified by flame test only sodium flame becomes visible as it masks the flame due to potassium, but when seen through blue glass only crimson light appears due to potassium.

Chemistry of the Reactions Involved

1. *Identification of Magnesium* The residue dissolves in dil. HCl and it gives magnessium chloride, which is soluble in water. Magnesium chloride forms a white crystalline ppt. of magnesium ammonium phosphate with disodiumhydrogen phosphate in the presence of NH_4OH.

$$MgCl_2 + Na_2HPO_4 + NH_4OH + 5H_2O \rightarrow \underset{\text{(white ppt.)}}{Mg(NH_4)PO_4} + 6H_2O + 2NaCl$$

2. *Identification of Potassium*

(i) With setureted solution of picric acid, K^+ ion forms yellow ppt. of potassium picrate.

$$\underset{\text{picric acid}}{C_6H_2(NO_2)_3OH} + K^+ \rightarrow \underset{\text{(yellow ppt.)}}{C_6H_2(NO_2)_3OK} + H^+$$

(ii) With sodium cobaltinitrite, K^+ ion form yellow ppt.

$$Na_3[Co(NO_2)_6] + 3K^+ \rightarrow \underset{\text{(yellow ppt.)}}{K_3[Co(NO_2)_6]} + 3Na^+$$

3. *Identification of Sodium*

(i) With zinc uranyl acetete, Na^+ ion forms yellow ppt.

$$Na^+ + Zn^{2+} + 3H_3COO^- + 3UO_2(CH_3COO)_2 + 9H_2O \rightarrow \underset{\text{(yellow ppt.)}}{NaZn(UO_2)_3(CH_3COO)_3.9H_2O}$$

(ii) With potassium pyroantimonate, Na^+ ion forms white ppt. of sodium pyrontimonate.

$$2Na^+ + K_2H_2Sb_2O_7 \rightarrow \underset{\text{(white ppt.)}}{Na_2H_2Sb_2O_7} + 2K^+$$

ANALYSIS OF INSOLUBLE MIXTURES

Some times the systematic analysis of the cations is not possible due to the presence of insoluble substances (insoluble in conc. HCl or conc. HNO_3 or even in aqua regia) in the mixture. Such mixtures are called insoluble mixtures. All insoluble substances can be analysed by using special treatment which is based mainly, on bringing them into solution by indirect methods. Insoluble substances have been classified according to their colour.

Colour	*Residue*
White	AgCl, $PbSO_4$, $BaSO_4$, $SrSO_4$, SnO_2, Sb_2O_3, Al_2O_3, CaF_2
Yellow	AgBr, AgI
Green	Cr_2O_3, $Cr_2(SO_4)_3$
Black	HgS
Red	Fe_2O_3
Violet	$CrCl_3$

The part which is not dissolved in conc. acids is filtered and washed with water. Analyse the insoluble residue in accordance with Table 3.13.

TABLE 3.13

Analysis of Insoluble Substances

Treat the insoluble residue with conc. ammonium acetete and acetic acid. Now heat and filter.

<table>
<tr>
<td rowspan="4">*Filtrate* It may have Pb^{2+}, Cl^-, Br^-, I^- and SO_4^{2-}. Confirm by usual tests.</td>
<td colspan="5">*Residue* It Pb^{2+} is present in the filtrate repeat the above treatment until filtrate give a negative test for Pb^{2+}. Now warm the residue with conc. KCN solution and filter.</td>
</tr>
<tr>
<td rowspan="3">*Filtrate* It may have Ag^+, Cl^-, Br^-, I^- and CN^-. pass H_2S gas through the filtrate. If a black ppt. is obtained, dissolve it in dil. HNO_3 and add dil. HCl. A white crudy ppt. confirms Ag^+.
If Ag^+ is present, take the original residue and add zinc piece and dil. H_2SO_4. Keep it for 10-15 min. Filter the solution and test for Cl^-, Br^- I^- in the filtrate by the usual tests.</td>
<td colspan="4">*Residue* Fuse the residue with an excess of the fusion mixture (Na_2CO_3 and KNO_3 in 3:1 by weight) in Pt or Ni crucible. Cool, extract the residue with water and filter.</td>
</tr>
<tr>
<td colspan="2">*Filtrate* It may have Cr^{3+}, Al^{3+}, Sn^{4+}, F^- and SO_4^{2-}.Add conc. HCl and evaporate to dryness. Treat it with conc. HCl add water heat and filter.</td>
<td colspan="2">*Residue* It may have Ba^{2+}, Sr^{2+}, Ca^{2+}, F^+, SnO_2, Sb_2O_3, Al_2O_3 and Fe_2O_3. Treet the residue with dil. HNO_3 and filter.</td>
</tr>
<tr>
<td>*Filtrate* It may have Sn^{4+}, Al^{3+} and Cr^{3+} Test for these cations as usual.</td>
<td>*Residue* It may have SiO_2. Test by microcosmic bead test as usual.</td>
<td>*Filtrate* It may have Ba^{2+}, Sr^{2+} Ca^{2+}, NO_3^-. Test these radicals by usual tests.</td>
<td>*Residue* If it is brown confirm iron in it by borax bead test, as usual. In order to confirm the other cations, fuse the residue.</td>
</tr>
</table>

Specimen Record of Mixture Analysis

The method to be adopted in recording results is illustrated in the following examples.

Experiment to analyse the given mixture

S. No.	*Experiment*	*Observation*	*Inference*
	Dry Tests		
1.	Note the colour of the mixture.	Bluish green colour	Cu, Ni may be present
2.	Heat the given mixture in a dry test tube.	White fumes with pungent smell, give thick white fumes with NH_4OH solution.	Cl^- may be present
3.	Perform the flame test with the given mixture.	Bluish-green flame	Cu may be present
4.	Perform the borax bead test with the mixture.	Green bead when hot, blue when cold	Cu may be present
5.	Heat the mixture with fusion mixture in charcoal cavity in the reducing flame.	Red scales	Cu may be present
6.	Did not perform the cobalt nitrate test because the residue was not white.		
7.	Add dil. H_2SO_4 to the small amount of the mixture.	No action	CO_3^{2-}, S^{2-}, SO_3^{2-}, NO_2^-, etc. absent
8.	Add conc. H_2SO_4 to the small amount of mixture.	Colourless gas with pungent odour (HCl) evolves and gives thick white fumes (NH_4Cl) with NH_4OH solution.	Cl^- may be present
	Wet Tests (Acid Radicals)		
9.	Prepare the clear and transparent solution.		

10. To portion of the solution, add dil. HNO_3 and $AgNO_3$ solution.	White ppt. soluble in NH_4OH solution	Cl^- confirmed
11. To the given mixture add solid $K_2Cr_2O_7$ + conc. H_2SO_4, heat the contents, pass the red vapours through NaOH solution (Chromyl-chloride test).	Yellow solution; add CH_3COOH and $Pb(CH_3COO)_2$ solution; yellow ppt.	Cl^- confirmed
12. To another portion of solution, add $BaCl_2$ solution.	White ppt. of $BaSO_4$ insoluble in any mineral acid	SO_4^{2-} confirmed
13. To the given mixture add conc. H_2SO_4 and ethyl alcohol. Ignite the vapours over the test tube.	A green-edged flame	BO_3^{3-} confirmed
Wet Tests (Basic Radicals)		
14. Heat the mixture with NaOH solution.	No NH_3 gas evolves	NH_4^+ absent
15. Prepare the clear and transparent solution in water or dil. or conc. HCl.		
16. Since the mixture is soluble in water, add dil. HCl to it.	No white ppt	Group I absent
17. Pass H_2S gas through solution.	Black ppt.	Group II present
18. Filter the black ppt. and dissolve in 50% HNO_3.	Ppt. dissolves	Hg^{2+} absent
19. To the part of the above solution add dil. H_2SO_4 and few drops of ethyl alcohol.	No white ppt.	Pb^{2+} absent
20. To the remaining portion of solution add NH_4OH solution in excess.	Deep blue colouration	Cu^{2+} may be present

21. To the above deep blue solution, add CH_3COOH and $K_4Fe(CN)_6$ solution.	Chocolate coloured ppt.	Cu^{2+} confirmed
22. In the filtrate of solution in expt. 17, pass H_2S gas again and again till there is no black ppt.	Chocolate coloured ppt.	Cu^{2+} confirmed
23. For the removal of BO_3^{3-} anion, boil off H_2S gas from the filtrate of Group II by evaporation and treat the residue with 3-4 times of conc. HCl. Dissolve the residue in dil. HCl and use it for Group III and others.		
22. Boil off the H_2S gas from the above solution, add solid NH_4Cl + conc. HNO_3, boil it, cool and add NH_4OH solution in excess.	White gelatinous ppt.	Al^{3+} may be present
25. Filter the white ppt. and dissolve the ppt. in dil. HCl.		
26. To the above solution add blue litmus solution, then drop by drop NH_5OH solution until the solution is just alkaline.	A blue-red lake	Al^{3+} confirmed
27. Pass H_2S gas through the filtrate of Group III.	Grey ppt.	Group IV present
28. Dissolve the ppt. in least amount of dil. HCl.	Ppt. dissolves	Zn^{2+} may be present

29. Boil off H_2S gas, add NaOH solution slowly in excess.	First a white ppt. is formed which dissolves in excess.	Zn^{2+} may be present
30. Pass H_2S gas in solution in expt. 29.	White ppt.	Zn^{2+} confirmed.

Result: The given mixture no. . . . contains

Acidic radicals Cl^-, SO_4^{2-}, BO_3^{3-}

Basic radicals Cu^{2+}, Al^{3+}, Zn^{2+}

VIVA-VOCE

Q. 1 Why is HCl employed in flame test?

Ans. The necessary condition for the flame test is that only the volatile compounds of cations impart colour to the flame. Only metal chlorides are volatile whereas their sulphates, nitrates, etc., are not. Thus, HCl is used to convert cations into their violatile chlorides.

Q. 2 What is the principle of flame test?

Ans. See text.

Q. 3 What type of flame is employed to perform the flame test? How is it obtained?

Ans. A non-luminuous flame is employed by keeping the holes of the burner open.

Q. 4 Why is a green flame not obtained in the case of barium sulphate or phosphate?

Ans. Barium sulphate and phosphate are not converted into chlorides easily. Therefore, the green flame is either indistinct or visible with difficulty.

Q. 5 Why is platinum were employed in the flame test?

Ans. Because platinum does not impart any colour to the flame, and the platinum wire is not attacked by conc. HCl even at a very high temperature.

Q. 6 Can we use iron or copper instead of platinum wire?

Ans. No. The reasons are:

(i) Both are attacked by conc. HCl.

(ii) Copper impart its own colour to the flame.

Q. 7 Do you know any substitute for platinum wire?

Ans. In place of a platinum wire, a short length nichrome wire may also be used. But it is not a satisfactory substitute.

Q. 8 A mixture of white colour when heated becomes yellow but becomes white again when cold. What does this indicate?

Ans. The mixture may contain zinc oxide or any zinc salt.

Q. 9 What is borax bead test?

Ans. See text.

Q. 10 What is the composition of the bead which is obtained in the borax bead test?

Ans. It consists of a mixture of sodium metaborate and boric anhydride.

Q. 11 Why is a small quantity of mixture used in the borax bead test?

Ans. Because otherwise the bead will become dark and opaque which in subsequent treatment cannot be recognized easily.

Q. 12 Name the cations whose oxides are not reduced in the charcoal cavity test?

Ans. These are Mg, Al, Sn and Zn because the oxides of all these metals glow in the cavity, are white in cold.

Q. 13 Then how are these tested?

Ans. By using the cobalt nitrate test.

Q. 14 What is this test?

Ans. This is a test generally performed if the white infusible residue is obtained in the charcoal cavity test. In this test, a drop of cabalt nitrate solution is added to the white infusible residue in the charcoal cavity. It is then heated by an oxidizing flame by means of a blow pipe. From the change in colour, the cation may be recognized.

Q. 15 What is decrepitation?

Ans. The crystals of certain substances containing an enclosed moisture or gases (e.g. rock salt, fluorspar, etc.) are burst by the quick expansion of the moisture of gases and pieces are scattered about with a sharp crackling sound. This is known as decrepitation.

Q. 16 What is deflagration?

Ans. Certain oxidizing agents like nitrates, chlorates, etc. cause a very rapid cumbustion of glowing charcoal. This is known as deflagration.

Q. 17 What is aqua-regia? Explain its functioning?

Ans. The mixture of 3 parts of conc. HCl and 1 part of conc. HNO_3 (by volume) is called aqua-regia.

$$HNO_3 + 3HCl \rightarrow H_2O + NOCl + 2Cl$$

(nitrosyl chloride)

In this reaction nitrogen is reduced (valency from +5 to +3) and chlorine is oxidized (valency from —1 to zero). It is good oxidizing agent.

Q. 18 Can H_2SO_4 be used instead of HCl for dissolving the mixture?

Ans. No we cannot use H_2SO_4 because (a) inoluble sulphates of Ba, Sr and Pb will be precipitated and will upset the whole scheme of qualitative analysis.

$$Ba^{2+} + SO_4^{2-} \longrightarrow BaSO_4$$

$$Sr^{2+} + SO_4^{2-} \longrightarrow SrSO_4$$

$$Pb^{2+} + SO_4^{2-} \longrightarrow PbSO_4$$

(b) When H_2S gas is passed through a solution containing H_2SO_4 reduction of the latter will produce a lot of sulphur which is difficult to handle.

$$H_2SO_4+H_2S \longrightarrow 2H_2O+5O_2+S$$

Q. 19 Can HNO_3 be used for dissolving the mixture?

Ans. Nitric acid will not interfere in first group but it will oxidize H_2S, the group reagent of second group into sulphur which is undesirable.

$$HNO_3+H_2S \longrightarrow 2H_2O+2NO_2+S$$

Q. 20 Why do you prefer dil. HCl for preparing original solution of basic radicals?

Ans. Because most of the salts are soluble in it except that of Group I. Further it does not interfere in the group analysis.

Q. 21 Can we test the basic radicals from the sodium carbonate extract residue?

Ans. Yes.

Q 22. How?

Ans. This can be used by dissolving the residue in dil. HCl and then proceeding as in the regular analysis.

Q. 23 Why does lead come in Group I as well as in Group II?

Ans. Lead is precipitated in Group I as $PbCl_2$. Since it is partly soluble in dil. HCl, a part of it goes into the filtrate which is to be tested for Group II radicals. Thus, on passing H_2S gas, it gives a black ppt. of PbS.

$$PbCl_2+H_2S \longrightarrow PbS+2HCl$$

Q. 24 How is H_2S gas prepared?

Ans. See text.

Q. 25 What do you understand by the term 'group reagent'?

Ans. A group reagent is a chemical substance or a mixture of chemical substances which is used in precipitation of a group of cations from their solutions. A group reagent contains an electrolyte having a common ion to that of the precipitated salt.

Q. 26 Name the group reagent for the various groups.

Ans. See text.

Q. 27 Can we use use conc. HCl in place of dil. HCl as group reagent for Group I?

Ans. No, because $PbCl_2$ is soluble in conc. HCl and therefore, it is not precipitated in Group I.

Q. 28 Why is it necessary to add HCl before proceeding to test Group II radicals?

Ans. HCl is added to suppress the ionization of H_2S. Thus, the lesser concentration of S^{2-} ions is available which is just sufficient to precipitate Group II radicals as their sulphides because their solubility products are low. On the other hand, the solubility products of Group IV radicals are very high and therefore they are not precipitated at all.

Q. 29 Explain why the sulphides of iron, zinc and manganese are not precipitated in Group II.

Ans. These sulphides are not precipitated because of their solubility products and of the presence of the acid in the solution. In the presence of HCl (a strong acid) the dissociation of H_2S is reduced (on account of the common ion effect) to such an extent that the concentration of the sulphide ion is insufficient to let the solubility products exceed. Since substances are precipitated only when their solubility products are exceeded, the sulphides of iron, zinc and manganese are not precipitated.

Q. 30 Why is the solution diluted in Group II before passing H_2S gas?

Ans. As the sulphides of Group II radicals are soluble in conc. HCl, they will not be completely precipitated if the solution is strongly acidic. For complete precipitation of Group II the solution must be sufficiently diluted with water.

Q. 31 Why is dilution necessary in the case of cadmium?

Ans. Cadmium generally creates difficulty as it is soluble partly even in dilute HCl. Its solution has thus to be diluted again and again and H_2S gas is passed until there is no precipitation.

Q. 32 How does yellow ammonium sulphide differ from ordinary ammonium sulphide?

Ans. The yellow ammonium sulphide $[(NH_4)_2S_n]$ contains a higher percentage of sulphur than ordinary ammonium sulphide.

Q. 33 How is it prepared?

Ans. It is prepared by passing H_2S gas in NH_4OH (1 vol. NH_3+2 vols. of H_2O) in which flowers of sulphur (10 g) are suspended, till a yellow solution is formed.

Q. 34 Why is white turbidity formed on diluting the solutions of $BiCl_3$ and $SbCl_3$?

Ans. These chlorides are hydrolyzed to their oxychlorides in excess of water, which are separated out as a white ppt. or turbidity.

$$MCl_3 + H_2O \rightarrow MOCl + 2HCl \quad [M = \text{Bi and Sb}]$$

(white ppt.)

Q. 35 Do you get ppt. on passing H_2S gas into any chloride of Bi, Sb or Sn?

Ans. Yes, their corresponding sulphides are precipitated.

$$2BiOCl + 2H_2S \rightarrow Bi_2S_3 + 2H_2O + 2HCl$$

(black ppt.)

$$2SbOCl + 3H_2S \rightarrow Sb_2S_3 + 2H_2O + 2HCl$$

(orange ppt.)

$$SnOCl_2 + 2H_2S \rightarrow SnS + H_2O + 2HCl$$

(yellow ppt.)

Q. 36 Why is it essential to remove assenic before testing phosphate radical?

Ans. Phosphate is tested by heating the mixture with conc. HNO_3 and ammonium molybdate when a *yellow ppt.* of ammonium phosphomolybdate indicates its presence. Arsenic also gives a *yellow ppt.* of ammonium arseno-molybdate under these conditions and hence interferes with this test. The test for phosphate should be performed after removing arsenic as As_2S_3 in Group II of the qualitative analysis.

Q. 37 How is sulphate tested in the presence of silver?

Ans. The test can be performed by preparing the solution of mixture in HNO_3 and treating with barium nitrate solution when only SO_4^{2-} will form a white ppt. of $BaSO_4$ and $AgNO_3$ will remain in solution.

Q. 38 Some times light yellow or white ppt. is obtained in the Group II even in the absence of the Group. Why, it is so?

Ans. The light yellow or white ppt. is due to the oxidation of H_2S into sulphur by certain oxidizing redicals, e.g. NO_2^-, SO_3^{--}, Fe^{3+}, etc.

$$2NaNO_2 + 2HCl + H_2S \rightarrow 2NaCl + 2NO + 2H_2O + S\downarrow$$

$$Na_2SO_3 + 2HCl + 2H_2S \rightarrow 2NaCl + 3H_2O + 3S\downarrow$$

$$2FeCl_3 + H_2S \rightarrow 2FeCl_2 + 2HCl + S\downarrow$$

Q. 39 Why is it essential to remove interfering radicals after Group II?

Ans. See text.

Q. 40 Why is it essential to boil off H_2S completely before proceeding to Group III?

Ans. If H_2S is not removed, the sulphides of the Group IV will also be precipitated along with Group III radicals.

Q. 41 Why is nitric acid added before the precipition of Group III?

Ans. Nitric acid is added to oxidize ferrous iron into ferric iron.

$$3FeSO_4 + 4HNO_3 \rightarrow Fe_2(SO_4)_3 + NO + 2H_2O$$

The oxidation of ferrous iron to ferric iron is essential due to the following reasons:

(a) Fe^{2+} is not completely precipitation as $Fe(OH)_2$ in presence of NH_4Cl by addition of NH_4OH whereas Fe^{3+} is completely precipitated as $Fe(OH)_3$ under the same conditions.

(b) Further $Fe(OH)_2$ is oxidized slowly to ferric hydroxide. Instead of getting a precipitate of a definite colour, the precipitate is differently coloured. Moreover, $Fe(OH)_2$ is green in colour like $Cr(OH)_3$ whereas $Fe(OH)_3$ is brown in colour. Thus, the colour of the precipitate of $Fe(OH)_3$ helps to distinguish it from $Cr(OH)_3$.

Q. 42 Why is a brownish ppt. obtained in Group III even if iron, aluminium and chromium are not present?

Ans. It is due to the precipitation of Mn as $MnO_2.H_2O$ which sometimes gets precipitated in the absence of sufficient NH_4Cl.

Q. 43 Why is ammonium chloride added before adding NH_4OH?

Ans. NH_4Cl suppresses the dissociation of NH_4OH to such an extent that solubility products of Group V are not reached and these are not precipitated alongwith the hydroxides of Group III radicals

$$NH_4Cl \rightleftharpoons NH_4^+ + Cl^-$$
$$NH_4OH \rightleftharpoons NH_4^+ + OH^-$$

Q. 44 Why is the large excess of NH_4OH avoided in Group III?

Ans. Because the hydroxides of Al and Cr are soluble in the large excess of NH_4OH. Therefore the large excess of NH_4OH is avoided.

Q. 45 Why can't you use $(NH_4)_2SO_4$ instead of NH_4Cl before adding NH_4OH in Group III of mixture analysis?

Ans. $(NH_4)_2SO_4$ cannot be used because if the mixture contains barium or strontium as radicals, they will be precipitated in Group III as insoluble sulphates. Thus, the scheme of the analysis will be upset.

Q. 46 Can we add NH_4OH first and then NH_4Cl?

Ans. No, because the role of NH_4Cl is lost. If you add NH_4OH before NH_4Cl, the radicals of Groups V and VI may be precipitated along with Group III.

Q. 47 Can we use NaCl and NaOH in place of NH_4Cl+NH_4OH as a group reagent for Group III?

Ans. No. As NaOH is a strong electrolyte, its ionization is not suppressed by NaCl. Hence, a larger concentration of OH^- ions is available which will exceed the solubility products of Group III along with Groups IV, V and VI hydroxides. Thus, Group IV, V and VI hydroxides will also be precipitated in Group III.

Moreover, NaOH will also dissolve the white ppt. of $Al(OH)_3$ and $Sn(OH)_2$ to form soluble $NaAlO_2$ and Na_2ZnO_2.

$$Al(OH)_3+NaOH \rightarrow NaAlO_2+2H_2O$$
$$Zn(OH)_3+2NaOH \rightarrow Na_2ZnO_2+2H_2O$$

Q. 48 Can we test chromium in $K_2Cr_2O_7$ by its usual tests?

Ans. No.

Q. 49 How will you test it?

Ans. In order to test it, H_2S gas a passed through acidified $K_2Cr_2O_7$ to reduce it to $Cr_2(SO_4)_3$ which can be tested for Cr as usual by adding NH_4OH in the filtrate.

$$K_2Cr_2O_7+3H_2S+4H_2SO_4 \rightarrow Cr_2(SO_4)_3+K_2SO_4+7H_2O+3S$$

Q. 50 What is the use of Na_2O_2 or Br_2 water and NaOH in the separation of Group III cations.

Ans. The ppt. of Group III cations are as hydroxides. NaOH has no action on $Fe(OH)_3$ but $Al(OH)_3$ and $Cr(OH)_3$ from soluble aluminate and chromite respectively.

$$M(OH)_3+NaOH \rightarrow NaMO_2+2H_2O$$
(where M=Al or Cr)

Na_2O_2 or bromine water oxidizes chromite into chromate (yellow colour solution) white aluminate remains unaffected.

$$Br_2 + 2NaOH \rightarrow NaOBr + NaBr + H_2O$$

$$2NaCrO_2 + 2NaOBr + 2NaOH \rightarrow Na_2CrO_4 + 2NaBr + H_2O$$

Q. 51 How will you explain the addition of excess of NH_4OH before passing H_2S in Group IV?

Ans. The solubility products of Group IV radicals are greater than those of Group II radicals. Therefore, a higher concentration of S^{2-} ions is required to preecipitate Group IV radicals as higher sulphides. Therefore, to get a higher concentration of S^{2-} ions, H_2S gas is passed in presence of NH_4OH The OH^- ions from NH_4OH neutralize the H^+ ions from H_2S to form undissociated water molecules. The removal the H^+ion causes more H_2S to dissociate or ionize, thus increasing the concentration of S^{2-} ions and so the product $[M^{2+}]$ $[S^{2-}]$ exceeds the solubility products of the sulphides of Zn, Mn, Ni and Co and hence they are precipitated.

$$(M = Zn, Mn, Co \text{ or } Ni)$$

$$2NH_4OH \rightleftharpoons 2NH_4^+ + 2OH^-$$

$$H_2S \rightleftharpoons 2H^+ + S^{2-}$$

$$2H^+ + 2OH^- \rightarrow 2H_2O$$

Q. 52 How can the formation of a colloidal precipitate be avoided in the zinc group?

Ans. Ammonium chloride must be present in sufficient amount. Large excess of H_2S should not be passed.

Q. 53 Why are all aqueous solutions of the cobaltous salts pink?

Ans. All aqueous solutions of cobaltous salts are pink due to the formation of $[Co(H_2O)_6]^{2+}$ion.

Q. 54 Suppose no black ppt. is obtained in Group IV, what does this indicate?

Ans. It means that Ni and Co are absent.

Q. 55 Sometime a black ppt. appears in Group IV even in the absence of Ni and Co. Explain it.

Ans. When $Fe^{3+}$is not precipitated completely in Group III it will be reduced to $Fe^{2+}$by H_2S which is then precipitated as black FeS in Group IV even when Co and Ni are absent.

$$FeCl_2+H_2S \rightarrow FeS+2HCl$$

Q. 56 Why is NH_4Cl essential in the precipitation of the calcium group?

Ans. Ammonium chloride prevents the precipitation of Mg^{2+}as $MgCO_3$ by the Group reagent $(NH_4)_2CO_3$ by lowering down its dissociation into NH_4^+ and CO_3^{2-} ions.

Q. 57 Does the excess of NH_4Cl interfere with the precipitation of the calcium group?

Ans. Yes, the concentration of CO_3^{2-} is decreased due to the reaction

$$2NH_4^+ + CO_3^{2-} \rightleftharpoons (NH_4)_2CO_3$$

to such an extent that the solubility products of Group V carbonates are not exceeded and therefore they are not precipitated.

Q. 58 How will you remove the excess of NH_4Cl before adding $(NH_4)_2CO_3$ for the precipitation of Group V?

Ans. This can be removed by heating the filtrate from Group IV to almost dryness with conc. HNO_3. Ammonium chloride is then decomposed according to the following equations:

$$NH_4Cl+HNO_3 \rightarrow NH_4NO_3+HCl$$

$$NH_4NO_3 \rightarrow N_2O+2H_2O$$

Q. 59 Why is $CaSO_4$ not precipitated on adding ammonium sulphate to a solution containing $Ca^{2+}$and Sr^{2+}ions?

Ans. $CaSO_4$ is not precipitated due to the formation of a complex with $(NH_4)_2SO_4$.

$$CaCl_2 + (NH_4)_2SO_4 \rightarrow CaSO_4 + 2NH_4Cl$$

$$CaSO_4 + (NH_4)_2SO_4 \rightarrow \underset{\text{(soluble complex)}}{(NH_4)_2[Ca(SO_4)_2]}$$

Q. 60 Why is NH_4OH added before adding $(NH_4)_2CO_3$, the precipitating agent for the calcuim group?

Ans. Ammonium hydroxide reacts with any bicarbonate present as impurity in $(NH_4)_2CO_3$.

$$NH_4HCO_3 + NH_4OH \rightarrow (NH_4)_2CO_3 + H_2O$$

The presence of bicarbonate is objectionable because the bicarbonates of Ba, Sr and Ca are soluble in water.

Q. 61 While precipitiating the calcium group, it is necessary to warm and not to boil the solution. Why.

Ans. Due to the presence of bicarbonate ion as an impurity in $(NH_4)_2CO_3$, $Ba^{2+}$and Sr^{2+} ions may form soluble bicarbonates. Warming decomposes these bicarbonates into normal carbonates which are precipitated.

$$Ca\,(HCO_3)_2 \rightarrow CaCO_3 + H_2O + CO_2$$

The solution must not be boiled otherwise insoluble carbonates with ammonium chloride are converted into soluble chlorides.

$$CaCO_3 + 2NH_4Cl \rightarrow CaCl_2 + (NH_4)_2CO_3$$

Q. 62 Why is it necessary to concentrate the filtrate of Group IV before testing for Group V radicals?

Ans. If the solution is not concentrated, $(NH_4)_2CO_3$ gets hydrolyzed.

Q. 63 Can we use Na_2CO_3 in place of $(NH_4)_2CO_3$ in Group V?

Ans. If Na_2CO_3 is used in place of $(NH_4)_2CO_3$, it will precipitate Group V radicals as well as magnesium radical. The reason for this is the high ionization of Na_2CO_3 in water into Na^+ and CO_3^{2-}. Now the higher concentration or CO_3^{2-} is available which exceeds the solubility products of Group V radicals as well as that of magnesium radical.

Q. 64 Why is it necessary to test Group V radicals in the order of Ba, Sr and Ca?

Ans. This order is selected on the basis of the following facts:

(a) Only the chromate of barium is insoluble in acetic acid whereas those of calcium and strontium are soluble in acetic acid.

(b) Both barium and strontium form sulphates but calcium does not.

(c) The oxalates of barium, strontium and calcium are insoluble.

Q. 65 Why is only accetic acid employed for dissolving the Group V ppt.?

Ans. It is due to the following reasons:

(a) If H_2SO_4 is used in place of acetic acid, Ba, Sr and Ca will be precipitated as their sulphates.

(b) If the ppt. is dissolved either in dil. HCl or in dil. HNO_3, calcium will not be precipitated by adding $(NH_4)_2C_2O_4$ because CaC_2O_4 formed gets dissolved in both dil. HCl and dil. HNO_3.

However, the use of CH_3COOH is free from the above difficulties. Hence, it is used for dissolving the Group V ppt.

Q. 66 How will you explain the solubility of calcium oxalate in dilute HCl?

Ans. When dilute HCl is added to calcium oxalate, the oxalate ions will combine with H^+ ions of HCl to form feebly ionized oxalic acid.

$$HCl \rightleftharpoons H^+ + Cl^-$$

$$\begin{array}{l} COO \\ | \\ COO \end{array}\!\!>\!Ca^+ 2H \rightleftharpoons \begin{array}{l} COOH \\ | \\ COOH \end{array} + Ca^{2+}$$

(feebly ionized)

Q. 67 What colours are produced in the flame by Ba, Sr and Ca?

Ans. These colours are as follows:

Radical	*Colour with naked eye*	*Colour through blue glass*
Ba	Persistent apple green	Bluish green
Sr	Crimson	Crimson
Cr	Brick red	Light green

Q. 68 Why are Group V radicals sometimes not precipitated, although present in the solution, on the addition of the Group reagent?

Ans. It generally happens if the filtrate for the Group V is very dilute. In such a case, $(NH_4)_2CO_3$ is hydrolyzed to NH_4OH and H_2CO_3.

$$(NH_4)_2CO_3 + 2H_4O \rightarrow 2NH_4OH + H_2CO_3$$

H_2CO_3 being a week acid does not ionize considerably and, therefore, the concentration of CO_3^{2-} ions in the solution remains quite low. Hence the solubility products of Group V carbonates are not reached and they are not precipitated.

Q. 69 **Why is a precipitate of magnesium carbonate not formed along with the carbonates of Ba, Sr and Ca in Group V?**

Ans. **For precipitation, Mg^{2+} requires a higher concentration of CO_3^{2-} to get itself precipitated as $MgCO_3$ which is insufficient in Group V due to the presence of NH_4Cl along with $(NH_4)_2CO_3$. The role of NH_4Cl is to suppress the ionization of $(NH_4)_2CO_3$, thereby resulting in a lower concentration of CO_3^{2-} ions due to the common ion effect.**

$$NH_4Cl \rightleftharpoons 2NH_4^+ + Cl^-$$
$$(NH_4)_2CO_3 \rightleftharpoons 2NH_4^+ + CO_3^{2-}$$

Q. 70 **How is magnesium precipitated in Group VI?**

Ans. **When the filtrate from Group V is treated with disodium hydrogen phosphate, a white crystalline ppt. of $Mg(NH_4)PO_4$ is obtained.**

$$MgCl_2 + Na_2HPO_4 + NH_3 \rightarrow MgNH_4PO_4 + 2NaCl$$

Q. 71 **What is a magneson reagent?**

Ans. **It is a 0.5 per cent solution of *p*-nitrobenzene-azo-resorcinol in 0.25 N NaOH solution.**

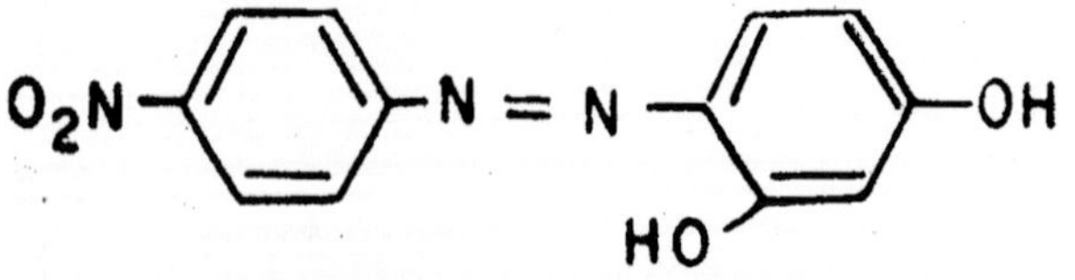

p-Nitrobenzene-azo-resorcinol

Q. 72 **What is the use of magneson reagent?**

Ans. **It is used for confirming Mg^{2+} ions. When magneson reagent is added to the filtrate obtained from Group V and then made alkaline with NaOH, a blue ppt. is formed.**

Q. 73 What is the formula of the blue ppt.?

Ans. With NaOH, Mg^{2+}ions present in the filtrate obtained from Group V yield a ppt. of magnesium hydroxide.

$$Mg^{2+} + 2OH^- \rightarrow Mg(OH)_2$$

On the ppt. of $Mg(OH)_2$, magneson dye is adsorbed to yield a blue coloured lake.

Magneson + Mg $(OH)_2$ → Blue lake.

Q. 74 Why are sodium, potassium and ammonium not precipitated in any of the Groups from I to VI?

Ans. Sodium, potassium and ammonium are not precipitated in any of the Groups from I to VI because these cations from soluble chlorides, sulphides, hydroxides and carbonates.

Q. 75 Why is a pair of cobalt glasses used in the flame test for K^+?

Ans. If sodium is present in the mixture even as an impurity, the reddish violet flame of potassium is masked by the intense yellow flame of sodium. Two thicknesses of cobalt glass completely absorb the yellow flame of sodium. Therefore, the flame of potassium is observed through a pair of cobalt glasses.

Q. 76 Do you know any chemical test for K^+?

Ans. Yes, If sodium cobaltinitirite $Na_3[Co(NO_2]_6$ is added to the filtrate from Group V, the formation of a yellow ppt. of potassium cobaltinitrite confirms the presence of K^+.

$$Na_3[Co(NO_2)_6] + 3KCl \rightarrow K_3[Co(NO_2)_6] + 3NaCl$$

4

SEMIMICRO QUALITATIVE ANALYSIS

Introduction

The purpose of the qualitative analysis of an inorganic mixture is to identify its constiuent ions—**anions** (also called **acid radicals**) and **cations** (also called **basic radicals**). The analysis may be performed by **physical**, **physico-chemical** and **chemical** methods. In chemical method of analysis, the constituent ion is usually converted into another compound of known characteristics and the parent ion is thereby inferred.

Various techniques employed in qualitative analysis depend upon the quantity of the samples used for analysis (Table 4.1).

Table 4.1

Method of analysis	*Amount of mixture used* (mg)
Micro	500-1000
Semimicro	10-100
Micro	1-10
Ultramicro	<1

Macro analsis and semimicro analysis are based essentially on similar principles. In semimicro analysis only the scale of

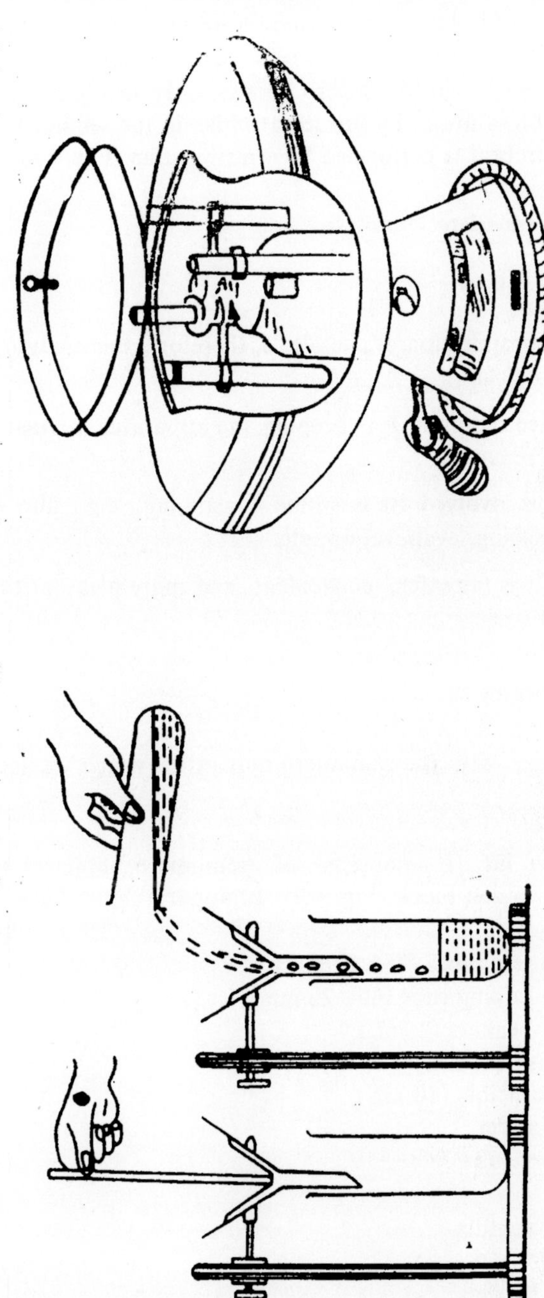

Separation of precipitate by filtration (macro analysis)

Separation ef residue by centrifugation (semimicro analysis)

Fig. 4.1. Separation of precipitate (residue).

operations is reduced with certain modifications in the general technique to suit the small quantities of solids and liquids to be handled. For example, in the macro analysis, the precipitate is removed from the solution by **filtration** while in the semimicro analysis the operation is performed by **centrifugation** (Fig. 4.1)

Advantages of Semimicro Qualitative Analysis

There are as follows:

(i) Lesser consumption of chemicals, therefore, this analysis is economical.

(ii) The space required for keeping the apparatus is considerably reduced.

(iii) The steps involved are less time consuming, e.g., filtration, washing, evaporation, etc.

(iv) Lastly, it is far safer, convenient and more pleasant to use.

Semimicro Apparatus

Let us get familiar with the semimicro apparatus which we use in the analysis.

1. **Semimicro kit.** It consists of semimicro apparatus mounted on a wooden block (Fig. 4.2). In apparatus, we have:

6 Semimicro test tubes (75×10 mm)
1 Semimicro boiling tube (60×25 mm)
2 Semimicro beakers (25mL)
1 Conical flask (10 mL)
1 Porcelain crucible (10 mL)
1 Test tube holder
1 Gas delivery tube
2 Droppers
1 Semimicro spatula
1 Glass rod (75×2 mm)

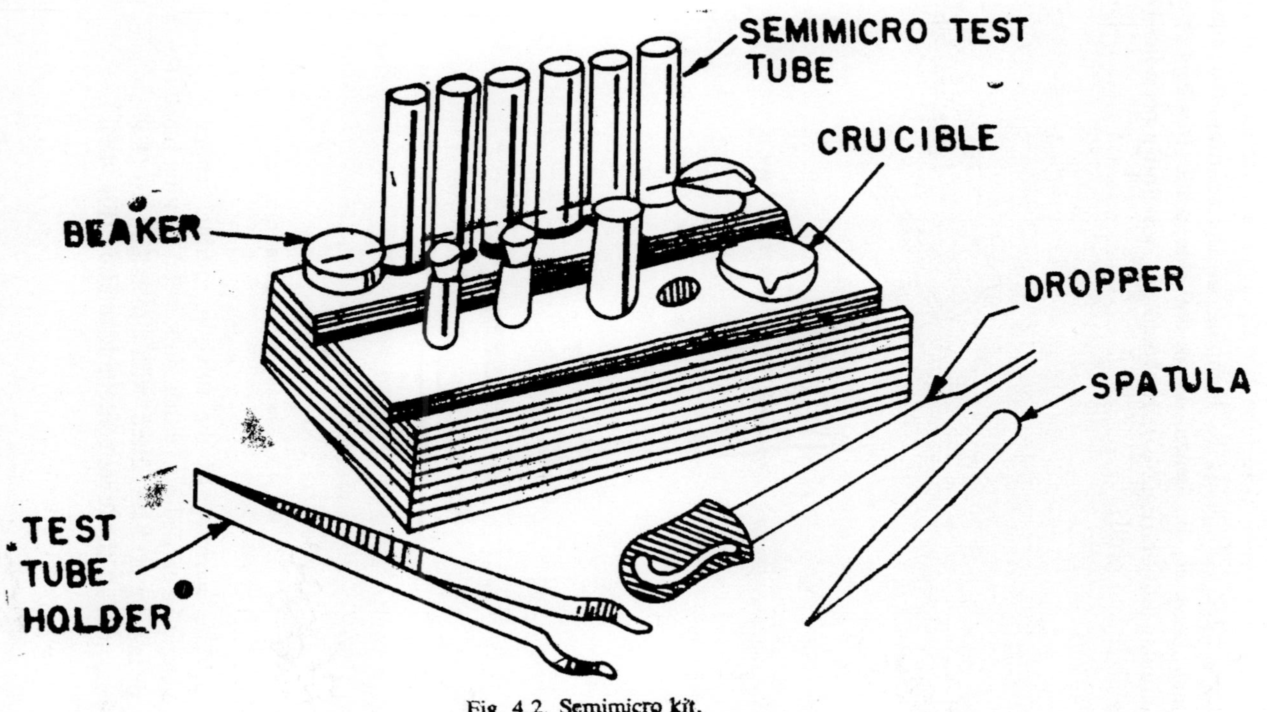

Fig. 4.2. Semimicro kit.

2. Heating block or water bath. Heating or boiling of the solution in a semimicro tube directly over the free flame should be avoided as it leads to bumping of the solution. The tube may, however, be heated from the side while it is kept in a circular motion (Fig. 4.3). It should be withdrawn periodically and shaken gently.

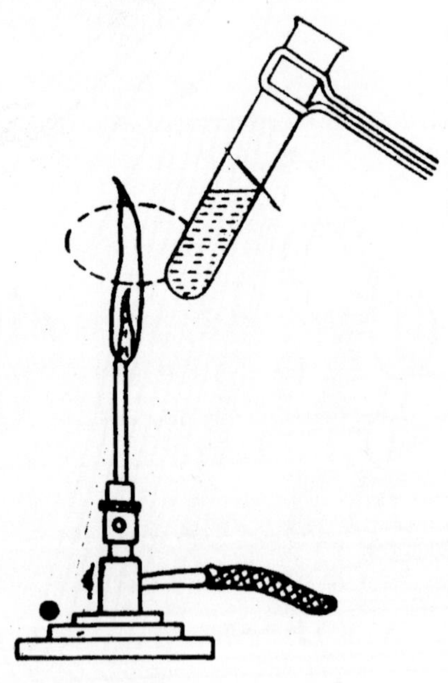

Fig. 4.3. Heating the solution from side.

The warming of the solution, during semimico analysis, should be carried out either in a metal heating block (Fig. 4.4) or in a water bath fitted with a metallic disc having holes to accomodate the tubes containing solution (Fig. 4.5)

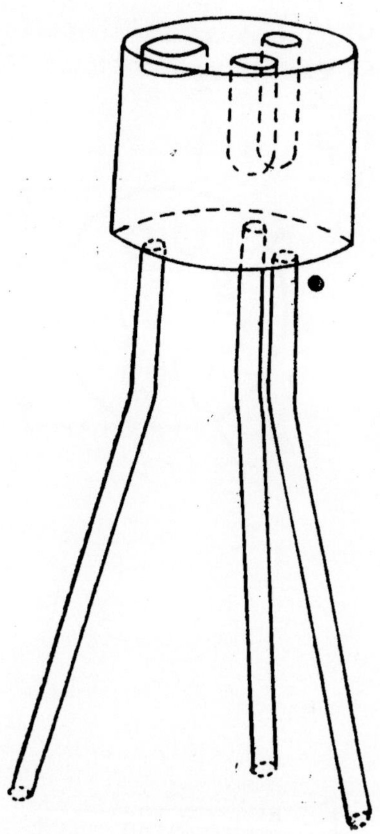

Fig. 4.4. Metal heating block.

3. Centrifuge machine. In semimicro analysis, the precipitate is separated by centrifugation instead of time-consuming filtration technique. For this purpose, we use a centrifuge machine which may be hand operated (Fig. 4.6) or electrically operated (Fig 4.1). Its operation is based on the principle of centrifugal force.

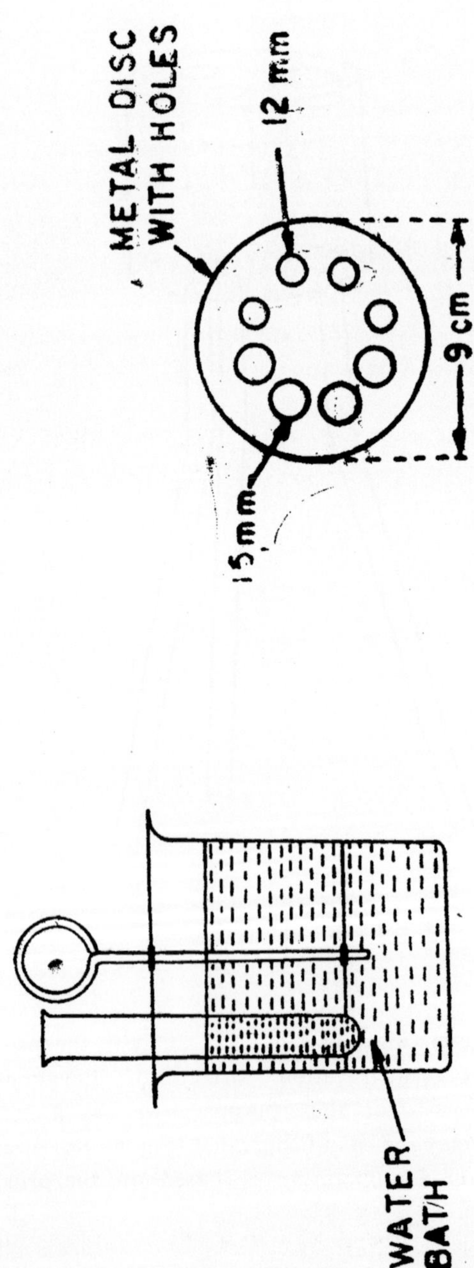

Fig. 4.5. Water bath fitted with a metal disc having holes.

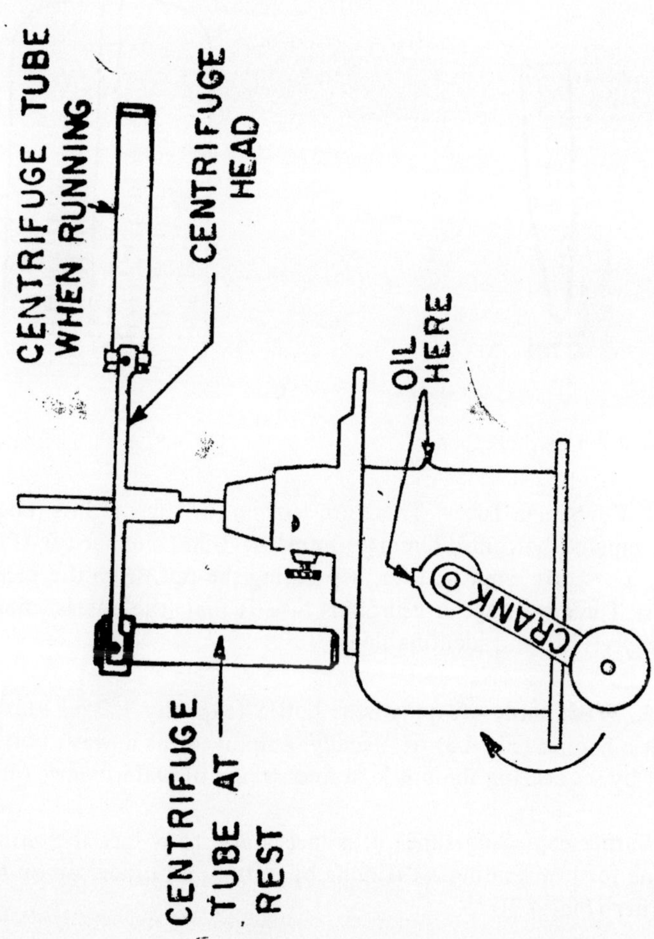

Fig. 4.6. Hand centrifuge machine.

Fig. 4.7. Centrifuge tube.

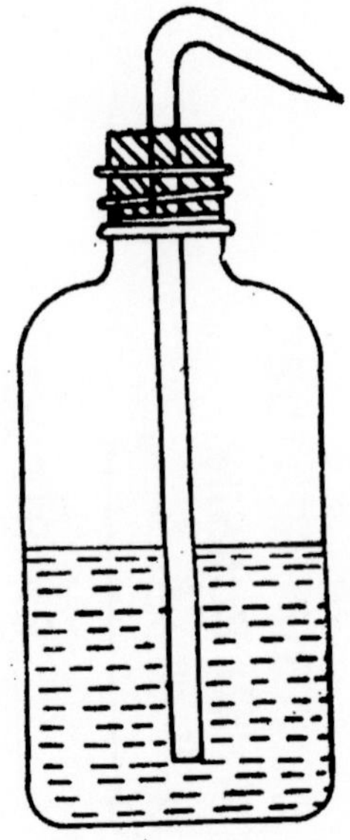

Fig. 4.8. A wash bottle.

4. **Centrifuge Tubes**. There are corning or pyrex glass tubes with tapered bottoms (70mm×10mm of 3-5mL capacity) (Fig 4.7). These are employed for separating the ppt. from the solutions. The advantage in using this tube is that the ppt. is more clearly visible and identifiable.

5. **Wash bottle**. A polythene bottle (capacity 250 mL) fitted with a fine jet (Fig 4.8) is usually employed as a wash bottle. Just by sequeezing the bottle, a fine stream of water comes out.

6. **Burner cap**. Sometimes it is necessary to reduce the burner flame for low heating. It is done by putting a burner cap on the burner (Fig. 4.9).

7. **Reagent bottles**. Cylindrical bottles (50 mL capacity) fitted with droppers and teats are used to kept the reagent solutions [Fig. 4.10, (*a*)]. Strong acids and solvents are kept in dropping bottles [Fig. 4.10, (*b*)].

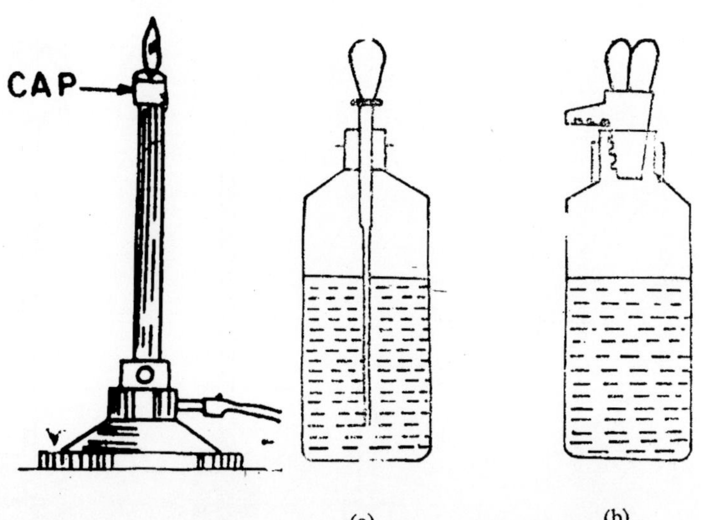

(a) (b)

Fig. 4.9. Burner with cap. Fig. 4.10. Reagent bottles.

8. H_2S Generator. Generally Kipp's apparatus [Fig. 4.11, (*a*)] with a tube having a fine capillary drawn at the end [Fig. 4.11, (*b*)] is used. The gas comes out under pressure and interacts with the test solution.

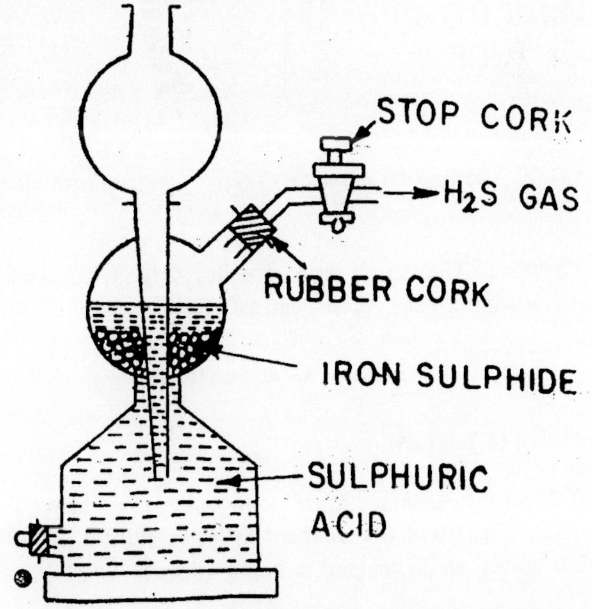

Fig. 4.11(a). Kipp's apperatus for generating H_2S gas.

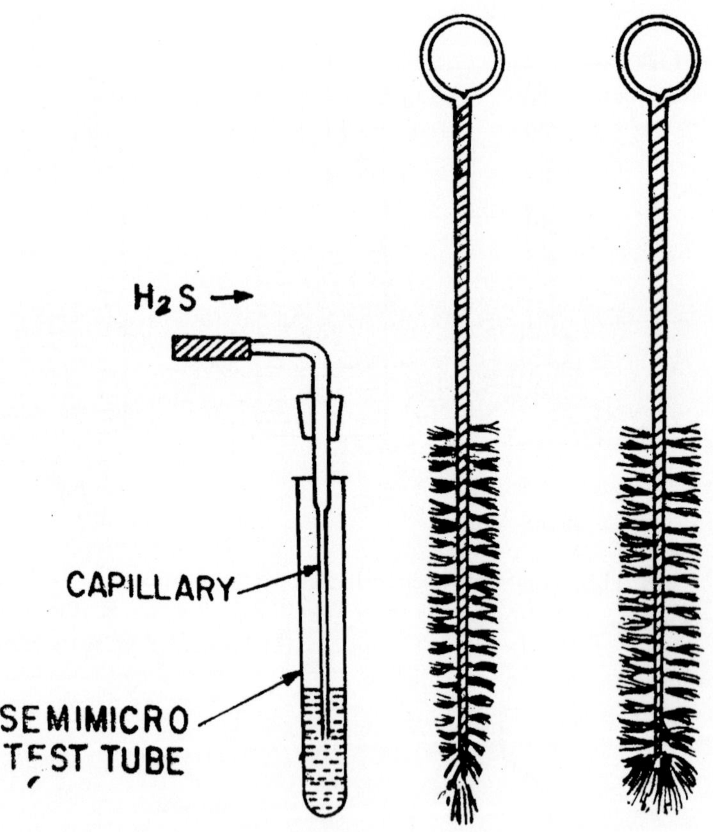

Fig. 4.11 (b). Capillary for passing H_2S gas. Fig. 4.12. Semimicro brushes.

9. Brushes. The small size brushes (Fig. 4.12) are used for cleaning semimicro test tubes, centrifuge tubes etc.

ANALYTICAL OPERATIONS

1. Addition of Reagent

(*a*) *Liquid reagents* Liquid reagents are always added drop-wise. The tip of the reagent dropper should not touch the reaction vessel, while reagent is being added.

(b) Solid reagents **Solid** reagents are added by a micro spatula.

2. Heating and Evaporation. The solution in a semimicro test tube or centrifuge tube cannot be heated over a free flame owing to the serrious chances of bumping in such a narrow tube. Therefore, heating block is used for the heating puposes. A number of solutions can be simultaneously heated on the heating block.

For evaporation, semimicro boiling tube or small crucible may be used and heated by placing over a proper place on the heating block.

3. Precipitation It is carried out in centrifuge tube or in semimicro test tube. During precipitation, the reagent should be added dropwise with the help of a dropper or reagent bottle.

4. Centrifugation The following points should be kept in mind during centrifugation.

(i) Fill centrifuge tube upto 2/3 of its height with the liquid and place in the bucket.

(ii) The balancing tube is prepared as above with water and placed in the bucket which is diametrically opposite to the first one.

(iii) The centrifuge should be started slowly and smoothly. Bring it to its maximum speed in a few seconds and keep it as such for half a minute.

(iv) Release the hand or switch off and allow the centrifuge to come to rest by self. Take out the centrifuge tube from the bucket.

Advantages of Centrifugation

(i) Centrifugation is quick while filtration is slow.

(ii) The precipitate gets concentrated in a small space in centrifugation and hence can be readily observed.

(iii) The washing of precipitate can be carried out repidly and efficiently.

5. Washing of the Precipitate After centrifugation the clear supernatant liquid is called centrifugate, which can be removed with the help of a capilary dropper. Now the ppt. is washed with distilled water. Add 5-10 drops of distilled water in the centrifuge containing the ppt. and mix thoroughly with stirring rod. The mixture is then centrifuged and the clear supernatant liquid is removed by a capillary dropper.

6. Dissolution and Transference of the Precipitate For dissolution, the reagent is added to the centrifuge tube containing the ppt. and warmed. If the ppt. does not dissolved completely the tube is warmed and undissoved substance is reparated by centrifugation. The ppt. is transferred from one tube to another by using a semimicro spatula.

ANALYSIS OF ACIDIC RADICALS

The acidic radicals are classified as in the case of marco analysis. The water extract (W.E.) and sodium carbonate extract (S.C.E.) of the mixture are prepared as follows:

Preparation of W.E.

Take 10-20 mg of the mixture in a test tube (t.t.). Add 1-2 mL of distilled water. Shake throughly, boil for about 1min and centrifuge. The centrifugate is called W.E.

Preparation of S.C.E.

Take 40-50 mg of the mixture in a boiling tube (or semimicro beaker). Mix it with 150-200 mg of Na_2CO_3. Add 5 mL distilled water and boil for 5 min. Centrifuge and the centrifugate is known as S.C.E.

Analysis of First Category Anions with Dil. H_2SO_4

Take 10 mg of the mixture in a t.t. Add to it 5 drops of 5 N H_2SO_4, stir well and observe the following:

(1) If a **colourless** and **odourless** gas evolves, CO_3^{2-} may be present

$$CO_3^{2-} + 2H^+ \longrightarrow \underset{\text{(colourless, odourless)}}{CO_2\uparrow} + H_2O$$

Confirmation of CO_3^{2-}

(a) Take 10 mg of the mixture on a watch glass. With the help of a dropper, add 2-3 drops of 5 N H_2SO_4 gently over the mixture (Fig. 4.13). Brisk effervascence with a hissing sound shows the presence of CO_3^{2-}.

(b) Take 10 mg of the mixture in a t.t. and a few drops of lime water in a gas trap (Fig. 4.14). Add 5-6 drops of 5 N H_2SO_4 in the t.t. and attach it with the gas trap. Heat gently when the lime water turns milky due to the formation of $CaCO_3$. On passing excess of CO_2, the milkiness disappears

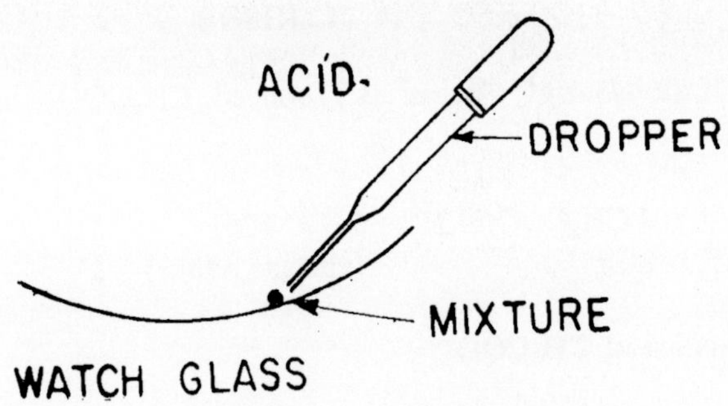

Fig, 4.13. Test for CO_3^{2-}

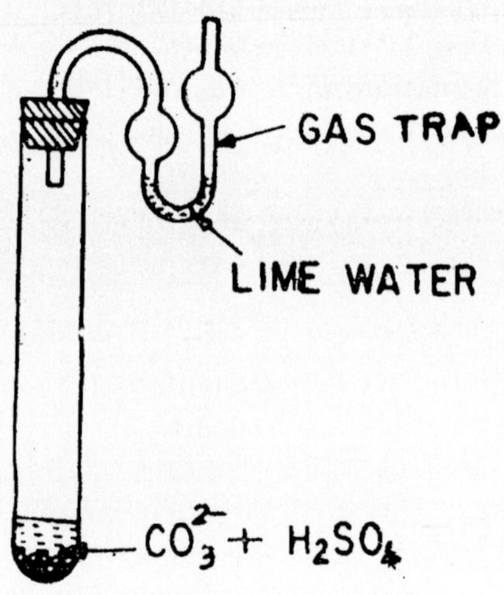

Fig. 4.14. Lime water test for CO_3^{2-}.

due to the formation of soluble $Ca(HCO_3)_2$. SO_3^{2-} also gives a similar test (*see combination tests* for distinction).

$$\underset{\text{lime water}}{Ca(OH)_2+CO_2} \rightarrow \underset{\text{(milkiness)}}{CaCO_3} + H_2O$$

$$CaCO_3+H_2O+\underset{\text{(excess)}}{CO_2} \rightleftharpoons \underset{\text{(soluble)}}{Ca(HCO_3)_2}$$

$$Ca(OH)_2+SO_2 \rightarrow CaSO_3+H_2O$$

$$CaSO_3+H_2O+SO_2 \rightleftharpoons Ca(HSO_3)_2$$

(2) If an **odour of vinegar** is produced, CH_3COO^- may be present.

$$CH_3COO^- + H^+ \rightarrow \underset{\text{(vinegar odour)}}{CH_3COOH}$$

Confirmation of CH_3COO^-

(*a*) To 5 drops of W.E. in a test tube add 2 drops of **neutral**

$FeCl_3$ solution when a red colour is produced due to the formation of ferric acetate.

$$3CH_3COO^- + Fe^{3+} \longrightarrow (CH_3COO)_3Fe$$
(red colour)

(*b*) To about 0.5 mL of W.E. in a t.t. add 0.5 mL of lanthanum nitrate solution followed by 0.5 mL of iodine solution and 4-5 drops of NH_4OH. Heat to boil when the appearance of blue colour confirms the presence of CH_3COO^-.

(3) If a **colourless gas** with a **smell of rotten eggs** is evolved, S^{2-} may be present.

$$S^{2-} + 2H^+ \longrightarrow H_2S\uparrow$$
(rotten egg smell)

Confirmation of S^{2-}

(*a*) Expose a small piece of filter paper soaked in a lead acetate solution to the ensuing gas. The paper turn blacks due to the formation of PbS.

$$(CH_3COO)_2Pb + H_2S \longrightarrow PbS + 2CH_3COOH$$
(black)

(*b*) Place one drop of S.C.E. on a spot plate and add to it 1 drop of sodium nitroprusside soln. A violet colour produced shows the presence of S^{2-}.

$$S^{2-} + [Fe(CN)_5NO)^{2-} \longrightarrow [Fe(CN)_5NOS]^{4-}$$
nitroprusside soln. (violet colour)

(4) If a **colourless gas** with a **suffocating odour** is evolved, SO_3^{2-} may be present.

$$SO_3^{2-} + 2H^+ \longrightarrow SO_2\uparrow \quad H_2O$$
(suffocating odour)

Confirmation of SO_3^{2-}

(*a*) Expose a small piece of filter paper dipped in acidified $K_2Cr_2O_7$ soln. to the ensuing gas. The paper turns green due to the formation of $Cr_2(SO_4)_3$.

$$Cr_2O_7^{2-}+3SO_2+2H^+ \longrightarrow Cr_2(SO_4)_3+H_2O$$

(5) If a **colourless gas** with a **suffocating odour** is evolved and a **white** or **yellow ppt.** of sulphur is deposited in the solution, $S_2O_3^{2-}$ is present.

$$S_2O_3^{2-}+2H^+ \longrightarrow SO_2+S\downarrow+H_2O$$

Confirmation of $S_2O_3^{2-}$

Take 4-5 drops of S.C.E. in a t.t. Acidify with dil. HCl, HNO_3 or CH_3COOH. Add 4-5 drops of $AgNO_3$ soln. A white ppt. rapidly changing to yellow, orange, brown and finally black is obtained. The colour changes are due to the formation of silver thiosulphate which subsequently decomposes to black silver sulphide.

$$S_2O_3^{2-}+2Ag^+ \longrightarrow Ag_2S_2O_3$$

$$Ag_2S_2O_3+H_2O \longrightarrow \underset{\text{(black)}}{Ag_2S} + H_2SO_4$$

(6) If **light brown fumes** with a **pungent odour** are evolved, NO_2^- may be present.

$$2NO_2^-+2H^+ \longrightarrow 2HNO_2$$

$$3HNO_2 \longrightarrow H_2O+HNO_3+2NO\uparrow$$

$$2NO+O_2 \longrightarrow \underset{\text{(brown)}}{2NO_2\uparrow}$$

Confirmation of NO_2^-

(*a*) Take 2 drops of W.E. in a grove tile. Add 2 drops each of sulphanilic acid and α-naphthylamine. Formation of a red azo dye confirms the presence of NO_2^-.

NO_3S- $-NH_2 + CH_3COOH + NO_2^- + H^+$

SULPHANILIC ACID

$\downarrow$

HO_3S- $-N=N-OOC.CH_3 + 2H_2O$

$-NH_2$

α-NAPHTHYLAMINE

$\downarrow$

HO_3S- $-N=N-$ $-NH_2 + CH_3COOH$

(RED AZO DYE)

(7) If a colourless gas with a smell of bitter almonds is evolved, CN^-, may be present.

$$CN^- + +H^+ \longrightarrow HCN \uparrow$$

Confirmation of CN^-

(*a*) Take 4-5 drops of S.C.E. in a t.t. Acidify with dil. CH_3COOH. Add 4-5 drops of NaOH and $FeSO_4$ solution,

Boil the solution and add dil. HCl followed by $FeCl_3$ solution. A blue colouration or ppt. confirms cyanide.

$$Fe^{2+}+6CN^- \longrightarrow [Fe(CN)_6]^{4-}$$

$$[Fe(CN)_6]^{4-}+4Fe^{3+} \longrightarrow Fe_4]Fe(CN)_6]_3$$
(blue)

Analysis of Second Category Anions with Conc. H_2SO_4

Take 10 mg of the mixture in a t.t. Add to it 3-4 drops of conc. H_2SO_4. Heat on a gentle flame and note the following:

(1) If a **colourless** and **pungent smelling** gas evolves, Cl^- may be present.

$$Cl^-+H^+ \longrightarrow HCl\uparrow$$

Confirmation of Cl^-

(a) Take 10 mg each of the mixture and solid MnO_2 in a t.t. Add 5 drops of conc. H_2SO_4 and heat on a gentle flame. A greenish yellow gas evolves showing the presence of Cl^-

$$MnO_2+4HCl \longrightarrow MnCl_2 \rightarrow 2H_2+Cl_2\uparrow$$
(greenish yellow)

(b) Acidify 2-3 drops of S.C.E. with dil. HNO_3 and add 2-3 drops of $AgNO_3$ soln. A curdy white ppt. of AgCl is formed which dissolves in NH_4OH soln.

$$Cl^-+Ag^+ \longrightarrow AgCl\uparrow$$
(white)

$$AgCl+2NH_4OH \longrightarrow [Ag(NH_3)_2]Cl+2H_2O$$
(soluble complex)

(c) **Chromyl chloride test** Mix 5 mg of the mixture with 10 mg of $K_2Cr_2O_7$ in a t.t. Add 3-4 drops of conc. H_2SO_4.

Hang a drop of NaOH soln. on the flattened of a glass rod (Fig. 4.15) and heat gently. The drop becomes yellow. Transfer the yellow drop in a test tube. Add 1 drop of 5 N CH_3COOH soln. warm and add one drop of lead acetate soln. A yellow ppt. of lead chromate is formed confirming the presence of Cl^- in the mixture.

$$4Cl^- + Cr_2O_7^{2-} + 6H_2SO_4 \longrightarrow \underset{\text{chromyl chloride}}{2CrO_2Cl_2} + 6HSO_4^- + 3H_2O$$

$$CrO_2Cl_2 + 4NaOH \longrightarrow \underset{\text{(yellow)}}{NaCrO_4} + 2NaCl + 2H_2O$$

$$Na_2CrO_4 + (CH_3COO)_2Pb \rightarrow \underset{\text{(yellow)}}{PbCrO_4 \uparrow} + 2CH_3COONa$$

(2) **If reddish brown** fumes with a **pungent odour** evolve, Br^- may be present.

$$2Br^- + 2H^+ + (O) \longrightarrow Br_2 \uparrow + H_2O$$

The fumes increase on addition of a pitch of MnO_2 to the reaction mixture.

Confirmation of Br^-

(a) Expose a small piece of filter paper dipped in fluorescein soln. to the ensuing fumes. If the yellow spot on filter paper turns red, Br^- is present. Brown vapours of NO_2 do not give this test but I^- interferes.

(b) Acidify 2-3 drops of S.C.E. with dil. HNO_3 and add 2-3 drops of $AgNO_3$ soln. A pale yellow ppt. of AgBr partially soluble in NH_4OH results.

$$Br^- + Ag^+ \longrightarrow \underset{\text{(pale yellow)}}{AgBr \uparrow}$$

$$AgBr + 2NH_4OH \longrightarrow [Ag(NH_3)_2]Br + 2H_2O$$

(c) Acidify 3-4 drops of S.C.E. with dil. HNO_3 and add 5 drops of a solvent like $CHCl_3$, CCl_4 or CS_2. Now add chlorine water while shaking. The solvent acquires an orange colour due to the extraction of bromine.

$$2Br^- + 2Cl_2 \longrightarrow 2Cl^- + \underset{\text{(orange)}}{Br_2}$$

(3) If **violet** fumes condensing on the sides of the t.t. evolve, I^- may be present.

$$2I^- + 2H^+ + (O) \longrightarrow I_2 + H_2O$$

Confirmation of I^-

(a) Expose a small piece of filter paper dipped in starch soln. to the evolving vapours. If it turns blue owing to the formation of starch-iodine complex, I^- is present.

(b) Adidify 2-3 drops of S.C.E. with dil. HNO_3 and add 2-3 drops of $AgNO_3$ soln. A yellow ppt. of AgI insoluble in NH_4OH results.

$$I^- + Ag^+ \longrightarrow \underset{\text{(yellow)}}{AgI \uparrow}$$

(c) Acidify 3-4 drops of S.C.E. with dil. HNO_3 and add 5 drops of a solvent like $CHCl_3$, CCl_4 or CS_2. Now add chlorine water while shaking. The solvent acquires a violet colour due to the extraction of iodine.

$$2I^- + Cl_2 \longrightarrow \underset{\text{(violet)}}{I_2} + 2Cl^-$$

(4) If **light brown** fumes evolve, NO_3^- may be present. The fumes neither condense on the sides of the t.t. nor respond to the fluourescein test (distinction from brown fumes evolving from Br^-).

$$NO_3^- + H^+ — HNO_3$$

$$4HNO_3 \longrightarrow \underset{\text{(brown)}}{4NO_2 \uparrow} + O_2 + 2H_2O$$

Confirmation of NO_3^-

(a) Take 10 mg of the mixture in a t.t. Add 5 drops of conc. H_2SO_4 and a piece of copper turning. Evolution of copious brown fumes shows the presence of NO_3^-.

$$NO_3^- + H^+ \longrightarrow HNO_3$$
$$Cu + 4HNO_3 \longrightarrow Cu(NO_3)_2 + 2NO_2\uparrow + 2H_2O$$

(b) **Brown ring test** Take 0.5 mL of W.E. in t.t. and add 0.5 mL of freshly prepared ferrous sulphate soln. followed by 3-4 drops of conc. H_2SO_4 by the side of the test tube. A brown ring forms at the junction of the two liquids.

$$6Fe^{2+} + 2NO_3^- + 8H^+ \longrightarrow 6Fe^{3+} + 2NO\uparrow + 4H_2O$$
$$Fe^{2+} + NO \longrightarrow \underset{\text{(brown)}}{[Fe(NO)]^{2+}}$$

(c) Take 2 drops of W.E. in a grove tile. Mix it with 10 mg of zinc dust (to reduce NO_3^- to NO_2^-). Now add 2 drops eash of sulphanilic acid and α-naphthylamine. Formation of a red coloured azo dye confirms the presence of NO_3^-.

(See reactions under NO_2^-).

(5) If **oily drops** are formed F^- may be present.

$$F^- + H^+ \longrightarrow HF$$

$$\underset{\text{(from t.t.)}}{SiO_2} + 4HF \longrightarrow \underset{\text{(oily drops)}}{SiF_4 + 2H_2O}$$

Confirmation of F^-

(a) Acidfy 5 drops of S.C.E. with 5 N CH_3COOH and add 2-3 drops of $CaCl_2$ soln. Heat for about 1 min when a white ppt. of CaF_2 appears showing presence of F^-.

$$2F^- + CaCl_2 \longrightarrow \underset{\text{(white)}}{CaF_2\downarrow} + 2Cl^-$$

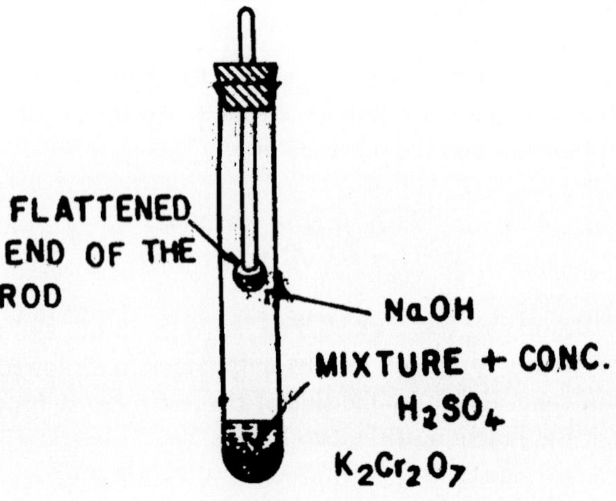

Fig. 4.15. Hanging drop device for testing Cl^-,

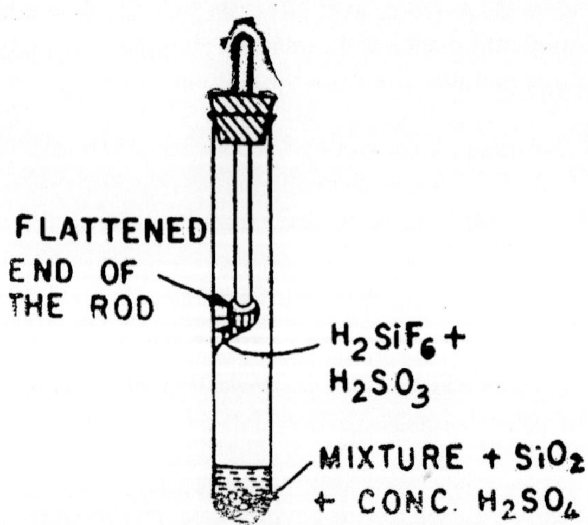

Fig. 4.16. Hanging drop device for testing F^-.

($C_2O_4^{2-}$ also gives a similar test. But the white ppt. of CaC_2O_4 is soluble in dil. H_2SO_4 and the clear soln. decolorizes $KMnO_4$ soln. CaF_2 does not respond to this test.)

(b) Take 10 mg of the mixture in a t.t. and mix with an equal amount of sand. Add 3-4 drops of conc. H_2SO_4 and heat. Hang a drop of water on the flattened end of a glass rod and expose it to the evolved gases. A white waxy deposit of a mixture of hydrofluosilicic acid (H_2SiF_6) and silicic acid (H_2SiO_3) formed on the glass rod (Fig. 4.16) shows the presence of F^-.

$$F^- + H^+ \longrightarrow HF$$

$$SiO_2 + 4HF \longrightarrow SiF_4 + 2H_2O$$

$$3SiF_4 + 3H_2O \longrightarrow \underset{\text{(white waxy deposit)}}{2H_2SiF_6 + H_2SiO_3}$$

(If a *colourless gas* is evolved, but burns with a *pale blue flame*, $C_2O_4^{2-}$ may be present.)

$$C_2O_4^{2-} + 2H^+ \rightarrow H_2O + CO + CO_2$$

Confirmation of $C_2O_4^{2-}$

(a) Take 10 mg of the mixture in a t.t. and add 5-10 drops of conc. H_2SO_4. Heat till the effervescence ceases. Add about 5 mg of MnO_2 when brisk and persistent effervescence indicates $C_2O_4^{2-}$.

$$C_2O_4^{2-} + 2H^+ \longrightarrow H_2C_2O_4$$

$$MnO_2 + H_2SO_4 + H_2C_2O_4 \longrightarrow MnSO_4 + 2H_2O + \underset{\text{(effervescence)}}{CO_2 \uparrow}$$

(b) Acidify 5 drops of S.C.E. with 5 N CH_3COOH and add 2-3 drops of $CaCl_2$ soln. Heat for about 1 min when a white ppt. of CaC_2O_4 appears. Centrifuge and wash the residue with 5 drops of water. Reject the washings. Dissolve the residue in 5 NH_2SO_4, heat and add 2-3 drops of very dilute (0.01 N) $KMnO_4$ soln. The disappearance of pink colour of $KMnO_4$ shows the presence of $C_2O_4^{2-}$.

$$C_2O_4^{2-} + CaCl_2 \longrightarrow \underset{\text{(white)}}{CaC_2O_4 \uparrow} + 2Cl^-$$

$$CaC_2O_4 + H_2SO_4 \longrightarrow CaSO_4 + H_2C_2O_4$$

$$2KMnO_4 + 3H_2SO_4 + 5H_2C_2O_4 \longrightarrow K_2SO_4 + 2MnSO_4 + 10CO_2 + 8H_2O$$

(7) If colourless gases are evolved with a smell of burnt sugar and mixture starts charring rapidly, tartrate, ($C_4H_4O_6^{2-}$) may be present.

Confirmation of $C_4H_4O_6^{2-}$

(a) Neutralize 5-10 drops of S.C.E. with 5 N CH_3COOH, heat and add NH_4OH till it smells of ammonia. Boil the solution to expel excess of NH_3.

Take 5 drops of $AgNO_3$ solution and add very dilute solution of NH_4OH until the ppt. Ag_2O is nearly redissolved.

Mix the above two solutions and warm. A bright silver mirror confirms $C_4H_4O_6^{2-}$.

$$2Ag^+ + 2OH^- \rightarrow Ag_2O + H_2O$$

$$5Ag_2O + C_4H_4O_6^{2-} \rightarrow 10Ag + 4CO_2 + H_2O + 2OH^-$$

(b) Neutralize 5-10 drops of S.C.E. as above and add 1 drop of $FeSO_4$ followed by 2 drops of 20 vol. H_2O_2 and 5-10 drops of NaOH solution and a drop of $FeCl_3$ solution. A deep violet or blue colouration confirms tartrate.

(8) If *colourless gases* are evolved with *slow charring* and *solution darkens slowly*, citrate ($C_6H_5O_7^{3-}$) may be present.

Confirmation of $C_6H_5O_7^{3-}$

(a) Citrate also gives silver mirror test as tartrate but citrate gives this test on boiling the solution.

(b) Neutralize 5-10 drops of S.C.E. as in tartrate and add

5-10 drops of $CaCl_2$ solution. On boiling the solution a crystalline white ppt. confirms citrate.

$$3Ca^{2+} + 2C_6H_5O_7^{3-} \longrightarrow Ca_3(C_6H_5O_7)_2$$

(9) If a yellow gas is evolved with a smell of Cl_2 gas in cold and on heating cracking sound is heard, chlorate (ClO_3^-) may be present.

$$3ClO_3^- + 2H^+ \longrightarrow 2ClO_2 + H_2O + ClO_4^-$$

Confirmation of ClO_3^-

(a) Neutralize 5-10 drops of S.C.E. with 5 N HNO_3 and add 2-4 drops of $AgNO_3$ and H_2SO_3 solution. A white ppt. confirms ClO_3^-

$$NaClO_3 + 2H_2SO_3 \longrightarrow NaCl + 2H_2SO_4$$

$$NaCl + AgNO_3 \longrightarrow AgCl + NaNO_3$$

(b) Take 5-10 drops of W.E. or S.C.E. and add 5 drops of conc. H_2SO_4 and 5-10 drops of aqueous solution of aniline sulphate. A deep blue colouration confirms ClO_3^-.

Analysis of Third Category Anions

(1) Identification of SO_4^{2-}

Acidify 2-3 drop of S.C.E. with 5 N HCl and add 2-3 drops of $BaCl_2$ soln. A white ppt. of $BaSO_4$ (insoluble in conc. HCl or conc. HNO_3) confirms the presence of SO_4^{2-}.

$$SO_4^{2-} + BaCl_2 \longrightarrow \underset{\text{(white)}}{BaSO_4\downarrow} + 2Cl^-$$

(2) Identification of BO_3^{3-}

Take 10 mg of the mixture in a t.t. and add 5 drops each of alcohol (methyl or ethyl) and conc. H_2SO_4. Fit the jet tube in the mouth of the t.t. Heat gently and bring the jet near the flame (Fig. 4.17). A green flame confirms the presence of BO_3^{3-}.

$$BO_3^{3-} + 3H^+ \longrightarrow H_3BO_3$$

$$H_3BO_3 + 3ROH \longrightarrow \underset{\text{(green)}}{B(OR)_3} \uparrow 3H_2O$$

(where $R = CH_3$ or C_2H_5)

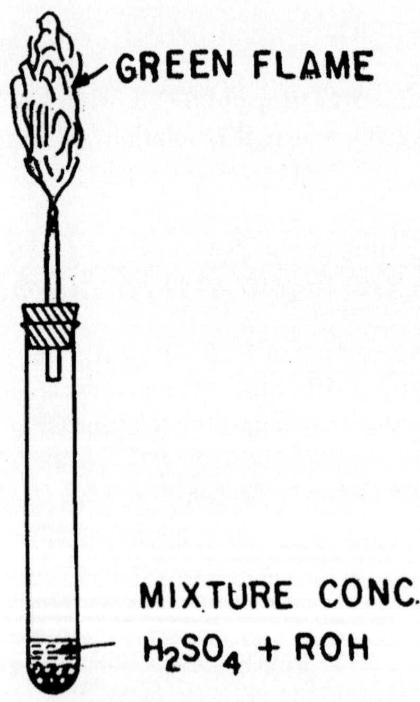

Fig. 4.17. Test for borate.

(3) Identification of PO_4^{3-}

(a) Add 5 drops of conc. HNO_3 to 2-3 drops of S.C.E. (or about 5-6 mg of the mixture). Heat to boiling when a canary yellow ppt. of ammonium phosphomolybdate appears slowly showing the presence of PO_4^{3-} in the mixture.

$$PO_4^{3-} + 3H^+ \longrightarrow H_3PO_4$$

$$H_3PO_4 + 12(NH_4)_2MoO_4 + 21HNO_3 \longrightarrow \underset{\text{(canary yellow)}}{(NH_4)_3P.Mo_{12}O_{40}} \downarrow + 21NH_4NO_3 + 12H_2O$$

(b) Neutralize 5 drops of S.C.E. with dil. HCl and add 3-4 drops of zirconyl nitrate soln. when a white ppt. of zirconyl phosphate appears confirming the presence of PO_4^{3-} in the mixture.

Combination Tests

As it has been said earlier that combination tests are performed when one anion interferes with the detection of other anion. Some such combination tests are given below:

(1) CO_3^{2-} in presence of SO_3^{2-}

Take 10 mg each of the mixture and $K_3Cr_2O_7$ in a t.t. Add 5 drops of 5 N H_2SO_4. Take lime water in a gas trap and fit it in mouth of the t.t. Heat the tube gently. It the lime water turns milky, CO_3^{2-} is present. On the other hand, SO_2 produced by the decomposition of SO_3^{2-} reduces $K_2Cr_2O_7$ to green coloured chromic sulphate.

(2) NO_3^- in presence of NO_2^-

Boil 1 mL of W.E. with 20 mg of NH_4Cl to decompose NO_2^-. Continue the boiling till effervescence ceases.

$$NO_2^- + NH_4Cl \longrightarrow N_2 \uparrow + 2H_2O + Cl^-$$

Test a drop of this soln. with acidified starch iodide paper for the complete removal of NO_2^-. In absence of NO_2^-, the paper does not acquire blue colour.

$$2I^- + 2NO_2^- + 2H^+ \longrightarrow 2NO + H_2O + I_2$$

$$I_2 + \text{Starch} \longrightarrow \text{Blue complex}$$

To the soln. in a grove tile, free from NO_2^-, add 10 mg of zinc dust (to reduce NO_3^- to NO_2^-). Now add 2 drops each of sulphanilic acid and α-naphthylamine. Formation of a red coloured azo dye shows the presence of NO_3^-.

(3) Cl^-, Br^- and I^- in presence of each other

(a) Take 5 drops of S.C.E. in a semimicro crucible or beaker. Acidify with dil. H_2SO_4 and add a few drops of conc. H_2SO_4 followed by 20 mg of $NaNO_2$. Heat till the entire iodine is given off (indicated by disappearance of violet colour). Now add Na_2CO_3 powder (to make the soln. alkaline to fix up HBr) followed by a few drops of conc. HNO_3. Brown fumes evolve if Br^- is present. Continue heating and adding HNO_3 dropwise till the soln. becomes colourless. Now add $AgNO_3$ soln. The appearance of white ppt. shows the presence of Cl^-.

(b) Neutralize 5 drops of S.C.E. with dil. HCl. Add a few drops of $CHCl_3$, CCl_4 or CS_2 followed by chlorine water with shaking. If the solvent acquires violet colour, I_2 is present. Continue adding more chlorine water dropwise and shaking till the violet layer disappears. If the layer assumes orange colour, Br^- is present.

(4) S^{2-}, SO_3^{2-}, $S_2O_3^{2-}$ and SO_4^{2-} in presence of each other

Take 10 drops of S.C.E. and shake it with 10 mg of $CdCO_3$. Heat for 1 min and centrifuge.

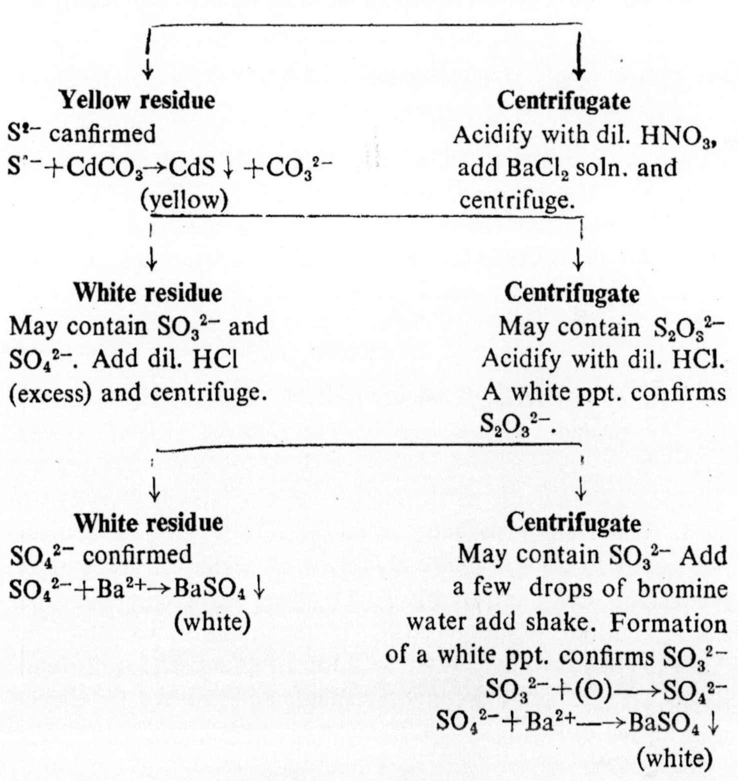

(5) NO_3^- in the presence of Br^- and/or I^-

(a) Take 5 drops of W.E. and boil the solution with excess of Cl_2 water in a semi-micro crucible till no more Br_2 or I_2 evolves. Now make ring test for NO_3^-.

(b) Take 5-10 drops of W.E. and add excess of ammoniacal silver sulphate solution. Filter the ppt. of AgBr or AgI. Perform ring test in the filtrate for NO_3^-.

(6) CO_3^{2-} in the presence of $C_2O_4^{2-}$

Take 20-25 mg of mixture and heat with excess of 5 N H_2SO_4 till there is no effervescence. Now add 15 mg MnO_2 powder, Fresh effervescence starts due to the decomposition of $C_2O_4^{2-}$.

(7) $C_2O_4^{2-}$ in the presence of F^-

Acidify 5-10 drops of S.C.E. with 5 N CH_3COOH and add 10 drops of $CaCl_2$ solution. A white ppt. of CaC_2O_4 and CaF_2 is obtained; centrifuge the ppt. The ppt. is treated with hot 5 N H_2SO_4 in which CaC_2O_4 is soluble. In centrifugate add 2 drops of $KMnO_4$ solution which is decolourised in the presence of $C_2O_4^{2-}$. The insoluble residue in 5 N H_2SO_4 is CaF_2.

Removal of Interfering Radicals (PO_4^{3-}, BO_3^{3-}, $C_2O_4^{2-}$ and F^-)
The interfering radicals can be removed by the following methods.

1. **Removal of phosphate : Zirconyl nitrate method** Evaporate nearly to dryness the centrifugate of Group II and extract the residue with 1 mL of 5 N HNO_3. Heat to boiling and add zirconyl nitrate solution until the precipitation is complete. Place the test tube in a water bath for 5 minutes and centrifuge. Reject the residue of zirconyl phosphate and proceed for Group III with the centrifugate.

Ferric chloride method Evaporate nearly to dryness the centrifugate of Group III and extract the residue with 1 mL of 5 N HCl. Boil 5 drops of this solution with 1 drop of conc. HNO_3 and use this solution for testing Fe^{3+} with $K_4Fe(CN)_6$ or KSCN solution, whereupon purssian blue or red colour respectively is produced. To the remaining solution, in HCl, add 5 N NH_4OH dropwise until a permanent turbidity appears. Now add 5 drops of glacial acetic acid and 10 drops of 3 N ammonium acetate soln. Finally add neutral ferric chloride solution dropwise till the solution acquires a permanent red tinge (excess of ferric chloride should be avoided). Heat the solution in a water bath for 5 minutes and centrifuge:

<table>
<tr><td rowspan="2">Residue ($FePO_4$, $AlPO_4$, $CrPO_4$ and $Fe(OH)_2 \cdot (CH_3COO)$). Test for Al^{3+} and Cr^{3+} as described in Table 4.6.</td><td colspan="2">Centrifugate. Add 10 drops of 5 N NH_4Cl and 5 N NH_4OH dropwise. If a ppt. is formed, remove it by centrifugation.</td></tr>
<tr><td>Residue Traces of $AlPO_4$. and $CrPO_4$. Test for Al^{3+} and Cr^{3+} as described in Table 4.6.</td><td>Centrifugate Use for Groups IV, V and VI.</td></tr>
</table>

2. **Removal of oxalate, fluoride and borate** Evaporate nearly to dryness the centrifugate of Group II. Add 10 drops of conc. HNO_3 in case of oxalate and 10 drops of conc. HCl or HNO_3 for fluoride and borate. Evaporate to dryness. (It should not be baked, heating should be stopped when a drop or two of the solution are left). Repeat the process twice and finally extract with about 1 mL of 5 N HNO_3 and proceed for Group III.

1. (*a*) **Reactions of phosphate ion,** PO_4^{3-} (removal by zirconyl nitrate method). Phosphate is eliminated as zirconyl phosphate.

$$ZrO(NO_3)_2 + 2Na_2HPO_4 + 2HCl \longrightarrow \underset{\text{(white ppt.)}}{ZrO(H_2PO_4)_2} + 2NaCl + 2NaNO_3$$

The excess of Zr^{4+} ions is eliminated by adding NH_4OH.

$$ZrO(NO_3)_2 + 2NH_4OH \longrightarrow \underset{\text{(white ppt.)}}{ZrO(OH)_2} + 2NH_4NO_3$$

(*b*) **Reactions of PO_4^{3-} (removal by $FeCl_3$ method** (*i*) The phosphates of Al, Cr and Fe are insoluble in acetic acid in the presence of ammonium acetate while phosphates of Groups IV, V and Mg are soluble.

(*ii*) The phosphates of other metals are removed as $FePO_4$, by adding neutral $FeCl_3$.

$$Fe^{3+} + PO_4^{3-} \longrightarrow FePO_4$$

(*iii*) The excess ion is removed as basic acetate by dilution and boiling.

$$(CH_3COO)_2Fe + 2H_2O \longrightarrow \underset{\text{(brown ppt.)}}{Fe(OH)_2(CH_3COO)\downarrow} + 2CH_3COOH$$

(*c*) **Reactions of removal of oxalate, fluoride and borate**

$$H_2C_2O_4 + 2NO_3^- + 2H^+ \longrightarrow 2CO_2 + 2NO_2 + 2H_2O$$

$$F^- + H^+ \longrightarrow HF\uparrow$$

(volatile with staem)

$$B_4O_7^{2-} + 2H^+ + 5H_2O \longrightarrow 4H_3BO_3$$

(volatile with steam)

Analysis of Basic Radicals

Basic radicals are analysed by wet test in semi-micro analysis. The classification of the basic radicals into 7 groups (zero to six) is the same as in macro analysis. The original solution is also prepared as in macro analysis. The analysis of the basic radicals is given below.

Identification of Zero Group Cation (NH_4^+ Radical)

Tests. (*i*) Take 10 mg of the mixture in a test tube and add 10 drops of 5 N NaOH. Attach filter tube in the mouth of the t.t. and place a small piece of moistened red litmus paper or mercurous nitrate paper. Heat the t.t.—odour of ammonia which turns (*a*) red litmus paper blue or (*b*) mercurous nitrate paper black, confirms NH_4^+.

(*ii*) Take 10-20 mg of mixture and to this add 10 drops of 5 N NaOH. Warm the solution and pass the vapours through

Nessler's reagent. A brown colouration or ppt. confirms the presence of NH_4^+ ion.

(iii) Take 10-20 mg of mixture. Warm this with 10 drops of 5 N NaOH. Bring a drop of conc. HCl carried at the top of a glass rod to the mouth of the tube. Dense white fumes of NH_4Cl will be formed if NH_3 is evolved. This confirms the presence of NH_4^+ ion.

Reactions (*i*) $(NH_4)_2SO_4+2NaOH \rightarrow Na_2SO_4+2H_2O +2NH_3\uparrow$

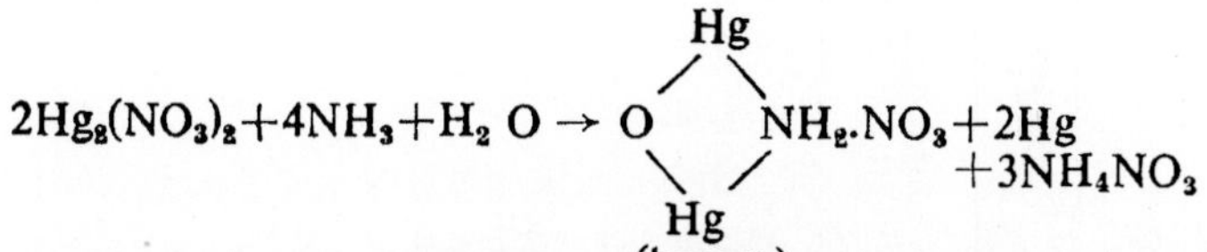

$$2Hg_2(NO_3)_2+4NH_3+H_2O \rightarrow O\begin{matrix} Hg \\ \diagup \quad \diagdown \\ \\ \diagdown \quad \diagup \\ Hg \end{matrix}NH_2.NO_3+2Hg+3NH_4NO_3$$

(brown)

(*ii*) $K_2HgI_4 \rightleftharpoons HgI_2+2KI$

Nessler's reagent

$$HgI_2+2NH_3 \rightarrow Hg\begin{matrix} \diagup NH_2 \\ \diagdown I \end{matrix} +NH_4I$$

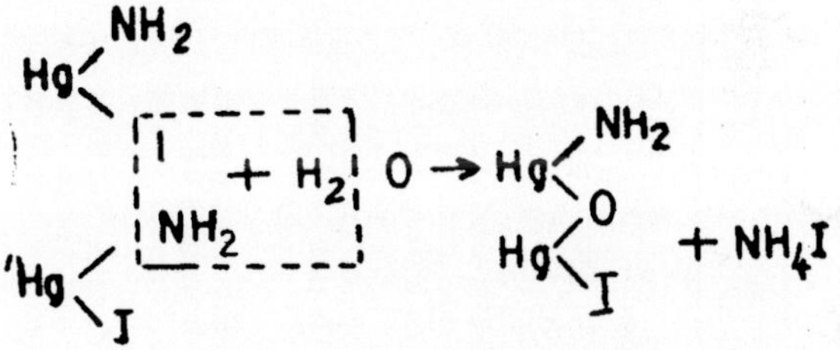

$$Hg\begin{matrix} \diagup NH_2 \\ \diagdown I \end{matrix} + Hg\begin{matrix} \diagup NH_2 \\ \diagdown I \end{matrix} + H_2O \rightarrow \begin{matrix} Hg\begin{matrix} \diagup NH_2 \\ \diagdown \end{matrix} \\ O \\ Hg\begin{matrix} \diagup \\ \diagdown I \end{matrix} \end{matrix} + NH_4I$$

oxydimercuric ammonium iodide (brown colour)

(*iii*) $NH_3+HCl \longrightarrow NH_4Cl$

(white fumes)

Systematic analysis of the cations of Groups I to VI are givenin Tables 4.2-4.9 as follows:

TABLE 4.2

Identification of Group I Cations (Pb^{2+}, Hg_2^{2+} and Ag^+)

<table>
<tr><td colspan="3">To 1 mL of the solution, add 3-4 drops of dil. HCl. If solution becomes turbid, boil for $^1/_2$ min. Cool it under tap water and then centrifuge.</td></tr>
<tr><td colspan="2">Residue (White) A gCl, $PbCl_2$ and Hg_2Cl_2. Wash the residue with 2 mL of cold water and reject the washings. Boil the residue with 1 ml of water and centrifuge.</td><td>Centrifugate Preserve it for subsequent groups.</td></tr>
<tr><td rowspan="2">Centrifugate. This may contain Pb^{2+}. Test portions as follows

(a) Take one drop of the centrifugate in a test tube and add one drop of KI Solution. The formation of a deep yellow ppt. confirms Pb^{2+}.
(b) Take one or two drops of the centrifugate in a test tube. To this add one drop of K_2CrO_4. The formation of a yellow ppt. confirms Pb^{2+}.
(c) Place one drop of the centrifugate on a spot plate, add one drop each of 5 N H_2SO_4 and alcohol. The formation of a white ppt. confirms Pb^{2+}.
(d) To 2 drops of centrifugate, add one drop of dithizone reagent and shake. The formation of red colouration confirms Pb^{2+}.

Pb^{2+}</td><td colspan="2">Residue. It may have Hg_2Cl_2 and AgCl. Wash it with hot water and treat it with 5 drops of 5 N NH_4OH and stir. Heat gently and centrifuge.</td></tr>
<tr><td>Centrifugate: Test for Ag^+.
(a) To one drop of the centrifugate add one drop of 5 N HNO_3. A white ppt. confirms Ag^+.
(b) Place one drop of the centrifugate on a spot plate and add one drop of $Mn(NO_3)_2$ solution and one drop of 5 N NaOH. A black ppt. confirms Ag^+.
(c) To one drop of the centrifugate, add few drops of KI solution. A pale yellow ppt. confirms Ag^+.

Ag^+</td><td>Residue (Black) Add one drop of conc. HNO_3 and three drops of conc. HCl. Evaporate to dryness and extract with 10 drops of water. Test as follows:
(a) To one drop of the solution, add one drop of $SnCl_2$ solution. A white ppt. turning black confirms Hg_2^{2+}.
(b) Place one drop of the solution on a spot plate and add one drop of KI solution. Brick red ppt. which dissolves on adding more of KI solution confirms Hg_2^{2+}.
(c) Take one or two drops of solution in a test tube. To this add 2 drops of gallic acid. Formation of an orange colour confirms Hg_2^{2+}.

Hg_2^{2+}</td></tr>
</table>

REACTIONS OF GROUP I CATIONS

1. Precipitation of group I cations

$$Pb^{2+} + 2Cl^- \longrightarrow \underset{\text{(white)}}{PbCl_2} \downarrow$$

$$Ag^+ + Cl^- \longrightarrow \underset{\text{(white)}}{AgCl} \downarrow$$

$$Hg_2^{2+} + 2Cl \longrightarrow \underset{\text{(white)}}{Hg_2Cl_2} \downarrow$$

2. Reaction of lead ion, Pb^{2+}

(*i*) $$PbCl_2 \underset{\text{heat}}{\overset{H_2O}{\rightleftharpoons}} Pb^{2+} + 2Cl^-$$

(*ii*) $$Pb^{2+} + 2I^- \longrightarrow \underset{\text{(deep yellow)}}{PbI_2} \downarrow$$

(*iii*) $$Pb^{2+} + CrO_4^{2-} \longrightarrow \underset{\text{(yellow)}}{PbCrO_4} \downarrow$$

(*iv*) $$Pb^{2+} + SO_4^{2-} \longrightarrow \underset{\text{(white)}}{PbSO_4} \downarrow$$

3. Reactions of silver ion, Ag^+

(*i*) $$\underset{\text{(insoluble)}}{AgCl} + 2NH_4OH \longrightarrow \underset{\text{(soluble)}}{[Ag(NH_3)_2]^+Cl^-} + 2H_2O$$

(*ii*) $$[Ag(NH_3)_2]^+Cl^- + 2HNO_3 \longrightarrow \underset{\text{(white)}}{AgCl} \downarrow + 2NH_4NO_3$$

(*iii*) $$2[Ag(NH_3)_2]^+ + Mn^{2+} + 4OH^- \longrightarrow \underset{\text{(black)}}{Ag} \downarrow + MnO_2 + 2NH_3 + 2H_2O$$

(*iv*) $$[Ag(NH_3)_2]^+ + I^- + 2H_2O \longrightarrow AgI + 2NH_4OH$$

TABLE 4.3

Identification of Group II Cations

(Pb^{2+}, Hg^{2+}, Bi^{1+}, Cu^{2+}, Cd^{2+}, As^{3+}, Sb^{3+} and Sn^{2+})

Dilute the centrifugate from Group I to 2 ml. Pass H_2S gas in a test portion of this. If a coloured ppt. is obtained, it reveals the presence of Group II. Now pass H_2S gas in the remaining solution slowly and steadily until the precipitation is complete. Centrifuge it.		
Residue (coloured) If it is coloured, this may contain HgS (black), PbS (black), Bi_2S_3 (brownish-black), CuS (black), CdS (yellow), As_2S_3 (yellow), Sb_2S_3 (orange) and SnS (brown or SnS_2 (yellow). Wash the residue with 5 drops of hot H_2S water containing a drop of NH_4NO_3 solution and reject the washings. Heat the ppt. with 10-20 drops of yellow ammonium sulphide solution for 3 minutes in a water bath and centrifuge.		*Centrifuge* Keep it for the analysis of subsequent groups.
Residue If it is coloured, this may contain Group IIA sulphide. Test this residue according to Table 4.4. II A	*Centrifugate* Analyse the centrifuge for Group II B according to Table 4.5. II B	

4. Reactions of mercurous ion, Hg_2^{2+}

(*i*) $Hg_2Cl_2 + 2NH_4OH \longrightarrow Hg(NH_2)Cl\downarrow + Hg\downarrow + NHCl_4 + 2H_2O$
(white) (black)

(*ii*) $Hg(NH_2)Cl + 2H^+ \longrightarrow Hg^{2+} + Cl^- + NH_4^+$

$Hg + 4H^+ + NO_3^- + Cl^- \longrightarrow Hg^{2+} + NOCl + 2H_2O$

(*iii*) $2Hg^{2+} + Sn^{2+} \longrightarrow Hg_2^{2+} + Sn^{4+}$
(white)

$Hg_2^{2+} + Sn^{2+} \longrightarrow 2Hg\downarrow + Sn^{4+}$
(black)

(*iv*) $Hg^{2+} + 2I^- \longrightarrow HgI_2\downarrow$
(brick red)

$HgI_2 + 2KI \longrightarrow K_2HgI_4$
(potassium mercuri iodide—soluble)

Reactions

$$M^{2+} + S^{2-} \longrightarrow MS$$

[M=Pb, Hg, Cu, Cd, Sn)

$$2M^{3+} + 3S^{2-} \longrightarrow M_2S_3$$

[M=Bi, As, Sb]

$$Sn^{4+} + 2S^{2-} \longrightarrow SnS_2$$

$$As_2S_3 + 3(NH_4)_2S + S \longrightarrow 6NH_4^+ + 2AsS_4^{3-}$$
thiarsenate ion

$$Sb_2S_3 + 3(NH)_{42}S + S \longrightarrow 6NH_4^+ + 2SbS_4^{3-}$$
thioantimonate ion

$$SnS + (NH_4)_2S + S \longrightarrow 2NH_4^+ + SnS_3^{2-}$$
thiostannate ion

TABLE 4.4

Identification of Group IIA Cations
(Hg^{2+}, Pb^{2+}, Bi^{3+}, Cu^{2+} and Cd^{2+})

Treat the residue for Group IIA with 1.5 mL of dil. HNO_3. Boil it for 2 minutes and centrifuge.

Residue Black due to HgS. Dissolve it in aqua regia and evaporate of aqua regia. Dilute it with water. Divide it into 3 parts. (*i*) To a drop of the solution add a drop each of amm. thiocyanate and sod. acetate followed by a drop of $Co(NO_3)_2$ solution. A deep blue colour or precipitate confirms mercury. (*ii*) To a drop of solution add a drop of NaOH solution A yellow precipitate confirms Hg^{2+}. (*iii*) To 5 drops of solution add 3 drops of $SnCl_2$ solution. A white ppt. turning grey confirms Hg^{2+}.	*Centrifuge* To a portion add a drop of dil. H_2SO_4 and alcohol. If a white precipitates appears, add 2 drops of alcohol and 5 drops of 5 N H_2SO_4 to the whole and boil till white fumes appear. Cool and add a drop of water and centrifuge.			
	Residue White due to $PbSO_4$. Dissolve in minimum amount of ammonium acetate solution. Now add 2 drops of K_2CrO_4 solution. A yellow precipitate of $PbCrO_4$ confirms Pb^{2+}.	*Centrifugate* Add amonia solution dropwise till the solution is alkaline. If precipitate appears, centrifuge.		
		Residue (White) Dissolve the precipitate in 2-3 drops of conc. HCl and heat. Add to this $^1/_2$ ml of water. (*i*) To 3 drops of solution add 2 drops of sodium stannite reagent. A black precipitate confirms Bi^{3+}. (*ii*) To 3 drops of solution add 2 drops of thiourea solution. A yellow colouration appears if Bi^{3+} is present.	*Centrifugate* Divided it in two parts. (*i*) Acidify 3 drops of solution with acetic acid and add 2 drops of $K_4Fe(CN)_6$. A brown precipitate confirms Cu^{2+}. (*ii*) To a drop of solution, add a drop of rubeanic acid reagent and a few drops of ammonia solution. A black. or greenish black colouration confirms Cu^{2+}.	If Cu^{2+} is present add KCN solution drop by till the solution is colurless. Pass H_2S. A yellow precipitate of CdS confirms Cd^{2+}.
Hg^{2+}	**Pb^{2+}**	**Bi^{3+}**	**Cu^{2+}**	**Cd^{2+}**

REACTIONS OF GROUP IIA CATIONS

1. Reactions of mercuric ion, Hg^{2+}

(*i*) $2HgS + 2HNO_3 + 6HCl \longrightarrow 2HgCl_2 + 3S\downarrow + 2NO\uparrow + 4H_2O$

(*ii*) $Hg^{2+} + Co^{2+} + 4SCN^- \longrightarrow Co[Hg(SCN)_4]$

(*iii*) $Hg^{2+} + 2OH^- \longrightarrow HgO + H_2O$

(*iv*) $2Hg^{2+} + Sn^{2+} + 2Cl^- \longrightarrow Hg_2Cl_2 + Sn^{4+}$
(white)

$Hg_2Cl_2 + Sn^{2+} \longrightarrow 2Hg + Sn^{4+} + 2Cl^-$
(black)

2. Reactions of lead ion, Pb^{2+}

(*i*) $3PbS + 8HNO_3 \longrightarrow 3Pb(NO_3)_2 + 2NO\uparrow + 3S\downarrow + 4H_2O$

(*ii*) $PbSO_4 + 2CH_3COONH_4 \longrightarrow (CH^3COO)_2Pb + (NH_4)_2SO_4$
$(CH_3COO)_2Pb + K_2CrO_4 \longrightarrow 2CH_3COOK + PbCrO_4$

3. Reactions of bismuth ion, Bi^{3+}

(*i*) $Bi_2S_3 + 8HNO_3 \longrightarrow 2Bi(NO_3)_3 + 2NO\uparrow + 3S\downarrow + 4H_2O$

(*ii*) $Bi^{3+} + 3OH^- \longrightarrow Bi(OH)_3\downarrow$
(white gelatinous)

(*iii*) $Bi(OH)_3 + 3HCl \longrightarrow BiCl_3 + 3H_2O$

(*iv*) $2Bi^{3+} + 3SnO_2^{2-} + 6OH^- \longrightarrow 2Bi\downarrow + 3SnO_3^{2-} + 3H_2O$
(black)

4. Reactions of cupric ion, Cu^{2+}

(*i*) $3CuS + 8HNO_3 \longrightarrow 3Cu(NO_3)_2 + 2NO\uparrow + 3S\downarrow + 4H_2O$

(*ii*) $Cu^{2+} + 4NH_3 \longrightarrow [Cu(NH_3)_4]^{2+}$
tetraamminecopper(II) ion

(*iii*) $[Cu(NH_3)_4]^{2+} + 4CH_3COOH \longrightarrow Cu^{2+} + 4CH_3COONH_4$

(*iv*) $2Cu^{2+} + [Fe(CN)_6]^{4-} \longrightarrow Cu_2[Fe(CN_6)] \downarrow$
cupric ferrocyanide
(chocolate colour)

5. Reactions of cadmium ion, Cd^{2+}

(*i*) $3CdS + 8HNO_3 \longrightarrow 3Cd(NO_3)_2 + 2NO \uparrow + 3S \downarrow + 4H_2O$

(*ii*) $Cd^{2+} + 4NH_3 \longrightarrow [Cd(NH_3)_4]^{2+}$
tetramminecadmium(II) cation
(colourless)

(*iii*) $[Cd(NH_3)_4]^{2+} + H_2S \longrightarrow CdS \downarrow + 2NH_4^+ + 2NH_3 \uparrow$
(yellow)

Separation of Cu^{2+} and Cd^{2+} with KCN

$2[Cu(NH_3)_4]^{2+} + 10KCN \longrightarrow 2K_3[Cu(CN)_4] + (CN)_2 + 8NH_3 + 4K^+$
potassium tetracyanocopper(I)
(colourless)

$(CN)_2 + 2NH_4OH \longrightarrow NH_4CNO + NH_4CN + H_2O$

$[Cd(NH_3)_4)^{2+} + 4KCN \longrightarrow K_2[CdCN)_4] + 2K^+ + 4NH_3 \uparrow$
potassium tetracyanocadium(II)
(colourless)

K_3 $[Cu(CN_4)]$ is comparatively stable. On the other hand, $K_2[Cd(CN)_4]$ furnishes sufficient concentration of Cd^{2+} and on passing H_2S in the solution, only CdS is precipitated.

REACTIONS OF GROUP IIB CATIONS

$2(AsS_4)^{3-} + 6H^+ \longrightarrow As_2S_5 + 3H_2S$
thioarsenate ion (yellow ppt.)

$2(SbS_4)^{3-} + 6H^+ \longrightarrow Sb_2S_5 + 3H_2S$
thioantimonate ion (orange ppt.)

$(SnS_3)^{2-} + 2H^+ \longrightarrow SnS_2 + H_2S$
thiostannite ion (yellow ppt.)

$Sb_2S_5 + 10H^+ + 4Cl^- \longrightarrow 2Sb^{3+} + 2Cl_2 + 5H_2S$

$SnS_2 + 4H^+ \longrightarrow Sn^{4+} + 2H_2S$

$As_2S_5 + H^+ \longrightarrow$ No reaction

TABLE 4.5

Identification of Group IIB Cations
(As^{3+}, Sb^{3+} and Sn^{2+})

To the centrifugate of Group IIB, and 5 NCl dropwise (until it is just acidic). If a coloured ppt. is obtained, it means that Group IIB is present. Centrifuge it. Reject the centrifugate and test residue for Group IIB cations.

Wash residue of Group IIB with 1 mL of hot water, centrifuge and reject washings. Add to the residue 1 mL of conc. HCl and boil gently for 2 minutes. Add 1 mL of water, stir and then centrifuge.

<table>
<tr><td rowspan="2">Residue Dissolve the residue by boiling it with 1 mL of conc. HNO_3. Divide it wo parts.
(i) To a part of the solution, add ammonium molybdate solution and heat. A yellow precipitate confirms As^{3+}.
(ii) Make second part alkaline with NH_4OH and add 1/2 mL of magnesia mixture. A white precipitate confirms As^{3+}</td><td colspan="2">Centrifugate It may have $SnCl_4$ and $SbCl_3$. Boil off H_2S. Add NH_4OH to make the centifugate alkaline. Add 3-4 crystals of oxalic acid, boil and pass H_2S. Centrifuge.</td></tr>
<tr><td>Residue (orange) Dissolve the precipitate in conc. HCl. Boil off H_2S. Divide it in two parts.
(i) To one part add NH_4OH in order to neutralize the solution. Dilute with large excess of water. A white precipitate or turbidity soluble in tartaric acid confirms Sb^{3+}
(ii) To another part of the solution. add a small tin piece and wait for some time. A grey spongy deposit indicates Sb^{3+}.</td><td>Centrifiugate It may contain $SnCl_4$. Boil off H_2S and add Zn dust and dil. HCl. Keep it for some time. Centrifuge and divide it into two portions.
(i) To one portion add ammonium molybdate solution. A deep blue colouration or precipitate indicates Sn^{3+}.
(ii) To second portion add 5 mg of Mg powder +2 drops of $FeCl_3$+2 drops of 5 per cent tartaric acid+1-2 drop of dimethylglyoxime solution and then add dil. NaOH solution. A red colour confirms Sn^{2+}.</td></tr>
<tr><td>As^{3+}</td><td>Sb^{3+}</td><td>Sn^{2+}</td></tr>
</table>

Reactions of As^{3+}

(i) The yellow residue of As_2S_5 dissolves in conc. HNO_3 forming arsrnic acid.

$$As_2S_5+4H^++10NO_3 \longrightarrow 2AsO_4^{3-}+10NO_2+5S+2H_2O$$
(soluble)

(ii) Ammonium molybdate yields a yellow ppt. with arsenic solution in presence of HNO_3.

$$AsO_4^{3-}+3NH_4^++12MoO_4^-+24H^+ \rightarrow (NH_4)_3AsO_412MoO_3+12H_2O$$
(yellow ppt.)

(iii) On adding magnesia mixture, a white crystaline precipitate is obtained.

$$H_3AsO_4+MgSO_4+3NH_4OH \longrightarrow Mg(NH_4)AsO_3+(NH_4)_2SO_4+3H_2O$$
(white ppt.)

(iv) H_3AsO_4 forms a yellow ppt. with $AgNO_3$ solution

$$H_3AsO_4+3AgNO_3 \longrightarrow Ag_3AsO_4+3HNO_3$$
(yellow ppt.)

Reactions of Sb^{3+}

(i) $Sn^{4+}+2H_2C_2O_4 \longrightarrow Sn(C_2O_4)_2+4H^+$

oxalic acid — (stable not decomposed by H_2S)

$$2Sb^{3+}+3H_2S \longrightarrow Sb_2S_3+6H^+$$
(orange ppt.)

(ii) Sb_2S_3 dissolves in HCl forming $SbCl_3$, on dilution milkiness is produced which is soluble in tartaric acid.

$$Sb_2S_3+6H^+ \longrightarrow 2Sb^{3+}+3H_2S$$

$$Sb^{3+} + Cl^- + H_2O \longrightarrow SbOCl + 2H^+$$

$$SbOCl + C_4H_6O_6 \longrightarrow \underset{\text{(soluble)}}{C_4H_5SbO_7} + H^+ + Cl^-$$

(iii) On putting tin foil in $SbCl_3$ solution, a black deposit of antimony is obtained.

$$2Sb^{3+} + 3Sn \longrightarrow 3Sn^{2+} + 2Sb$$

Reactions of Sn^{4+}

(i) Addition of zinc dust to the solution reduces $SnCl_4$ to $SnCl_2$.

$$Sn^{4+} + Zn \longrightarrow Sn^{2+} + Zn^{2+}$$

(ii) Mercuric chloride is reduced to Hg_2Cl_2 (white ppt.) and finally to grey or black precipitate of mercury.

$$Sn^{2+} + Hg^{2+} + 2Cl^- \longrightarrow Sn^{4+} + \underset{\text{(white ppt.)}}{Hg_2Cl_2}$$

$$Hg_2Cl_2 + Sn^{2+} \longrightarrow Sn^{4+} + \underset{\text{(grey)}}{2Hg} + 2Cl^-$$

(iii) Ammonium molybdate forms a blue colour or precipitate with $SnCl_2$ solution.

$$Sn^{2+} + 3MoO_4^{2-} \longrightarrow \underset{\text{(blue)}}{Mo_3O_8} + Sn^{4+} + 5H_2O$$

TABLE 4.6

Identification of Group III Cations (Fe^{3+}, Al^{3+} and Cr^{+3})

Boil off H_2S from the centrifugate. Add 1 drop of conc. HNO_3 and boil. Add about 200 mg of NH_4Cl and boil. Cool and add NH_4OH dropwise until the solution is ammoniacal. Centrifuge.

Residue may have $Fe(OH)_3$, $Cr(OH)_3$, $Al(OH)_3$ and MnO_2xH_2O. Wash the residue thrice with 5 drops portion of water containing a drop of NH_4NO_3 solution. Mix the first washings with the centrifugate and reject others. Add 1 mL of 5 N NaOH and 5 to 6 drops of H_2O_2. Boil and centrifuge.

Residue (Brown) Dissolve the residue in 1 ml of 5 N HCl and divide it in 3 parts.	*Centrifugate* If colourless, Al is present and/or is absent ; if yellow Cr is definitely present. Divide solution in two portions.	
	Tests for Cr^{3+}	Tests for Al^{3+}
(*i*) Place 1 drop of the yellow solution on a spot plate and add 1 drop of $K_4Fe(CN)_6$—*a prussian blue colour or ppt*. confirms Fe^{3+}.	(*i*) Acidify a part of this portion with acetic acid and add lead acetate solution. A bright yellow precipitate soluble in NaOH confirms Cr^{3+}.	(*i*) To one part add 1 mL of amm. acetate solution and $^1/_2$ mL of aluminon+excess of $(NH_4)_2CO_3$ solution. A bright red lake confirms Al^{3+}.
(*ii*) Place 1 drop of the yellow solution on a spot plate and add 1 drop of KSCN solution—*a blood red colour* confirms Fe^{3+}. Fe^{3+}	(*ii*) Acidify another part with dil. H_2SO_4 and add ether. Add 2-3 drops of H_2O_2 and shake. A blue colour in tehereal layer ccnfirms Cr^{3+}.	(*ii*) Add a few crystals of NH_4Cl to the second part and boil. A white gelationous precipitate confirms Al^{3+}.
(*iii*) To the third part add 3 drop of conc. HNO_3, 10 mg of bismuthate solution and sdake. A *purple violet precipitate* confirms Mn^{2+}.		(*iii*) *Charcoal Cavity Test* Place 2 drops of the solution and 10 mg of Na_2CO_3 in the charcoal cavity. Heat in an oxidizing flame. Add 1 drop of $Co(NO_3)_2$ to the dry mass and heat again —*a blue mass* (Thenard's blue) confirms Al^{3+}.
Mn^{2+}	Cr^{3+}	Al^{3+}

Reactions

(i) $M^{3+}+3OH^- \longrightarrow M(OH)_3$

(M=Fe, Cr, Al)

(ii) $Na_2O_2+H_2O \longrightarrow 2NaOH+(O)$

$$Al(OH)_3+NaOH \longrightarrow NaAlO_2+2H_2O$$

$$2Cr(OH)_3+4NaOH+3(O) \longrightarrow 2Na_2CrO_4+5H_2O$$

(iii) Sometimes the formation of hydrated manganese dioxide ($MnO_2.H_2O$) takes place due to the oxidation of $Mn(OH)_2$ by air and also by nitric acid.

$$Mn(OH)_2+(O) \longrightarrow MnO_2.H_2O$$

Reactions of Fe^{3+} and Mn^{3+}

(i) $Fe(OH)_3+3HCl \longrightarrow FeCl_3+3H_2O$

(ii) $4FeCl_2+3K_4Fe(CN)_6 \longrightarrow \underset{\text{ferri-ferrocyanide}}{Fe_4[Fe(CN)_6]_3}+12KCl$

(iii) Ammonium thiocyanate yields with ferric ions a deep red colouration.

$$FeCl_3+3NH_4SCN \longrightarrow \underset{\text{(deep red)}}{Fe(SCN)_3}+3NH_4Cl$$

(iv) Manganese dioxide in presence of HNO_3 is oxidized by PbO_2 or sodium bismuthate into permaganic acid (pink).

$$PbO_2+2HNO_3 \longrightarrow Pb(NO_3)_2+H_2O+(O)$$

$$2MnO_2+H_2O+3(O) \longrightarrow \underset{\text{(pink)}}{2HMnO_4}$$

$$NaBiO_3+4HNO_3 \longrightarrow NaNO_3+Bi(NO_3)_3+2H_2O+(O)$$

$$2\,MnO_2.H_2O+3(O) \longrightarrow \underset{\text{(pink)}}{2HMnO_4}$$

TABLE 4.7

Identification of Group IV Cations

(Co^{2+}, Ni^{2+}, Zn^{2+} and Mn^{2+})

Add NH_4OH dropwise to the centrifugate from Group III until it smells of ammonia. Now pass H_2S gas through this solution until the precipitation is complete. Centrifuge it. Preserve the centrifugate for the subsequent groups. Residue may contain CoS, NIS, MnS and ZnS.

Wash the residue with 1 mL of NH_4Cl. Centrifuge and reject the washings. To the residue add 2 mL of water followed by 1 ml of dil. HCl. Stir the mixture and then centrifuge.

<table>
<tr>
<td rowspan="2">Residue Black residue may have NiS, CoS. Dissolve the residue in aqua regia (6 drops of HCl+2 drops of HNO_3). Evaporate it to dryness. Note the colour of the residue. If it is blue, it indicates cobalt. If it is yellow, it indicates nickel. If green, both cobalt and nickel may be present.

Extract the residue with 2 mL of water and divide into five parts.</td>
<td colspan="2">Centrifugate It may have Zn^{2+} and Mn^{2+} .Boil off H^2S and add 10 drops of 5 N NaOH and 4 drops of H_2O_2 or Br_2 water. Centrifuge.</td>
</tr>
<tr>
<td>Residue It may be brown to black due to $Mn(OH)_2$ or MnO.OH. Dissolve the ppt. in 10 drops of 5 N</td>
<td>Centrifugate. If may have Na_2ZnO_2. Divide this into four parts.</td>
</tr>
</table>

(*i*) Place 1 drpp of the solution on the spot plate and add 1 drop each of 5 N NH_4OH and dimethylglyoxime solution—*a red ppt.* confirms Ni^{2+}. (*ii*) Take 5 drops of the solution, add 5 drops of NaOH and 2 drops of Br_2 water. A black precipitate confirms Ni^{2+} **Ni^{2+}**	(*i*) To 2 drops of the solution add 1 drop of NH_4SCN solution and 5 drops of amyl alcohol-*a blue coloured amyl alcohol layer* confirms Co^{2+}. (*ii*) To 5 drops of solution add acetic acid (3 drops) followed by 3 drops of α-nitroso β-naphthol. A red-brown precipitate confirms the presence of Co^{2+}. Co^{2+}	HNO_3 and 1 drop of H_2O_2. Heat to decompose excess of H_2O_2. Divide this into four parts: (*i*) To part I add 3 drops of Br_2 water and 3 drops of NaOH. Boil. A black precipitate confirms Mn^{2+}. (*ii*) To part II add 50 mg of PbO_2 and $^1/_2$ mL of conc. HNO_3. Boil, cool and dilute the contents. A pink colouration confirms Mn^{2+}. (*iii*) To part III, add a pinch of solid sodium bismuthate. Formation of a purple colour confirms Mn^{2+}. (*iv*) To parts IV, add 2 drops of dil. NaOH and 1 drop of benzidine reagent. A blue colour confirms Mn^{2+}. **Mn^{2+}**	(*a*) In part I, pass, H_2S gas. A white ppt. confirms Zn^{2+}. (*b*) Acidify part II with 5 N H_2SO_4. Place one drop of this solution on a spot plate and add one drop each of 0.1% $CuSO_4$ and ammonium mercury-thiocyanate reagent. Stir. A violet ppt. confirms Zn^{2+}. (*c*) Place part III upon potassium cyanocobaltate test paper. Dry the paper over a flame and ignite in a small crucible. Observe the colour of the ash against a white background. A part of it will be green, if Zn^{2+}. (*d*) Acidify part IV with 5 N HCl and add $K_4Fe(CN)_6$. A bluish white ppt. confirms Zn^{2+}. **Zn^{2+}**
Test for Co^{2+} add Ni^{2+} if present together. Take 5 drops of the solution in a dish. To this add $NaHCO_3$ and Br_2 water dropwise Shake the dish, If an apple green colour is obtained in cold, it confirms CO^{2+}. If on heating a black colour appears, it confirms Ni^{2+}.			

Reactions of Cr^{3+}

(i) Dil. acetic acid neutralizes excess of NaOH. Lead acetate forms with sodium chromate solution a yellow precipitate of $PbCrO_4$.

$$CrO_4^{2-} + Pb^{2+} \longrightarrow PbCrO_4 \downarrow$$

$$PbCrO_4 + 4OH^- \longrightarrow PbO_2^{2-} + CrO_4^{2-} + 2H_2O$$

(ii) With acidified chromate solution, H_2O_2 forms a blue peroxide of chromium which is stable in ether medium.

$$2CrO_4^{2-} + 4H^+ + 3H_2O_2 \longrightarrow \underset{\substack{\text{perchromic acid} \\ \text{(blue)}}}{2HCrO_5} + 4H_2O$$

Reaction of Al^{3+}

(i) On adding NH_4Cl to one part and heating, $Al(OH)_3$ is precipitated.

$$AlO_2^- + NH_4^+ + H_2O \longrightarrow Al(OH)_3 \downarrow + NH_3$$

(ii) The white precipitate of $Al(OH)_3$ is dissolved in dil. HCl (minimum quantity).

$$Al(OH)_3 + 3H^+ \longrightarrow Al^{3+} + 3H_2O$$

On adding a few drops of litmus solution, a pink colour is obtained. Now, on addition of NH_4OH dropwise (till it becomes alkaline), precipitate of $Al(OH)_3$ reappears. The precipitate of $Al(OH)_3$ adsorbs the blue colouring matter of litmus and turns blue.

(iii) *Charcoal cavity test*

$$2\ Co(NO_3)_2 \xrightarrow{\text{heat}} 2\ CoO + 2NO_2 \uparrow O_2$$

$$CoO + Al_2O_2 \longrightarrow \underset{\substack{\text{cobalt aluminate} \\ \text{(Thenard's blue)}}}{Co(AlO_2)_2}$$

Reactions

(i) $M^{2+} + 2Cl^- \rightarrow MCl_2$
(M=Mn, Zn)

Reactions of Co^{2+} and Ni^{2+}

(i) The precipitate containing NiS and CoS on treatment with aqua regia forms their corresponding chlorides.

$$NiS + 2HCl + 3(O) \longrightarrow NiCl_2 + SO_2 + H_2O$$

$$CoS + 2HCl + 3(O) \longrightarrow CoCl_2 + SO_2 + H_2O$$

(ii) $CoCl_2$ forms a yellow precipitate with potassium nitrite and acetic acid.

$$CoCl_2 + 7KNO_2 + 2CH_3COOH \longrightarrow K_3[Co(NO_2)_6] \downarrow \\ 2KCl + 2CH_3COOK$$

(iii) A blue complex ammonium tetrathiocyanatocobaltate-(III) is formed with NH_4SCN which is soluble in acetone.

$$CoCl_2 + 4NH_4SCN \longrightarrow (NH_4)_2[Co(SCN)_4] + 2NH_4Cl$$
amm. tetrathiocyanatocobaltate(III)

(iv) Potassium ferricyanide yields a reddish brown precipitate.

$$3CoCl_2 + 2K_3Fe(CN)_6 \longrightarrow Co_3[Fe(CN)_6]_2 + 6KCl$$

(v) Nickel in alkaline solution forms a scarlet red precipitate chelate with dimethylglyoxime. (See p. 182)

(vi) $NiCl_2$ in presence of $NaHCO_3$ and bromine water yields a black precipitate.

$$NiCl_2 + 2NaHCO_3 \longrightarrow NiCO_3 + 2NaCl + H_2O + CO_2$$

$$NiCO_3 + 3H_2O + (O) \longrightarrow Ni(OH)_3 \downarrow + 2CO \uparrow$$

$$2Ni(OH)_3 \longrightarrow Ni_2O_3 + 3H_2O$$
(black ppt.)

Formation of scarlet red chelate of bis(dimethylglyoximato)nickel(II) when nickel(II) reacts with dimethylglyoxime in ammoniacal medium

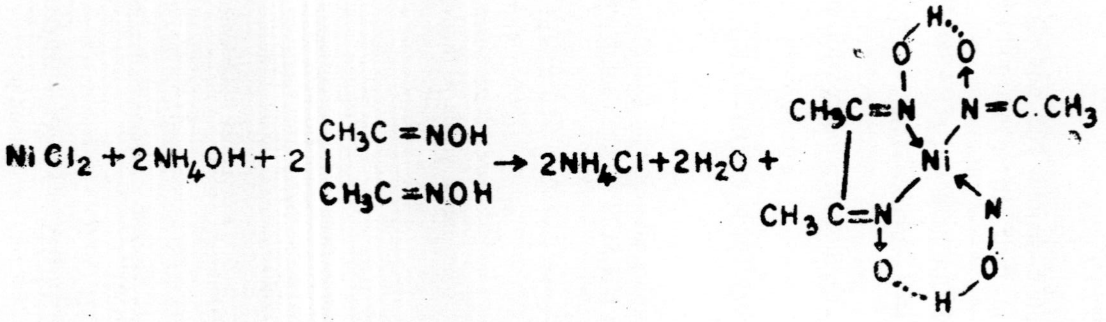

$$NiCl_2 + 2NH_4OH + 2\begin{array}{l} CH_3C{=}NOH \\ | \\ CH_3C{=}NOH \end{array} \rightarrow 2NH_4Cl + 2H_2O + \text{[bis(dimethylglyoximato)nickel(II) complex]}$$

dimethylglyoxime

bis(dimethylglyoximato)-
nickel(II) complex
(scarlet red ppt.)

Reactions of Zn^{2+} and Mn^{2+}

(i) The filtrate containing $MnCl_2$ and $ZnCl_2$ when treated with NaOH solution yields precipitate of $Mn(OH)_2$ and $Zn(OH)_2$.

$$MnCl_2+2NaOH \longrightarrow Mn(OH)_2+2NaCl$$

But the precipitate of $Zn(OH)_2$ dissolves in excess of NaOH forming sodium zincate.

$$Zn(OH)_2+2NaOH \longrightarrow Na_2ZnO_2+2H_2O$$

(ii) The precipitate of $Mn(OH)_2$, in excess of NaOH, turns brown in air.

$$\underset{}{2Mn(OH)_2}+\underset{\text{(air)}}{(O)} \longrightarrow \underset{\text{(brown precipitate)}}{2MnO(OH)}$$

(iii) Brown precipitate of MnO(OH) on boiling with PbO_2 and conc. HNO_3, yields a pink colouration on dilution.

$$PbO_2+3HNO_3 \longrightarrow Pb(NO_3)_2+H_4O+(O)$$

$$2MnO_2+H_2O+O \longrightarrow \underset{\text{(pink)}}{2HMnO_4}$$

(iv) Br_2 water in NaOH solution oxidizes $Mn(OH)_2$ to a black ppt.

$$Mn(OH)_2+(O) \longrightarrow \underset{\text{(black)}}{MnO.(OH)_2}$$

(v) On passing H_2S through Na_2ZnO_2 solution, ZnS is precipitated.

$$Na_2ZnO_2+H_2S \longrightarrow ZnS+2NaOH$$

(vi) On adding $CuSO_4$ and ammonium mercuric thiocyanate solution to zinc solution, a blue ppt. of $Zn[Hg(SCN)_4]$ and $Cu[Hg(SCN_4)]$ is obtained.

TABLE 4.8

Identification of Group V Cations
(Ba^{2+}, Sr^{2+} and Ca^{2+})

Take the centrifugate after precipitation of Group IV in a semimicro boiling tube or crucible. Boil off H_2S completely and concentrate to 1 mL. Transfer this solution to another semi micro test tube. To this add 1 mL of ammonium carbonate solution followed by 2 drops of conc. NH_4OH solution. Warm gently (do not boil) and centrifuge. Analyse the residue for Group V and centrifugate for Group VI.

Wash the residue with 2 drops of water. Reject the washings. Dissolve the ppt. in 5 N CH_3COOH. Boil the solution to drive off CO_2. To 5 drops of this solution, add 1 drop of K_2CrO_4 solution and warm. If a yellow ppt. appears, add K_2CrO_4 solution to the remaining solution also. Warm and centrifuge (if no yellow ppt. appears, Ba^{2+} may be taken as absent and test for Sr^{2+} and Ca^{2+} in the remaining solution without adding K_2CrO_4 solution).

<table>
<tr>
<td rowspan="2">Residue Pale yellow residue indicates Ba^{2+}. Wash the residue with warm water and confirm the residue for Ba^{2+} as follows:
(a) Dissolve a portion of the residue in minimum amount of conc. HCl and apply the flame test. An apple green flame confirms Ba^{2+}.
(b) Dissolve a portion of residue in minimum amount of 5 N HCl. Place a drop of this solution on a filter paper. To this add 1 drop of H_2O_2, 1 drop of NH_4Cl, 2 drops of NH_4OH and finally 1 drop of 0.5 per cent solution of sodium rhodizonate solution. A red brown strain confirms Ba^{2+}.</td>
<td colspan="2">Centrifugate To this add 1 mL of $(NH_4)_2SO_4$ solution followed by NH_4OH dropwise until mixture becomes alkaline. Warm and keep it for one minute and contrifuge.</td>
</tr>
<tr>
<td>Residue White residue indicates the presence of Sr^{2+}. Dissolve the residue in minimum amount of conc. HCl and perform flame test. A crimson red flame (persistent) confirms Sr^{2+}.</td>
<td>Centrifugate Add 5 drops of $(NH_4)_2C_2O_4$ solution and water. A white ppt. of CaC_2O_4 confirms Ca^{2+}.
Further confirm Ca^{2+} by flame test on the residue A brick red flame (non-persistent) confirms Ca^{2+}.</td>
</tr>
<tr>
<td>Ba^{2+}</td>
<td>Sr^{2+}</td>
<td>Ca^{2+}</td>
</tr>
</table>

REACTIONS OF THE CATIONS OF GROUP V

1. Action of acetic acid

$$MCO_3 + 2CH_3COOH \longrightarrow (CH_3COO)_2M + CO_2\uparrow + H_2O$$
$$(M = \text{Ba, Sr, Ca})$$

2. Reaction of barium ion, Ba^{2+}

$$Ba^{2+} + CrO_4 \longrightarrow BaCrO_4\downarrow$$

barium chromate (yellow)

3. Reaction of strontium ion, Sr^{2+}

$$Sr^{2+} + SO_4^{2-} \longrightarrow SrSO_4\downarrow$$

strontium sulphate (white)

4. Reaction of calcium ion, Ca^{2+}

$$Ca^{2+} + C_2O_4^{2-} \longrightarrow CaC_2O_4\downarrow$$

calcium oxalate (white)

Reactions of Mg^{2+}

(*a*) Titan yellow is a water-soluble dyestuff. It is adsorbed by magnesium hydroxide producing a deep red colour or ppt.

(*b*) A white crystalline ppt. of magnesium ammonium phosphate is formed.

$$Mg^{2+} + NH_3 + HPO_4^{-} \longrightarrow Mg(NH_4)PO_4$$

(*c*) Magneson is a dyestuff. It is adsorbed by magnesium hydroxide to give a blue colour or ppt.

(*d*) $$CoO + MgO \longrightarrow MgCoO_2$$

(pink)

TABLE 4.9

Identification of Group VI Cations
(Mg^{2+}, K^+ and Na^+)

Evaporate the centrifugate from Group V with 0.5 mL of conc. HNO_3 in a crucible to almost dryness. Continue heating of the dry mass until fumes of ammonium salt ceases to evolve. Treat the residue with 1 mL of water. Stir and transfer to a semimicro tube, centrifuge and separate the clear liquid.

Residue Dissolve the residue in 5-6 drops of 5 N HCl Divide the solution into four parts: (*a*) Place one drop of the solution on spot plate and one drop each of the titan yellow and 5 N NaOH. A red ppt. confirms Mg^{2+}. (*b*) Take 3 drops of the solution in a test tube. To this add one drop of sodium hydrogen phosphate solution and 2 drops of ammonia. Scratch the walls of test tube with a glass rod. A white crystalline ppt. confirms Mg^{2+}. (*c*) Place a drop of solution on a spot plate. To this add 1-2 drops of magneson reagent and then a drop of 5 N NaOH. A blue ppt. confirms Mg^{2+}. (*d*) *Charcoal cavity test*. A pink mass is obtained.	*Centrifugate* Evaporate to dryness and bake to decompose ammonium salts completely. Cool and extract the residue with 5-7 drops of 5 N CH_3COOH. Divide the solution into two portions. **I portion** (*a*) To part I, add 3 drops of $Na_3Co(NO_2)_6$ solution. A yellow ppt. confirms K^+. (*b*) To part II, add 3 drops of perchloric acid or sodium perchlorate solution. A white ppt. confirms K^+. (*c*) *Flame test*. Further confirm K^+ by flame test using cobalt blue glass. A crimson flame results. **II portion** Divide it into three parts. (*a*) To part I, add 3 drops of potassium pyroantimonate solution, white ppt. confirms Na^+. (*b*) To Part II, add 3 drops of zinc uranyl acetete, warm. A yellow crystalline ppt. confirms Na^+. (*c*) With Part III perform the flame test. A golden yellow flame confirms Na^+.
Mg^{2+}	**Na^+**

Reactions of K^+

(*a*) $$3K^+ + [Co(NO_2)_6]^{3-} \longrightarrow K_3[Co(NO_2)_6]$$
(yellow ppt.)

(*b*) $$K^+ + ClO_4^- \longrightarrow KClO_4$$
(white ppt.)

Reactions of Na^+

(*a*) $$2Na^+ + H_2Sb_2O_7^{2-} \longrightarrow Na_2H_2Sb_2O_7$$
(white ppt.)

(*b*) $$Na^+ + Zn^{2+} + 3CH_3COO^- + 3UO_2(CH_3COO)_2 + 9H_2O \longrightarrow NaZn(UO_2)_3(CH_3COO)_9.9H_2O$$
(yellow ppt.)

5

SPOT TEST ANALYSIS

(Micro Qualitative Analysis)

Introduction

In micro analysis (commonly called as spot test analysis) the masses and volumes for analysis are about 5 mg and 0.1 mL, i.e. 1-2 drops. Tananaev (1920) introduced this technique and Fiegl extended its scope to such an extent that it occupies very important position in the modern qualitative analysis. Selective and charactristic spot tests for inorganic and organic compounds are known which detect with certainty the individual cations present in a mixture.

Procedure

(i) The spot test is carried out either on a plate called spot plate or on a Whatmann filter paper No. 120 or Schleicher and Schull paper No. 601. On the plate it is confined to a small area and takes the shape of spot.

(ii) Take 1-2 drops of the original solution on spot plate followed by systematic addition of the reagent.

(iii) The detail of the test is given in the test of individual cation.

Advantages

(i) These are quicker and easier to carry out.

(ii) These can be interpreted more readily.

(iii) These are less susceptible to slight variation of experimental conditions.

Notes

(i) The analytical grade reagents must be used.

(ii) The test should be performed strictly according to the instructions provided in a test.

A systematic analysis of the cations, in order of the groups, is given in the following pages.

Group I (Pb^{2+}, Ag^{+} and Hg_2^{2+})

Test for Pb^{2+}

(*a*) *Benzidine Reagent*

$$H_2N-C_6H_4-C_6H_4-NH_2$$

This reagent produces benzidine blue on oxidation with lead oxide. The interference is due to Bi^{3+}, Ce^{4+}, Mn^{2+}, Co^{2+}, Ni^{2+}, Ag^{+} and Tl^{+}, but in alkaline medium only Tl^{+} interferes.

Test Place 1 drop of the test solution on a filter paper and add 2 drops of 3 N NaOH and 1 drop of saturated Br_2 water. Now add 2 drops of 50 per cent ammonia solution. Dry the spot and add 2 drops of the benzidine solution (0.05% in 10% CH_3COOH).

A blue colour develops that indicates lead, the limit of identification being 1 μg Pb; conc, limit, 1 in 50,000.

(*b*) *Dithizone* (*or Diphenylthiocarbazone*) *Reagent*

$$S = C\begin{matrix} \diagup NH.NH.C_6H_5 \\ \diagdown N = NC_6H_5 \end{matrix}$$

Lead salts form brick-red complex with this reagent. The interference is due to Ag^+, Hg^{2+}, Cu^{2+}, Cd^{2+}, Sb^{3+}, Ni^{2+} and Zn^{2+}. But in the presence of much alkali cyanide, the interference may be eliminated.

Test Take 2 drops of the test solution in a semi-micro test tube and add few crystals of KCN. Now add 2 drops of the reagent solution (5 mg in 100 mL of CCl_4).

The green colour of the reagent changing to red indicates lead, the limit of identification being 0.1 μg Pb; conc. limit, 1 in 1,250,000.

Tests for Ag^+

(*a*) *p-Dimethylamino-benzylidenerhodanine Reagent*

$$\begin{matrix} HN & — & C=O & & \\ | & & | & & \\ SC & & C & = CH - C_6H_4 - & N(CH_3)_2 \\ & \diagdown S \diagup & & & \end{matrix}$$

Silver salts form red-violet salt in faintly acidic solution with the reagent (Ag replaces H of NH group). The interference is due to Hg, Cu, Au, Pt and Pd.

Test Place 1 drop of the test solution on spot plate, add 1 drop of N HNO_3 followed by a drop of the reagent solution (0.03% solution in alcohol or acetone).

A red-violet ppt. indicates Ag, the limit of identification being 0.02 μg Ag; conc. limit, 1 in 2,500,000.

(*b*) *Potassium chromate Reagent*

$$K_2CrO_4$$

Silver salts form red ring with the reagent.

Test Place a drop of the test solutlon on spot plate, add one drop of $(NH_4)_2CO_3$ solution and stir. Remove one drop of the clear liquid and place it on filter paper and add one drop of the reagent solution (1% solution in N CH_3COOH).

A red ring indicates Ag, the limit of identification being 2 μg Ag; conc. limit, 1 in 25,000.

Tests for Hg_2^{2+}

(*a*) *Dithizone Reagent*

$$C_6H_5-N=N-\underset{}{\overset{S}{\overset{\|}{C}}}-\overset{H}{\overset{|}{N}}-\overset{H}{N}-C_6H_5$$

Mercury salts form yellow colour at pH above 7 with the reagent. The interference is due to CN^-, SCN^-, $S_2O_3^{2-}$ and $[Fe(CN)_6]^{3-}$.

Test Take 1 drop of the test solution in a semi-micro test tube and add 10 drops of 3 M $CCl_3.COOH$ solution and 3 drops of 10 per cent oxalic acid solution. Now extract the colour in 1 mL of *n*-butyl acetate. Place 3-4 drops of the *n*-butyl acetate layer in a second semi-micro test tube and add 2-3 drops is a 0.002 per cent solution of reagent in $CHCl_3$.

A yellow solution indicates mercury, the limit of identification being 2.5 μg Hg.

(b) Gallic acid Reagent

Mercury salts form orange colour with the reagent.

Test Take 1 drop of the test solution in a semi-micro test tube and add 1 drop of the reagent solution (1% alcoholic solution).

Orange colour becomes yellow on dilution indicates mercury.

Group II (Hg^{2+}, Pb^{2+}, Bi^{3+}, Cu^{2+}, Cd^{2+}, As^{3+}, Sb^{3+}, Sn^{2+})
Tests for Hg^{2+}

(a) Diphenylcarbazone Reagent

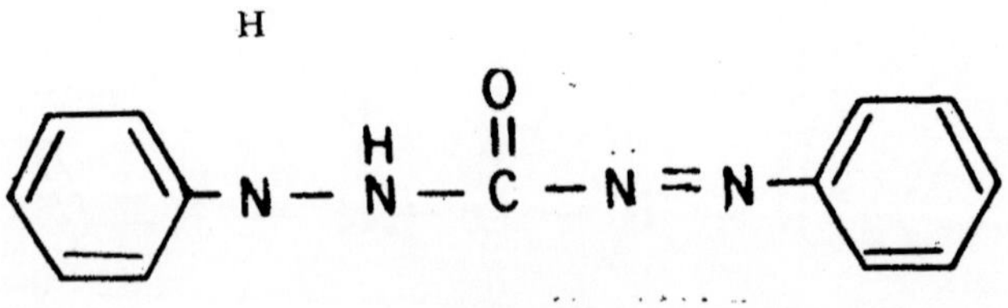

$$C_6H_5-\overset{H}{N}-\overset{H}{N}-\overset{\overset{O}{\|}}{C}-N=N-C_6H_5$$

Mercury salts form an insoluble violet to blue complex with the reagent. The metals like Cu, Fe and Co give coloured compounds, but in 0.2 N HNO_3 the reaction is specific for mercury.

Test Place 1 drop of the test solution on a filter paper and add 1 drop of a 1 per cent solution of reagent in ethanol.

A violet ring indicates mercury, the limit of identification being 0.05 μg Hg; conc. limit, 1 in 50,000.

Tests for Pb^{2+} Same as given above.

Tests for Bi^{3+}

(*a*) ***Thiourea***

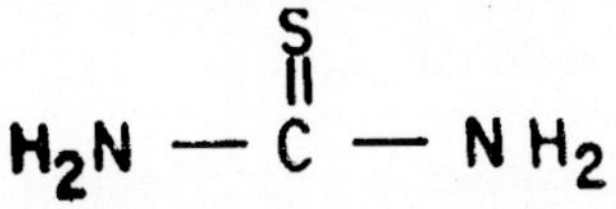

$$H_2N-\overset{\overset{\displaystyle S}{||}}{C}-NH_2$$

Bismuth salts give a yellow solution with the reagent in acid solution. The interference is due to Sb^{3+}, Hg_2^{2+}, and Ag^{+}.

Test Place 1 drop of the test solution on a spot plate and add 1 drop of a 10 per cent aqueous solution of reagent and one drop of dil. HNO_3.

A yellow solution indicates bismuth, the limit of identification being 2.5 μg Bi; conc. limit, 1 in 30,000.

(*b*) *Cinchonine potassium iodide Reagent*

Bismuth salts form orange red colour with the reagent in faintly acid solution. The interference is due to Pb, Cu and Hg.

Test Place 1 drop of the test solution on a spot plate and add 1 drop of the reagent solution (1 g of cinchonine in 100 mL of hot water containing a few drops of HNO_3, after cooling, 2 g of KI are added).

An orange red spot indicates bismuth, the limit of identification being 0.15 μg Bi; conc. limit, 1 in 350,000.

Tests for Cu^{2+}

(*a*) *Benzoin α-oxime* (*Cupron*) *Reagent*

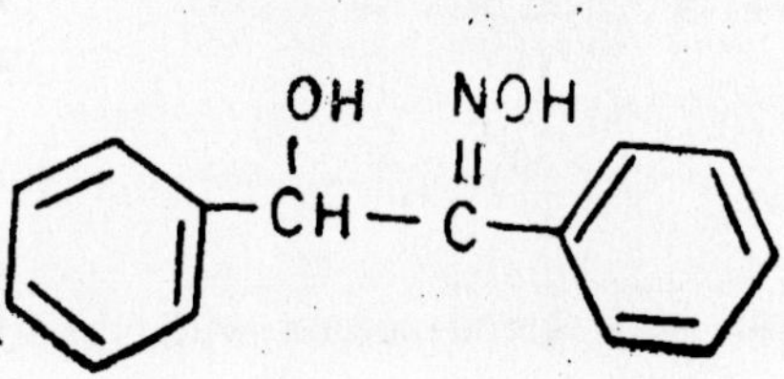

$$C_6H_5-\overset{\overset{\displaystyle OH}{|}}{C}H-\overset{\overset{\displaystyle NOH}{||}}{C}-C_6H_5$$

Copper salts form a green ppt. in the presence of ammonium tartrate, other metals do not interfere.

Test Impregnate filter paper with a solution of 5 per cent cupron in ethanol and dry it. Now add 1 drop of a 10 per cent aqueous solution of potassium hydrogen tartrate and a drop of the test solution. Hold the paper over ammonium hydoxide.

A green colour indicates copper, the limit of identification being 0.1 μg Cu; conc. limit, 1 in 500,000.

(*b*) *Salicylaldoxime*

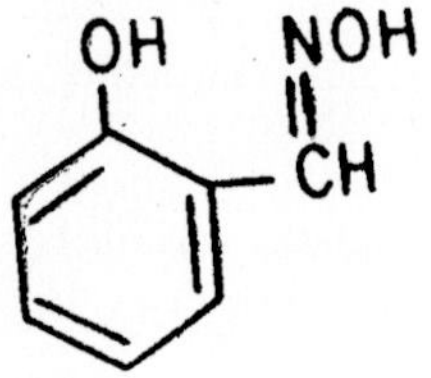

OH NOH
‖
CH

Copper salts give a yellow-green ppt. with reagent in acetic acid solution.

Test Take 2 drops of the test solution in a semi-micro test tube and slightly acidify it with acetic acid. Add 1 drop of the reagent solution (1 g reagent is dissolved in 5 mL ethanol and pour the solution dropwise into 95 mL of water, shake and filter. Use filtrate as a reagent solution).

A yellow-green ppt. indicates copper, the limit of identification being 0.5 μg Cu; conc. limit, 1 in 100,000.

(*c*) *Dithio-oxamide* (*Rubeanic acid*) *Reagent*

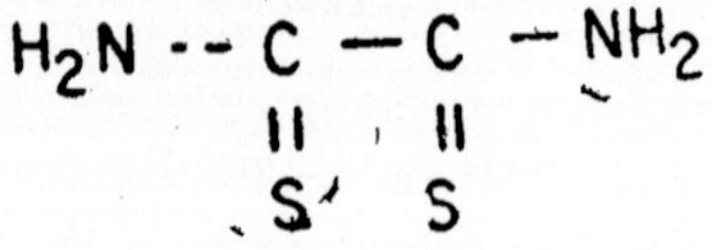

$$H_2N-\underset{\underset{S}{\|}}{C}-\underset{\underset{S}{\|}}{C}-NH_2$$

Copper salts form dark green colour with the reagent. The

interference is due to Ag^+ and Au^{3+}. But by adding 1-2 drops of 5 per cent NaCl solution before the test, Ag^+ does not interfere.

Test Place 1 drop of the test solution on filter paper and add 1 drop of 20 per cent malonic acid solution. Now add 1 drop of a reagent solution (1.3% in methanol).

A black to dark green colour indicates copper, the limit of identification being 0.025 μg Cu; conc. limit, 1 in 2,500,000.

Tests for Cd^{2+}

(*a*) *Diphenylcarbazone Reagent*

$$C_6H_5-\overset{H}{N}-\overset{H}{N}-\overset{O}{\overset{\|}{C}}-N=N-C_6H_5$$

Cadmium salts forms dark purple colour with the reagent.

Test Place 2 drops of the test reagent on filter paper, add 2 drops of the reagent solution (1.5% solution in ethanol) and 1 drop of 3 per cent sodium tetraborate solution. Now add 4 drops of ethanol slowly to the spot and allow the paper to dry.

A dark purple ring indicates cadmium.

(*b*) *Dinitro-p-diphenylcarbazide reagent*

$$O=C\begin{cases} NH.NH.C_6H_4-NO_2-p \\ NH.NH.C_6H-NO_2-p \end{cases}$$

Cadmium hydroxide is coloured brown by the reagent which rapidly becomes greenish blue with H.CHO.

Test Take 2 drops of the test solution in a semi-micro test tube. Add 1 drop of 10 per cent NaOH solution, 1 drop of 10 per cent KCN solution, 1 drop of the reagent solution (0.1% solution in ethanol) and 2 drops of 40 per cent HCHO solution.

A brown ppt. changing readily to greenish blue indicates cadmium, the limit of identification being 0.8 μg Cd; conc. limit, 1 in 60,000.

Tests for As^{3+}

(*a*) ***Mercuric bromide reagent***

Arsenic salts form orange or yellow colour with the reagent.

Test Take zinc powder in a semi-micro test tube and add dil. H_2SO_4. To this add arsenic compound. Hold $HgBr_2$ paper over the month of test tube.

A yellow or orange colour indicates arsenic.

(*b*) *Bettendorff's Test*

Arsenic salts give brown or black colour or ppt. in this test.

Test Place 2 drops of the test solution in a semi-micro crucible and add 1-2 drops of liq. ammonia, 2 drops of '20-vol.' H_2O_2 and 2 drops of 10 per cent $MgCl_2$ solution. Evaporate the solution till fumes cease. Treat the residue with 2 drops of $SnCl_2$ solution in conc. HCl and warm.

A brown or black ppt. or colour indicates arsenic, the limit of identification being 1 μg As; conc. limit, 1 in 50,000.

Tests for Sb^{3+}

(*a*) ***Rhodamine B (or Tetracthyl-rhodamine) Reagent***

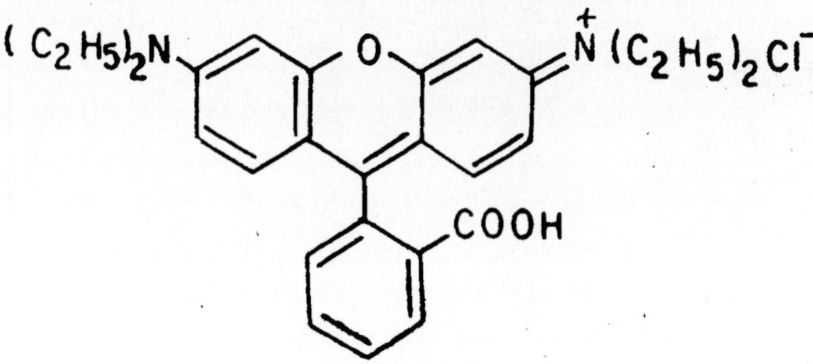

$(C_2H_5)_2N$ — $\overset{+}{N}(C_2H_5)_2Cl^-$ — O — COOH

Antimony(V) salts form violet benzene layer with the reagent. Thus the Sb(III) salts must be oxidized by adding $NaNO_3$ in the presence of conc. HCl in the test solution.

Test Place 5 drops of 1:3 dil. H_2SO_4 in a semi-micro test tube and add one drop of the test solution. Now add 1 drop of 10 per cent KI solution and 1 mL benzene, shake the solution well and take 2 drops of this solution on a spot plate. Add one drop of the reagent solution (0.2 per cent aqueous solution).

A violet benzene layer indicates antimony, the limit of identification being 0.25 μg Sb; conc. limit, 1 in 100,000.

(*b*) *Gallocyanine Reagent*

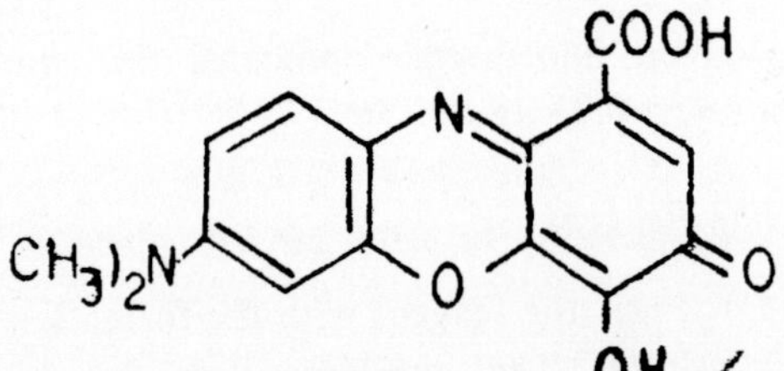

COOH — N — $(CH_3)_2N$ — O — O — OH

Antimony salts give blue colour with the reagent.

Test Take 1 drop of the test solution on a spot plate and add 1 drop or the reagent solution (0.05% solution in 1 N HCl).

A change from wine red colour to blue indicates antimony.

Tests for Sn^{2+}

(*a*) *Morin*

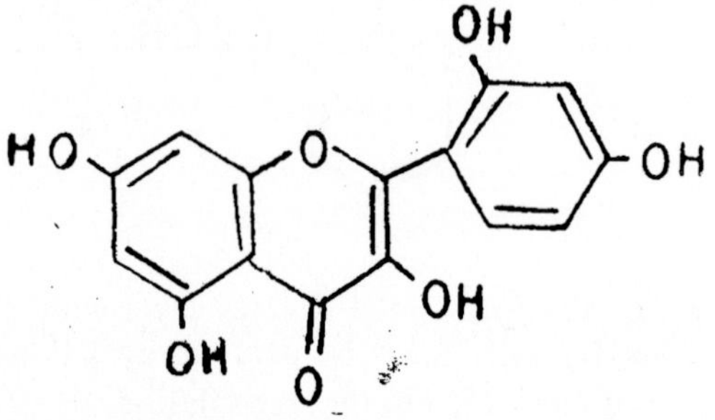

Tin salts form yellow-green solution with the regent in sulpho-alkaline solution.

Test Treat the test solution with an excess of yellow ammonium sulphide solution and filter. Take 2 drops of the filtrate in a semi-micro test tube and add 5 per cent H_2O_2 solution, wait for 1-2 minutes and place 1 drop of this solution on filter paper and hold the paper over ammonia solution. Add 1 drop of a 0.02 per cent solution of the reagent in acetone. Bathe the filter paper in a 1:20 glacial acetic acid-ethanol mixture for 10 minutes and examine under u.v. light.

A yellow-green fluorescence indicates tin, the limit of identification being 0.05 μg Sn.

(*b*) *Cacotheline Reagent*

Tin(II) salts reduce the reagent with the formation of a violet coloured compound. The interferance is due to H_2S, Sb^{3+}, SO_3^{2-} and $S_2O_3^{2-}$.

Test Impregnate a piece of filter paper with a saturated solution of the reagent (0.6% aqueous). Before the paper is quite dry, add a drop of the test solution.

A red to violet ring surrounded by a pale yellow to colourless zone on the yellow paper indicate tin, the limit of identification being 0.5 lig Sn, conc. limit: 1 in 2,50,000.

(c) *Dithiol Reagent*

Stannous salts form red ppt. with the reagent in acid solution. The interference is due to Ag, Pb, Hg, Cd, As, Sb, Cu, Ni, Co, Bi, PO_4^{3-} and NO_2^-.

Test Take 2 drops of the test solution in a semimicro crucible, acidified with dil HCl and add 3 drops of the reagent solution (0.2 g of reagent in 100 ml. of 1 per cent NaOH solution and adding 0.3—0.5 g of thioglycollic acid) to facititate the reduction of Sn^{+4} to Sn^{2+})-

A red ppt. of colour indicates tin, conc. limit: 1 in 5,00,000.

Group III (Fe^{3+}, Al^{3+} and Cr^{3+})

Tests for Fe^{3+}

(*a*) *2,2′-Dipyridyl Reagent*

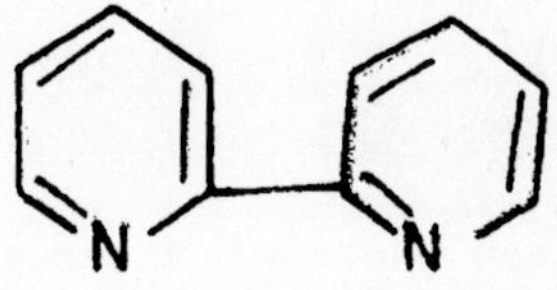

Iron(II) salts form deep red colour with the reagent. Therefore iron(III) must be reduced first with hydroxylammonium chloride or thioglycollic acid.

Test Take 2 drops of the test solution in a semi-micro test tube, add 3-4 drops of hydroxylammonium chloride and acidily the solution. Place 1 drop of this solution on spot plate and add 1 drop of the reagent solution (2% solution in ethanol).

A deep red colour of the solution indicates iron, the limit of identification being 0.25 μg Fe; conc. limit, 1 in 1,666,000.

(b) *o-Phenanthroline Reagent*

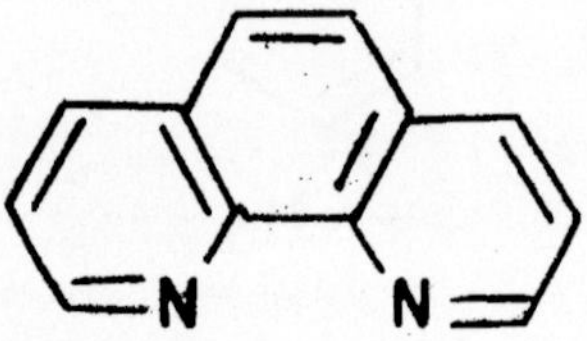

Iron(II) salts give red colour with the reagent in fanity acidic solution. Reduce iron(III) to iron(II) as above.

Test Place 1 drop of reduced iron(III) on the spot plate and add 1 drop of the reagent solution (0.1% aqueous solution).

A red colour indicates iron, the conc. limit, 1 in 1,50,000.

(c) ***Ferron Reagent***

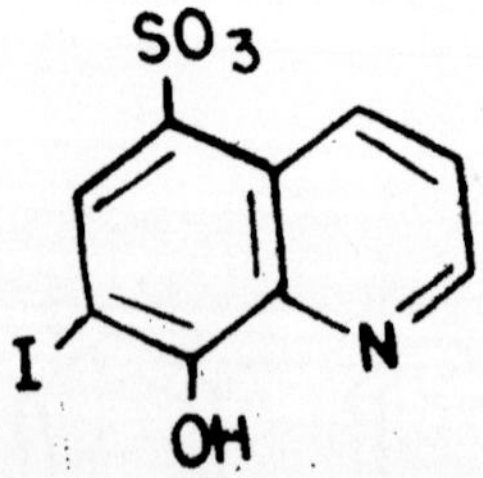

Iron(III) salts give green colour with the reagent at pH 3.5.

Test Place 1 drop of the test solution (pH 3.5) on a spot plate and add 1 drop of the reagent solution (0.1% aqueous solution).

A green colour indicates iron, the limit of identification being 0.5 μg Fe.

Tests for Al^{3+}

(*a*) *Aluminon Reagent*

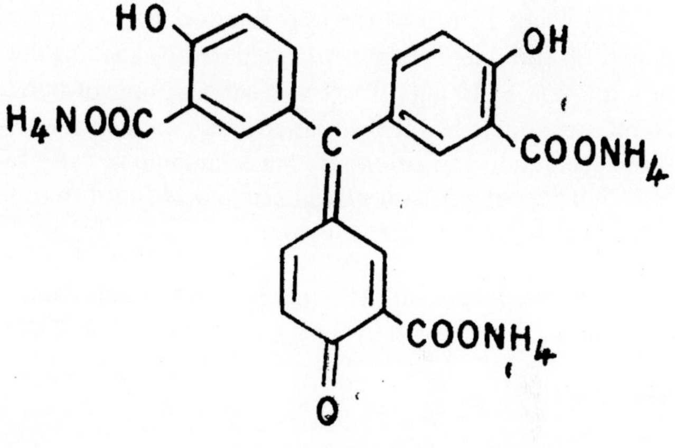

Aluminium hydroxide precipitated in the presence of this reagent yields a red lake. The interference is due to Cu, Fe, Ni, and Be.

Test Place one drop of test solution (pH about 6.3) on filter paper and add 1 drop of the reagent (0.1% aqueous) solution and wait for 30 seconds. Rinse paper with water.

A red spot indicates aluminium, the limit of identification being 0.5 μg Al.

(*b*) *Quinalizarin Reagent*

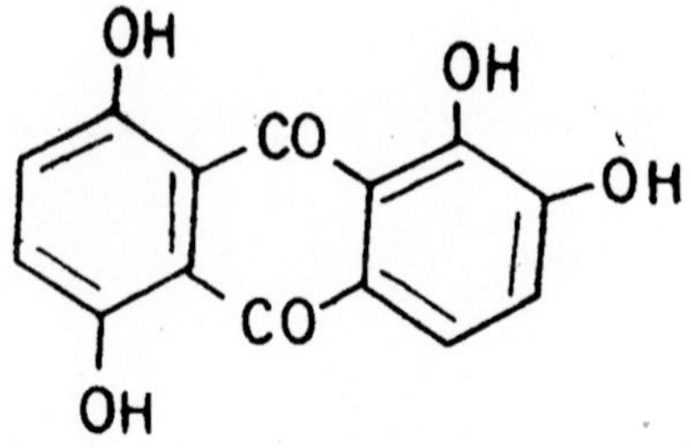

[Structure of quinalizarin: anthraquinone (two CO bridges) with OH groups at positions 1, 4 on one ring and 1, 2 (adjacent OH, OH) on the other ring]

Aluminium salts give red-violet colour with the reagent.

Test Place 1 drop of the test solution on a prepared filter paper. (A suitable filter paper is prepared by soaking filter paper in a solution of 10 mg of the reagent in 2 mL of pyridine and 20 mL acetone). Hold the paper over ammonia when it will turn blue due to formation of the ammonium salt of the dye. Now hold the paper over glacial acetic acid until the unmoistened paper regains its brown colour.

A red-violet spot on the paper indicates aluminium, the limit of identification being 0.01 μg Al; conc. limit, 1 in 2,000,000.

Tests for Cr^{3+}

(*a*) *sym-Diphenylcarbazide Reagent*

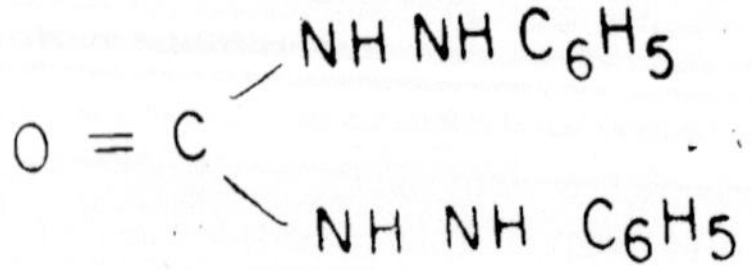

$$O=C\begin{matrix} \diagup NH\,NH\,C_6H_5 \\ \diagdown NH\,NH\,C_6H_5 \end{matrix}$$

Chromium salts give violet colour with the reagent. The interference is due to Co, Cu, Ni, and Fe.

Test Place 1 drop of the test solution on a spot plate and add 1 drop of saturated solution of potassium persulphate.

Now add 1 drop of 2 per cent $AgNO_3$ solution. After waiting for a few seconds, add 1 drop of conc. H_2SO_4. Add 1 drop of reagent solution (1% solution in ethanol).

A violet colour indicates chromium, the limit of identification being 0.5 μg Cr; conc. limit, 1 in 2,000,000.

(*b*) *Alizarin S Reagent*

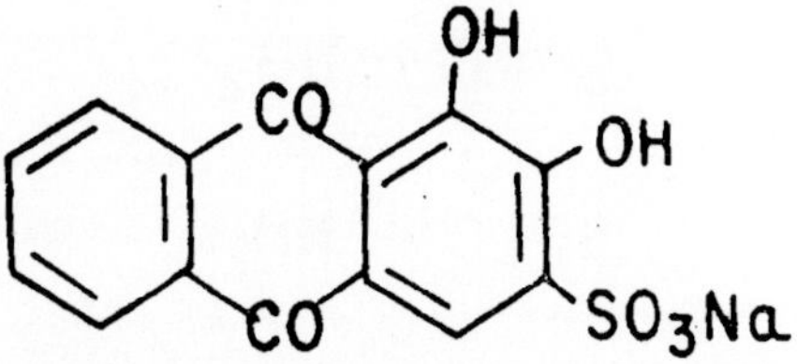

Chromium salts give red ppt. or colour with the reagent.

Test Take a drop of test solution (alkaline with NaOH) and treat with a drop of reagent solution (0.1% aqueous), followed by acetic acid until the violet colour disappears and then with a further drop of acetic acid.

A red colour or ppt. which intensifies on standing indicates chromium.

Group IV (Ni^{2+}, Co^{2+}, Mn^{2+}, and Zn^{2+})

Tests for Ni^{2+}

(*a*) *Dimethylglyoxime Reagent*

$$\begin{array}{l} H_3C-C=NOH \\ \qquad\;\; | \\ H_3C-C=NOH \end{array}$$

Nickel salts give red colour or ppt. with the reagent in alkaline medium. The interference is due to Fe^{2+} which can be prevented by the presence of EDTA.

Test Place 1 drop of test solution on filter paper and add 1 drop of reagent solution (1% ethanolic solution). Expose the paper to ammonia fumes.

A pink or red spot indicates nickel, the limit of identification being 0.25 μg Ni; conc. limit, 1 in 300,000,

(*b*) *Dithio-oxamide Reagent*

$$\begin{array}{l} S=C-NH_2 \\ \quad\;\; | \\ S=C-NH_2 \end{array}$$

Nickel salts give blue colour with the reagent in alkaline medium. The interference is due to Cu, Cd, Co, Cd and Zn.

Test Place one drop of the test solution on filter paper, Expose the filter paper to ammonia fumes. Now add 1 drop of the reagent solution (1% ethanolic solution).

A blue to blue-violet spot indicates nickel, the limit of identification being 0.01 μg Ni; conc. limit, 1 in 1,250,000.

(*c*) *α-Furil-dioxime Reagent*

$$\begin{array}{l} C_4H_3O-C=NOH \\ \qquad\qquad\;\; | \\ C_4H_3O-C=NOH \end{array}$$

Nickel salts give red ppt. with the reagent in slightly ammoniacal solution. The interference is due to Fe^{++} and should be oxidized and alkaline tartrate solution added before applying the test.

Test Place 1 drop of the test solution on a filter paper. Expose it to ammonia fumes. Now add 2 drop of the reagent solution (10% ethanolic solution).

A red colour or ppt. indicates nickel, the limit of identification being 0.02 μg Ni; conc. limit, 1 in 6,000,000.

Tests for Co^{2+}

(*a*) ***α-Nitroso-β-naphthol Reagent***

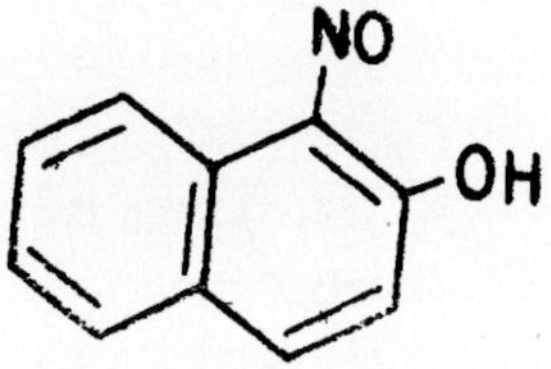

Cobalt salts give red-brown ppt. with the reagent. The interference is due to Cu, Fe and Pd.

Test Place 1 drop of the test solution on filter paper and add 1 drop of the reagent solution (0.1 g reagent in 20 mL water and 1 mL dil NaOH and diluting to 200 mL with water).

A pink ring indicates cobalt, the limit of identification being 0.05 μg Co; conc. limit, 1 in 1,000,000.

(*b*) *Nitroso-R-salt Reagent*

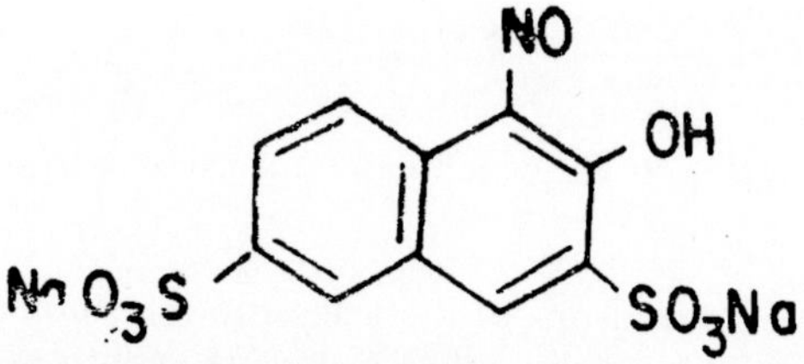

Cobalt salts give deep red colour with the reagent. The interference is due to Sn and Fe. The interference due to iron can be prevented by the addition of an alkali fluoride.

Test Place 1 drop of the neutral test solution (buffered with CH_3COONa) on a spot plate, add 2-3 drops of the reagent solution (1% aqueous solution).

A red colour indicates cobalt, conc. limit. 1 in 500,000.

Tests for Mn^{2+}

(*a*) *Tetra-base Reagent*

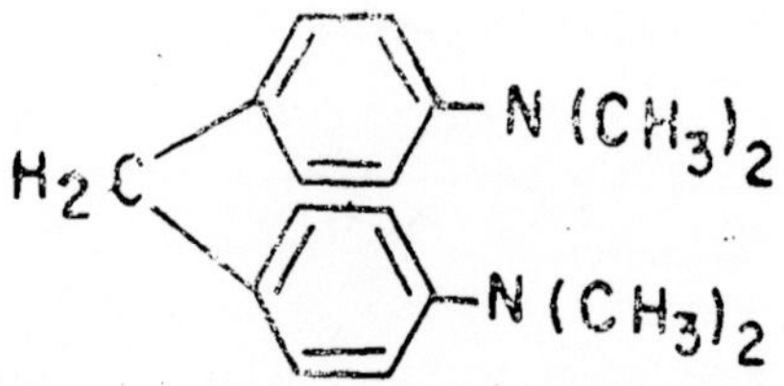

H_2C $N(CH_3)_2$ $N(CH_3)_2$

Manganese salts give blue colour with the reagent. The interference is due to Fe and Hg.

Test Place 1 drop of the test solution on a spot plate and add 1 drop of saturated solution of KIO_4. Now add 1 drop of the reagent solution (42% solution in glacial acetic acid).

A blue colour indicates manganese, the limit of identification being 0.05 μg Mn; conc. limit, 1 in 50,000,000.

(*b*) *Formaldoxime Reagent*

HCH=NOH

Manganese salts give red colour with the reagent. The interference is due to Cu which can be overcome by the use of KCN.

Test Take a few drops of the test solution in a semi-micro test tube and add 2 drops of 4 N NaOH solution. Now add one drop of the reagent solution (2.5% aqueous solution).

A red colour indicates manganese, the limit of identification being 0.25 μg Mn; conc. limit, 1 in 20,000,000.

Tests for Zn^{2+}

(*a*) *Dithizone Reagent*

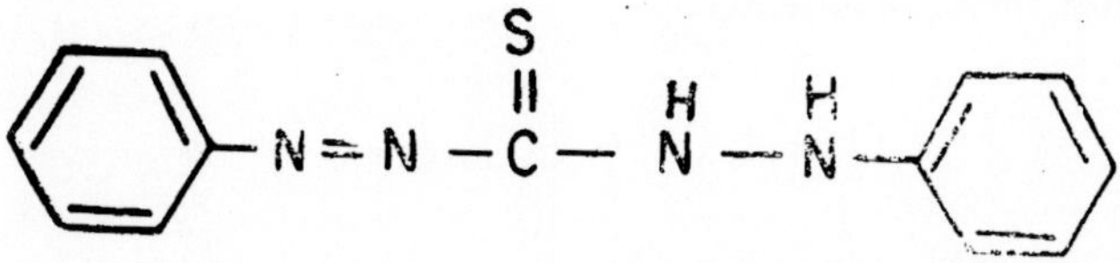

$$C_6H_5-N=N-\overset{\overset{\displaystyle S}{\|}}{C}-\overset{H}{N}-\overset{H}{N}-C_6H_5$$

Zinc salts give red colour in carbon tetrachloride with the reagent. The interference due to heavy metals are climinated by the use of NH_4CN.

Test Take 1 drop of the test solutiod (pH 4.0-5.5) in a semi-micro test tube, add 2 drops of 10 per cent $Na_2S_2O_3$ solution and 1 drop of 2 M NH_4CN. Now add 5 drops of a 0.002 per cent solution of reagent in carbon tetrachloride and shake.

A red colour in CCl_4 layer indicates zinc. The limit of identification is 0.06 μg Zn.

(*b*) *Quinaldic acid Reagent*

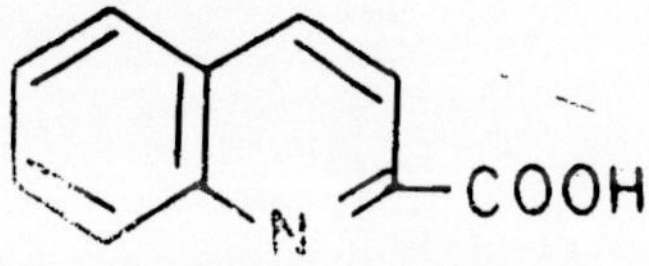

Zinc salts form white ppt. with the reagent. The interference is due to Cu, Cd, Fe and Cr.

Test Take 2 drops of the test solution in a semi-micro test tube and add 2 drops of the reagent solution (1 g of the reagent is neutralized with NaOH and then diluted to 100 mL with distilled water).

A white ppt. indicates zinc.

Group V (Ba^{2+}, Sr^{2+}, and Ca^{2+})

Tests for Ba^{2+}

(*a*) *Sodium rhodizonate Reagent*

```
CO — CO — C.ONa
|         ||
CO — CO — C. ONa
```

Barium salts give red-brown colour with the reagent. The interference is due to Fe, Pb, Sr and S^{2-}. These ions must be removed before the test is applied, but Sr^{2+} can be distinguished from Ba^{2+} by exposing the red-brown spot to HCl fumes, the colour of the spot will be discharged if it was produced by Sr^{2+}.

Test Place 1 drop of the test solution (neutral or very slightly acidic) and one drop of the reagent solution (freshly prepared 0.2 per cent aqueous solution) on a filter paper. Expose the filter paper to ammonia fumes.

A red-brown colour indicates barium, the limit of identification being 0.25 μg Ba; conc. limit, 1 in 200,000.

Tests for Sr^{2+}

(*a*) *Sodium rhodizonate Reagent*

As discussed above the reagent can be used for the detection of Ba^{2+} and Sr^{2+}. Therefore in the presence of Ba^{2+}, barium is converted to insoluble chromate.

Test Place 1 drop of the neutral test solution on filter paper impregnated with K_2CrO_4 solution. After a minute, add a drop of reagent solution.

A brown-red spot indicates strontium, the limit of identification being 3.9 μg Sr (in the presence of 80 times as much as Ba); conc. limit, 1 in 13,000.

Test for Ca^{2+}

(*a*) *Picrolonic acid Reagent*

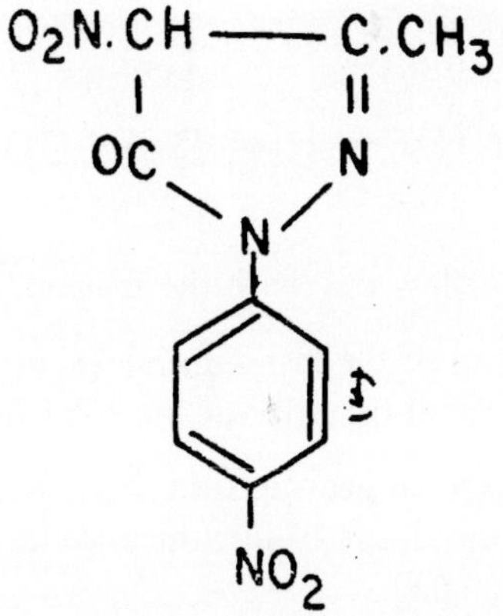

$O_2N.CH$ — $C.CH_3$

OC N

N

(I)

NO_2

Calcium salts form characteristic crystalline ppt. with the reagent.

Test Place 1 drop of a cold saturated (1% aqueous) solution of reagent on a warm microscope slide, add 1 drop of the test solution.

Characteristic rectangular crystals indicate calcium, the limit of identification being 0.01 μg Ca; conc. limit, 1 in 50,000.

(*b*) *Sodium rhodizonate Reagent*

In the absence of Ba^{2+}, Sr^{2+} and Pb^{2+}, Ca^{2+} may be detected by means of the reagent.

Test Place 1 drop of the test solution (neutral or weakly acidic) on a spot plate. Add 1 drop of the reagent solution (freshly prepared 0.2% aqueous solution). Now add 1 drop of 0.5 N NaOH solution and mix.

A violet ppt. indicates calcium, the limit of identification being 1 μg Ca.

(*c*) *Sodium dihydroxytartrate osazone Reagent*

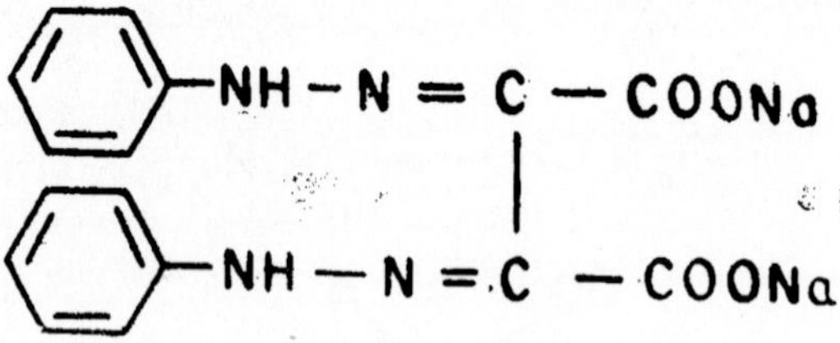

Calcium salts form yellow ppt. with the reagent.

Test Take a drop of the test solution (neutral) on a black watch glass. Add a small quantity of the solid reagent.

A white film or ppt. appearing over the surface of the liquid indicates calcium, the limit of identification being 0.01 μg Ca; conc. limit, 1 in 5,000,000.

Group VI (Mg^{2+}, Na^+ and K^+)

Tests for Mg^{2+}

(*a*) *Magneson Reagent*

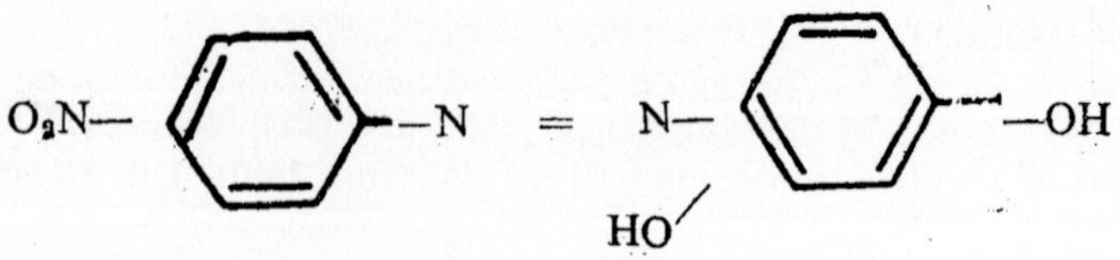

Magnesium hydroxide forms sky-blue lake with the reagent. A number of ions interfere with test.

Test Place 1 drop of the test solution (alkaline medium) on a spot plate. Now add 1 to 3 drops of the reagent solution (0.001 g of the reagent in 100 mL 2 N NaOH solution).

A sky-blue ppt. or lake in a mauve liquid indicates magnesium. the limit of identification being 0.5 μg Mg; conc. limit, 1 in 100,000.

(b) Titan yellow Reagent

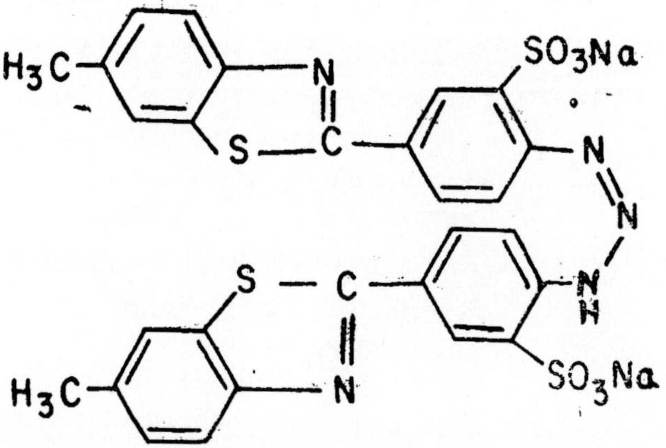

Magnesium salts form bright red ppt. in caustic alkaline solution in the presence of CN^-. The interference is due to Cu and Mn. But these ions can be removed by precipitating as sulphides with Na_2S.

Test Place 1 drop of the test solution on a spot plate. Add 2 drops of 5 N KCN solution and 1 drop of 4 N NaOH solution. Stir the solution thoroughly and now add 1 drop of the reagent solution (0.1% aqueous solution).

A bright red ppt. or colour indicates magnesium, the limit of identification being 1.5 μg Mg; conc. limit, 1 in 33,000.

Tests for Na^+

(a) Uranyl zinc acetate Reagent

Sodium salts form yellow colour or ppt. with the reagent.

Test Take 2 drops of the test solution on a black watch glass and add 8 drops of the reagent solution.* Stir the solution with the glass rod.

*The reagent is prepared as follows:
Dissolve 10 g of $UO_2(CH_3COO)_2$ in 6 g of 30 per cent CH_3COOH, and dilute with water to 50 mL (solution A).
In a separate measuring flask, dissolve 30 g of $Zn(CH_3COO)_2$ in 3 g of 30 per cent CH_3COOH and dilute with water to 50 mL. (solution B)
Mix the two solutions A and B and add a small quantity of NaCl. Allow to stand for 24 h, and filter; filtrate contains uranyl zinc acetate.

A yellow colour or ppt. indicates sodium, the limit of identification being 12.5 μg Na; conc. limit, 1 in 4,000.

Test for K^+

(*a*) *Dipicrylamine Reagent.*

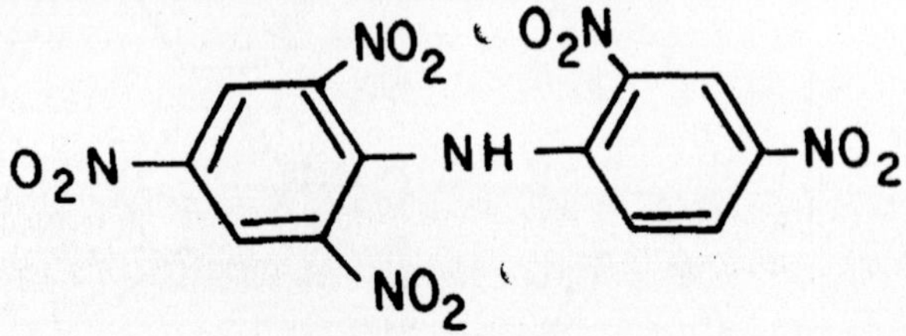

Potassium salts form orange red colour with the reagent. The interference is due to NH_4^+.

Test Take 1 drop of the test solution (neutral) on a filter paper and add 1 drop of the alkaline solution of the reagent (Dissolve 200 mg of the reagent in 20 mL of boiling 0.1 N Na_2CO_3, filter and cool the filtrate).

An orange red colour indicates potassium, the limit of identification being 3 μg K; conc. limit, 1 in 10,000.

Test for NH_4^+

(*a*) *p—Nitrobenzenediazonium chloride Reagent*

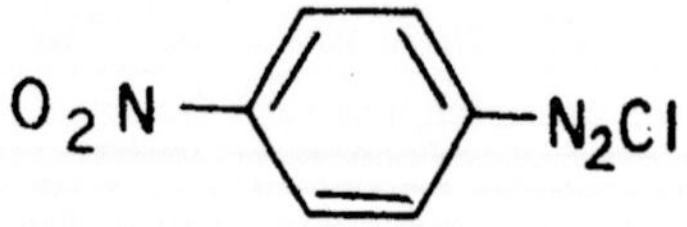

Ammonium salts form red zone around the CaO with the reagent.

Test Place a drop of the test solution (neutral or slightly acidic) on a spot plate, followed by 1 drop of the reagent and a fine granule of CaO between the two drops.

A red zone around the CaO indicates ammonium. The limit of identification being 0.7 μg NH_4^+; conc. limit, 1 in 75,000.

APPENDIX

Preparation of Reagent Solutions

Reagent	*Approximate normality*	*Preparation of 1 litre solution*
Ammonium acetate	3 N	Dissolve 231 g in water and dilute to volume.
Ammonium carbonate	4 N	Dissolve 160 g in a mixture of 140 ml of conc. ammonia and 860 mL of water.
Ammonium chloride	5 N	Dissolve 270 g in water and dilute it to volume.
Ammonium nitrate	1 N	Dissolve 80 g in water and dilute it to volume.
Ammonium oxalate	0.5 N	Dissolve 34 g in water and dilute it to volume.
Ammonium sulphate	2 N	Dissolve 132 g in water and dilute it to volume.
Ammonium sulphide (yellow)	6 N	Pass H_2S gas through 150 mL of concentrated ammonia solution in cold until it is saturated; add 10 g of flowers of sulphur and 250 mL of conc. ammonia solution. Shake the mixture until the sulphur is dissolved and finally dilute with distilled water to volume.
Barium chloride	0.5 N	Dissolve 61 g in water and dilute it to volume.
Calcium chloride	0.5 N	Dissolve 55 g in water and dilute it to volume.
Cobalt nitrate	0.3 N	Dissolve 44 g in water and dilute it to volume.
Copper sulphate	0.5 N	Dissolve 125 g in about 500 mL water containing 3 mL of conc. H_2SO_4. Make up the volume.

Reagent	*Approximate normality*	*Preparation ot 1 litre solution*
Ferric chloride	0.5 N	Dissolve 135 g in about 500 mL of water containing 20 mL of conc. HCl. Make up the volume.
Iodine solution	0.1 N	Dissolve 12.7 g iodine in a solution containing 20 g of KI in 30 mL of water and finally dilute with water to volume.
Lead acetate	0.5 N	Dissolve 95 g in water containing conc. HCl and dilute it to volume.
Mercuric chloride	0.2 N	Dissolve 27 g in water and dilute it to volume.
Potassium chromate	0.5 N	Dissolve 49 g in water and dilute it to volume.
Potassium ferricyanide	0.033 M	Dissolve 10.98 g in water and dilute it to volume.
Potassium ferrocyanide	0.025 M	Dissolve 10.5 g in water and dilute it to volume.
Potassium iodide	0.5 N	Dissolve 83 g in water and dilute it to volume.
Potassium permanganate	0.1 N	Dissolve 3.2 g in water, dilute to volume and finally filter through glass wool.
Potassium thiocyanate	0.5 N	Dissolve 49 g in water and dilute it to volume.
Silver nitrate	0.1 N	Dissolve 17 g in water and dilute it to volume.
Sodium hydrogen phosphate	1 N	Dissolve 120 g in water and dilute it volume.
Stannous chloride	0.5 N	Dissolve 56 g in 100 mL of conc. HCl and then dilute with water to 1 litre. Add a few pieces of tin metal.
Neutral $FeCl_3$ solution		Add NaOH solution dropwise to $FeCl_3$ solution until a slight ppt. persists on shaking. Now add dil. HCl in drops until the ppt. just dissolves.
Nessler's reagent		Dissolve 23 g of mercuric iodide and 16 g of KI in distilled water (free of NH_3) and dilute to 1000 mL. Then add 100 mL of 6 N NaOH solution.

Solid Reagents Aluminium powder, Ammonium chloride, Borax, Calcium chloride, Lead dioxide, Magnesium metal, Potassium nitrite, Potassium permanganate, Potassium bisulphate, Potassium dichromate, Potassium iodide, Sodium nitrate, Sodium bicarbonate, Sodium nitrite, Sodium peroxide, Sodium bisulphate, Zinc metal, Zinc chloride, α-naphthol.

Indicators

Phenolphthalein solution Dissolve 5 g of phenolphthalein in 50 mL of rectified spirit and 500 mL water with constant stirring. Filter, if necessary.

Litmus solution (blue) Dissolve 10 g of the solid in 1000 mL of water.

Litmus solution (red) To 1 per cent blue litmus soln. prepared above, add a few drops of HCl until the solution acquires a red colour.

Methyl orange solution Dissolve 1 g of solid in one litre of hot water and filter.

Methyl red solution Dissolve 1 g of solid in 0.5 litre of alcohol and dilute with water to one litre.

International Atomic Masses*

Element	*Symbol*	*Atomic number*	*Atomic mass (amu)*
Aluminium	Al	13	26.9815
Antimony	Sb	51	121.75
Arsenic	As	33	74.9216
Barium	Ba	56	137.34
Bismuth	Bi	83	208.280
Boron	B	5	10.811
Bromine	Br	35	79.909
Cadmium	Cd	48	112.40
Calcium	Ca	20	40.08
Carbon	C	6	12.01115
Chlorine	Cl	17	85.453
Chromium	Cr	24	51.996
Cobalt	Co	27	58.9332
Copper	Cu	29	63.54
Fluorine	F	9	18.9984
Gold	Au	79	196.967
Hydrogen	H	1	1.00797
Iodine	I	53	126.9043
Iron	Fe	26	55.847
Lead	Pb	82	207.19
Lithium	Li	3	6.939
Magnesium	Mg	12	24.312
Manganese	Mn	25	54.9380
Mercury	Hg	80	200.59
Nickel	Ni	28	58.71
Nitrogen	N	7	14.0067
Oxygen	O	8	15.9994
Phosphorus	P	15	30.9738
Platinum	Pt	78	195.09
Potassium	K	19	39.102
Silicon	Si	14	28.086
Silver	Ag	47	107.870
Sodium	Na	11	22.9898
Strontium	Sr	38	87.62
Sulphur	S	16	32.064
Tin	Sn	50	118.69
Uranium	U	92	238.03
Zinc	Zn	30	65.37

*Values are based on the C-12 standard.